CAR

CW01023374

Sean Costello

# THE CARTOONIST

**PAN BOOKS**
London, Sydney and Auckland

First published in the USA 1990 by Pocket Books, a division of
Simon & Schuster Inc., New York
This edition published 1991 by Pan Books Ltd,
Cavaye Place, London SW10 9PG
9 8 7 6 5 4 3 2 1
© Sean Costello 1990
ISBN 0 330 31338 X

Printed in England by Clays Ltd, St Ives plc

For my girls, Carole and Candace

And for "Granny" and "Gramps",
You were the best
I love you

# Acknowledgments

I'm one of those writers who, once he's got an idea, will talk a person's ear off about it. For me, it seems to help. So I thought I'd thank a few people who are now missing ears. Jake "The Snake" Abourbih, speed reader, gentle critic, peerless pal. My brother, Marty, who didn't laugh. My mother, who laughed (just kidding, Mom, but it fits). And Lita McDonald, who makes me laugh ... and who is a gifted writer just waiting to be discovered. Bob Gibson (in memory) and Sue Gibson, who were generous with their ideas. Charles and MaryAnn de Lint, for their constant encouragement and friendship. Ely Kish, for drawing covers and sharing dreams. Richard Curtis, for everything. Paul McCarthy, for everything else. And finally, Stephen King, who stood with me at the junction of the Knights' Hill Road and Route 302 and gave me the best advice a pro could give a beginner: "Read a lot and write a lot; it really works." Thanks, Steve. It worked.

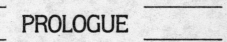

# PROLOGUE

### Sunday, July 12, 1972

There were three of them: Brian Horner and Scott Bowman in the front, Jake Laking in the back. Scott was driving. It was 5:35 A.M. In the east a flat arc of crimson widened like a sleepy eye. The driver's-side window was rolled all the way down, and from time to time Scott leaned his face into the cool rush of air. He was beginning to have some real difficulty concentrating on the road, which was slick from an earlier drizzle.

"Come on, Jake," Scott said in weary exasperation. "I'm beat, half-pissed, and I sure as Christ shouldn't be driving. So where *are* we, huh?"

An inebriated cackle drifted up from the back seat of the Volkswagen Beetle. The interior light was snapped on and a map of the southeastern New England states was wrestled noisily open.

"I haven't got a clue," Jake said after a considering pause. Jake was in charge of navigation—or, at least, he was supposed to be. They had turned north off I-90 just

1

outside of Boston in the hopes of finding a campground or a cheap motel, but that had been well over two hours ago. "Lost, I guess." He cackled again.

"That's great," Scott said, hammering the wheel with the butt of one hand. Beside him, Brian slouched in a drunken drowse. "That's just great!"

"Lighten up," Jake replied sharply, the good humor gone from his voice. "Who gives a shit where we are? We're boogyin', right?" He reached into the hip pocket of his wash-faded Levi's and produced a flattened plastic Baggie. "Besides, I've got a bit of a treat in store." He wagged the thing in the air next to Scott's right ear.

"What's that?" Scott asked warily, trying to see whatever it was in the rearview mirror. His eyes shifted back to the narrow roadway in time to correct for a tight, unmarked turn.

"I purchased this little number in that bar back in Boston," Jake said with a slur. "A few toots of this particular herb and you won't give a damn where you are."

"Dope?!" Scott exploded. "That tears it, man. I thought you gave that up in high school. You know what color of shit we'd be in if we got caught with that stuff in the car? We're in the *States* now, dickhead. This isn't Canada. We'd lose our spots in medical school, and that would be the least of it."

Scott shook his head, partly in disgust, but mostly in an effort to clear his vision. He'd had more to drink than he was accustomed to, and now his alertness was dwindling dangerously. The interstate had been okay, the kind of wide, unbending strip you could navigate pretty much on autopilot. But wherever they were now, he needed every ounce of concentration he could muster. The road was unlit and winding, really treacherous in places.

An awkward silence settled in the car. Only Brian, his hulking, linebacker's body shifting slackly in the shotgun seat, was oblivious of its weight. Jake couldn't see the harm in a little combustible cheer. They were getting it on, celebrating their acceptance into medical school.

That had been the point of the trip in the first place—
that and visiting the universities each of them had been
admitted to.

But it was Scott's car, and Scott was the serious one.

They rolled on. To Scott, the winding rural road
seemed endless. There had been no signs of habitation in
almost an hour, and the only roadsign had been so badly
buckshot it was illegible. At this point all he wanted to do
was stop someplace quiet and sleep it off.

In the back seat Jake lit up. Scott could hear him
inhaling and then stifling a cough. After a moment the
joint's glowing tip stitched like a firefly across the rearview mirror. Then it was under Scott's nose.

Scott pushed it away. "I'm driving," he said flatly, and
the joint vanished into the back again.

The weed made Scott nervous. He had worked too
hard and too long to lose it all over something as juvenile
as a bag of grass. Banking into another curve, he mar-
veled at the paradox that was Jake Laking. Moody,
brilliant beyond anyone Scott had previously encountered, Jake could regress without warning into the kind of
redneck yo-yo you'd expect to find haunting the strip
joints by night and the welfare lines by day.

In the back seat Jake broke into a chorus of his old high
school song.

> "Yellow and blue, yellow and blue,
> What we want we always do . . ."

The road jagged hard to the left. As Scott eased into the
curve, the headlights flickered off a badly canted
roadsign.

"Old Burwash Road," he said, reading the sign aloud.
"See if you can find it on the map."

The happy minstrel in the back ignored him. Brian
grunted awake from his stupor.

> "Rick-a-rack-a, rick-a-rack-a,
> Ziss-boom-ba."

Genuinely angry now, Scott glared into the rearview mirror. He was about to chew Jake out when Brian shouted, "Heads up!" and seized the wheel, cranking it hard to the right.

Scott looked out in time to see a kitten dart onto the blacktop from the tall grass bordering the roadway. Tail straight up, eyes flicking back an eerie red reflex from the glare of the oncoming headlights, its tawny body froze in the middle of the lane and waited for the killing impact. Shoving Brian's hand away, Scott continued the rightward veer, edging the starboard wheels into the loose dirt of the shoulder and just missing the terror-stricken animal. The dirt caught and held, tugging at the car like a giant hand.

The child's head appeared first, popping out through the curtain of grass like the head of the world's tiniest vaudeville performer. Her body followed, and then she was standing there, not a dozen feet away, rigid with fear as the kitten had been only a heartbeat before. She wore a frilly white dress and polished white shoes and she couldn't have been much older than ten. Her hair was like spun silver, and it riffled prettily in the breeze. Her eyes, round and terrified, locked on Scott's in an unwavering death grip that burned with the same red fire as the kitten's eyes had when it froze in the middle of the road. Pale in the glare of the headlights, she seemed somehow transparent, spectral, unreal.

But the sound she made when the Volkswagen scooped her up, a sound like hailstones pelting tin, was more than real.

It was mortal.

It took only seconds, yet during that catastrophic interval Scott Bowman learned what an arbitrary concept Time really is. Somehow an eternity in the cruelest reaches of hell got crammed into those few seconds, and it never ended.

It just went on and on and on.

The Beetle's low chrome bumper took her just above the knees, folding her onto the steeply sloping hood like a

4

well-hit bowling pin. Her head struck the hood with a metallic *thunk,* a dull death-sound that would waken Scott from numberless future nightmares. Then she was rolling upward, her slender legs pitched bonelessly to the right, her arms pinwheeling in small, futile circles. Now her face was in front of Scott's, bare inches away, her eyes glazed but still fixed on his even though she was almost certainly already dead.

*She's looking at me,* he thought wildly, *oh, dear God, she's looking right at me!*

Then her face struck the windshield with a sharp, wet splintering sound and glass was rocketing inward, glittering shards that stung like angry hornets. There followed an instant when it seemed she would hang there forever, her lifeless eyes peering in at him accusingly. Then she was gone, over the side and down into the pale, receding night.

The car fishtailed twice, first to the left, then to the right, then heeled back onto the blacktop before juddering to a halt across the faded center line. There was a jagged, fist-sized hole in the windshield. Next to it, running off thinly to the left, was a small, almost inconsequential smear of blood. Cool air found its way through that hole and struck Scott's shock-whitened face.

It smelled of slaughter.


He closed his eyes and tried to wind back the clock; a few seconds was all he needed. He would return to the instant the kitten had appeared and run the witless creature over, drive on without sparing it even a single backward glance. Frantic phrases like prayers streaked through his mind, staccato verses directed at any god, pagan or otherwise, who might hear his pleas.

*o god let her live please do anything but please let her live i beg of you . . .*

Scott's body trembled convulsively, its every fiber riddled with horror. His fingers went to his chin and found blood, his own blood, running in a rivulet from a pea-sized wound caused by a bullet of flying glass.

*a dream let it be a dream . . .*

Slowly he opened his eyes. He didn't look at his friends. He looked instead at the windshield in the desperate hope that it would be intact, that the spiderweb fracture with the fist-sized hole would be gone, that the runny smear of blood would have vanished.

But the hole was there . . . and the blood.

Reality skewed.

The harsh *clunk* of a door.

Low, shocky, overlapping voices.

Then Scott was drifting out of the car, following the hunched figures of his friends, gliding toward that small, crumpled shape in the road. He fell to his knees beside her even as the others shrank away. He was no doctor, not yet, but he knew she was dead just as surely as he knew that a part of him had died along with her. He placed a hand behind her neck and her head lolled slackly toward him. Her eyes were still open, still gazing blankly into his.

"Don't touch her!" Brian cried into the flat morning air. "You could damage her spinal cord!"

"She's dead, you asshole," Jake said coldly.

At the sound of Jake's voice Scott looked up—and his heart lurched into his throat.

Jake's eyes, usually a soft, pallid green, seemed to emit their own amber light as they swept the roadway in both directions, then shifted to the bordering woods. He stood with his shoulders hunched and his head cocked intently to one side, and for an instant Scott imagined a coiled, predatory cat, scenting danger and preparing to disembowel it.

And in that same instant Scott knew his friend's thoughts, clearly and absolutely.

Because they were his own thoughts, too.

Brian Horner, his huge frame weaving against the indigo sky, stared down dumbly at the child and started to blubber. For him, what had happened was only now beginning to sink in.

Scott turned again to the child and realized she was an albino. It explained the ghostly pallor, the snow-white hair . . . and those eyes, devoid of pigment, reflecting red in the glare of the headlights.

Her blood was red, too. It was on his hand, tacky and warm, and a pool of it was spreading around her ruined head like some terrible satanic halo.

The world tilted crazily, the darkness that had been so rapidly receding returning, spilling into Scott's vision like fountain ink. There was a voice, harsh and reproachful—Jake's voice—and clawed fingers gouging into his shoulder . . . but the voice seemed far away and hollow, reaching him from the bottom of a dark, dry well.

Now he was falling into that well . . . down . . . down . . . spiraling down.

At the bottom was the child's white face.

And its eyes were on fire.

# PART
# ONE

# CHAPTER 1

### August 15, 1988

On the morning of his thirty-seventh birthday, Scott Bowman awoke with a muffled cry. He sat straight up in bed, tugging the sheets in clenched fists and exposing his wife's naked back. There was a panicky feeling in the pit of his stomach, and to his bewilderment, tears were coursing down his stubbled cheeks. As he sat there, disoriented and damp with sweat, a single tear found its way over his lip and into his mouth. It tasted salty on his tongue, a warm, private taste he had all but forgotten. There had been no call for tears in a long time.

He realized then that he'd been dreaming, and immediately tried to call back the images, which only moments before had been so disturbingly vivid. But, as so often happened, other thoughts and perceptions funneled rapidly in, forcing the memory to the outer reaches of recall.

He closed his eyes and tried to concentrate. There had been a sterile white room, windowless and hot, and an

oppressive feeling of being trapped, forgotten, left alone
. . . but that was all he could catch.

He opened his eyes and gazed at his wife's tanned
back, the slow respirations of her slumber. Then, as if
doubting her existence, he touched her. Krista stirred,
moaning softly, then settled back into sleep. Scott smiled
a little then, thinking that Krista could probably sleep
through a bomb blast. She claimed it was because she had
a clear conscience, nothing rattling around bothersomely
in her head while she was supposed to be recharging life's
batteries.

Moving his hand away, it occurred to Scott that he had
actually needed that tactile connection, like a firm pinch,
as reassurance that this was the real part—Krista, the
bedroom, their life together—and not the barren cubicle
in his dream. Because in the dream, which had seemed so
concrete, so horribly plausible, none of his normal life
had existed anymore. Abruptly, cruelly, it had all been
snatched away. . . .

And in that instant the images came back to him with
startling clarity. He swung his legs off the bed and sat
rigidly, curled fists buried into the fabric of the mattress.
A light morning breeze, damp after crossing the lake,
whispered through the peach-colored sheers, making
them caper like insubstantial ghosts. Looking out, Scott's
eyes swept the misty surface of the lake.

But he saw only the bleakness of the dream.

The white room, that was the key image; but it wasn't
just a room, it was a padded cell. That had been his single
irrational fear as a psychiatrist-in-training: being sane,
but ending up locked in a padded cell. There had been
such a cell in the basement of the hospital Scott had
trained in, a hot, gloomy chamber with six-inch padding
covering its every surface, the reek of stale sweat and
spent rage oozing from its four grimy corners. It had
smelled like an animal's den, and on the few occasions
Scott had been required to go down there alone, he had
done so with the trepidation of a child approaching a

closet from which only moments before he had heard scratching sounds, and a low, ravening growl.

In the dream he had been incarcerated inside such a cell—the images were very clear now—his arms lashed across his chest, his veins shot full of mind-numbing drugs. His family had abandoned him, led to believe he'd been stricken incurably mad, and the people outside, the people in charge, were faceless and aloof. Nothing he said was of any consequence, and everything he said was considered insane. But it wasn't insane, and if he wasn't allowed out soon, it was going to be too late for . . . for . . .

*For what?*

But that part of it remained solidly out of reach. And in the warm yellow light of this mid-August dawn, he wasn't sure he wanted to know the rest. It had been only a dream, after all.

But the feeling it had left in its wake—a dark tangle of fear, loneliness, and a very real sensation of physical illness—was on him like a wet blanket. It was a cold but not unfamiliar feeling, one he had last experienced ten years earlier, when the telephone woke him in the midnight quiet of his intern's-wages apartment and a relative's voice announced that his parents had been burned alive while they slept, their big old Rockliffe mansion reduced to coals.

*Morbid,* Scott thought, shivering. Why had he awakened on such a dismal note?

He glanced again at the sleeping shape next to him, letting the warm reality of his wife and his home envelop him. *I'm in my own place with my own people,* he told himself. The empty feeling in his heart was absurd, born of a dream, and he decided to bury it.

He grabbed his bathrobe from its hook behind the door and wrestled it on. The alarm was set for seven-thirty, but it was still only quarter of six. Not wanting to sleep again, he switched off the alarm and left the room. He padded along the hardwood hallway to the stairwell—

then, responding to some nameless instinct, he stopped and took the few steps back to his daughter's room. Silently, he pushed the door open and peeked inside.

Ghostbusters wallpaper assaulted his eyes, shade after grinning shade, each snow-white inside its slashed red circle. Kath's brass bed gleamed richly in the morning light. The glass top of the vanity was littered in tiny plastic Smurfs and, in almost tragic counterpoint, the trappings of Kath's approaching adulthood—mascara, eyeliner, costume jewelry—only toys now, but soon, too soon, very serious concerns indeed. Kath, ten, lay bundled on her side beneath her summer comforter, one tanned arm wrapped lovingly around Jinnie, her Cabbage Patch doll. From the doorway Scott could see the loose curls of her fine, sun-gilded hair.

He tiptoed into the room and leaned over his daughter's bed. Kath's mouth was open, a small dark oval edged in vermilion, and her turned-up nose was bent against her pillow. Her precious round face beamed with high summer color, and the love Scott felt for her at that moment was almost painful in its intensity. He placed a gentle, almost shy kiss on the swell of her cheek, then backed quietly away.

Pulling the door shut behind him, he was startled again by a nearly uncontainable rush of emotion. He had been unable to pass Kath's room without checking . . . to make sure she was really there, he admitted to himself. It was weird—he was still caught up in the subtle dislocation of the dream.

Downstairs, Scott fixed himself a light toast-and-coffee breakfast, then thumped back upstairs to shower and shave, accomplishing all of this with considerably more noise than was necessary. He felt a small pang of disappointment when the ruckus of these ablutions failed to waken his wife or his daughter. For a delicious, delinquent moment he considered calling in sick, taking a French leave, crawling back into bed and waking Krista with Mister Happy. After all, it *was* his birthday.

But the voice of his conscience interjected with its

usual stubborn intolerance. Today was a heavy clinic day until two, then he had a group of medical students to babysit. On this latter account he knew he deserved no sympathy. Every year he promised himself he would drop his university affiliation, and every year he smilingly accepted reappointment.

So he decided to buck up, meet his responsibilities. After all, there was tonight's "surprise" party to look forward to, and he took strength from that. Krista always arranged some sort of birthday bash for him, and he saw no reason for his thirty-seventh (*middle age,* an inner voice heckled) to be any different. It was a comfortable certainty, and Scott found himself grinning at the thought of it. This was not to suggest that Krista Bowman was predictable. In some ways she was—loving, caring, mothering, sexy—but for the most part there was just no second-guessing Mrs. Draper's youngest gal, Krista Marie.

At the door before setting out on the twenty-minute drive to the Health Sciences Centre in Ottawa, Scott had the barely containable urge to shout and waken the entire household, maybe the whole damned lake. But he didn't. He went out to the garage, climbed into the car, and nudged a tape into the deck, trying as he motored up the unpaved hill to think about tonight's party and the fun they would all have together.

But that dream-born feeling, dark and strangely prescient, refused to leave him. It remained like a low-grade fever throughout most of that day.

# CHAPTER 2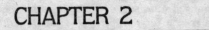

By four-thirty that afternoon Scott had pretty much forgotten his early-morning dream and the funk it had kindled inside of him. In fact, as he stood in the hallway on Two Link and addressed his students, a growing part of his mind was already home, lounging on the deck, sipping a beer almost too cold to hold. It was hot, tacky, and the smell of the chronic ward was none-too-sweet. The students, six of them, each done up in a bleached-and-pressed intern's jacket, stood attentively around him in a tight horseshoe. They had already seen and briefly reviewed five patients, and Scott felt that was more than enough. Mrs. Stopa would be the last.

He loosened his tie and set about this final task.

"Mrs. Stopa is ninety-three," Scott said, taking the hand of the stuporous old Pole seated on the commode in front of him. "She has garden-variety senility, or simple deterioration, as the textbooks call it." The object of the afternoon's exercise was to introduce the students to the

16

wonders of aging, specifically, senescence. "As you can see, she's totally vegged-out. Complete mental destitution."

In truth, Mrs. Stopa was a study in apathy. She stared vacantly into her lap. She drooled. Her jaws worked continuously, but only rude chomping noises came out. There was really little else Scott could say about the old gal, and when she suddenly broke wind, the group edged discreetly away.

"Well, gang," Scott said expectantly. "It's Friday. Shall we call it a day—"

"Hey, everyone! Come look at this!"

It was one of the students, an attractive young lady, calling to the group from across the hallway. She was staring excitedly over the shoulder of an elderly gent whose chest had been crisscrossed in canvas restraints to prevent him from toppling out of his wheelchair. At first glance, the old man appeared to have little more going for him than his ward-mate, Mrs. Stopa. His scrawny frame was clad in the accustomed attire of the senile— sleeveless undershirt, hospital-blue pajama bottoms, fuzzy brown slippers—and there was the familiar reek of ammonia about him. His face was sharp and heavily lined, and drool trailed from his chin to his food-spotted bib. His eyes, small and so deeply brown they appeared black, punctuated his barren expression like the button eyes of a rag doll.

But as Scott drew closer, a light flickered in those eyes that hinted at something deeper. It was fleeting, gone so quickly it might not have been there. But in the space of that single breath, Scott felt certain he'd seen something . . . lurking in those wrinkle-webbed eyes. What the old man was doing with his hands added to the feel of mystery. With his left, he steadied a clipboard against his knees, and with the pencil in his right, he drew.

Scott had heard about this old boy, but had not yet seen him in person. His attending physician, Vince Bateman, who was also the chief of psychiatry, had presented the old man at Wednesday morning rounds as a "diagnostic dilemma." Clinically, the patient satisfied most of the criteria needed for a diagnosis of senility; and yet, according to Bateman, his artistic ability approached the incredible. He had arrived by ambulance, unconscious and with no ID, and Bateman had christened him "the Cartoonist."

"C'mere, gang," the student prompted excitedly. "Check this out. It's amazing!"

The rest of the group gathered round, gawking curiously at the pad and the brisk, apparently haphazard path of the pencil. With an impatient glance at the time, Scott joined them.

Unmindful of the intrusion, the old man continued his pencil scratching. As he drew, he rocked to the music coming from the radio on the wheelchair beside him. It was one of those old-fashioned transistor models that had been so popular some twenty years back, prior to the advent of the Walkman and the ghetto-blaster. Its cracked and battered casing was held together with strips of masking tape, grubby with age.

Scott glanced at the old man's pad . . . and when he did, his impatience vanished. As a kid Scott had been an avid comic-book fan, all of them, everything from *Sergeant Rock* down to *Richie Rich.* But he had never seen anything like this.

The artist had created a series of action drawings, squared-off in classic comic-book style, which depicted two men boxing. In the last of these, one man lay face-down on the mat. The other stood with his legs spread apart and his arms triumphantly upthrust. Lead-black blood trickled from the loser's ear; the old man was just in the process of detailing his vanquished body. The pencil moved with remarkable accuracy and speed, and the drawings were of a professional quality. No, Scott thought, it was more than that. They seemed almost alive.

"Who is he, Dr. Bowman?" one of the students asked.

"Well, no one knows for sure," Scott replied, switching back in his memory to Bateman's presentation. "A

nameless vagrant, found unconscious in the park bordering the QE Parkway. He's not my patient, but if memory
serves me he's shown none of the classic signs of alcohol-
ism, which is the usual case with these unidentified
derelicts."

Scott glanced at the man in the wheelchair and, for just
a second or two, found the scratching of his pencil
unnerving.

"He's amazing," the girl who'd discovered him said.
"Look at how fast he goes. And he hardly even seems to
be looking at the page!"

"He is not really senile," said another student, a
soft-spoken East Indian. "Is he?"

Scott opened his mouth to reply when a high, effemi-
nate voice cut in behind him.

"Well, he pretty much fits the bill, Doctors."

Scott and his entourage turned to face Vince Bateman,
who had been passing by in the hall and had overheard
the question.

Scott felt a familiar stab of dislike for the man. As a
clinical psychiatrist, Bateman had few peers. The trouble
was that he knew it, and his ego, as huge and ungainly as
a grizzly, made him nigh on insufferable to work with. He
took over the discussion without so much as a confirming
glance at Scott.

"When this gentleman came to us two weeks ago," he
began professorially, "all he had were his tattered clothes
and a knapsack containing that clipboard, a bunch of old
drawings, and a bundle of lead pencils." He adjusted his
Gucci tie, then flicked an annoying bit of lint from the
sleeve of his herringbone jacket. "Before the medical
people could come up with a diagnosis, the old fellow
regained consciousness and started producing these
drawings. One of my residents saw him in consultation,
quite properly tagged him as senile, and had him transferred up here. He'll remain on the chronic ward until he
can be placed in a more appropriate center—Saint
Vincent's, or someplace like that."

"But what about his drawings?" the East Indian said

wonderingly. "An artist like this cannot be senile . . . can he?"

Perplexity crossed Bateman's face like a swift-moving cloud. He stroked pensively at his mustache before speaking, and when the words came, they seemed to cause him physical pain. It was that hard for Vince Bateman to be indefinite.

"I have to admit being at a loss to explain the art-work," he said flatly. "It could be an unconscious carry-over from his past, something he was previously capable of doing with little or no thought. Another possibility, since senility is a cyclical condition, is that he draws only when more or less lucid. The fact that he doesn't commu-nicate during these periods could be due to some sepa-rate form of pathology, such as aphasia secondary to stroke . . . or he might simply be choosing to ignore his external environment."

The perplexity had left Bateman's face and now it clouded the faces of the students. Typical of Bateman, he was talking way over their novice heads.

Scott, irked and anxious to leave, decided to elucidate.

"What Dr. Bateman is saying, group, is that we haven't got a clue to what makes this old boy tick. In some ways he fits neatly into a diagnostic slot, and in other, very fundamental ways he does not."

Bateman flushed. The only thing he hated more avidly than disorder was being paraphrased. Scott had to turn his head to conceal a self-satisfied smirk.

"There's a batch of his artwork right here," Bateman said curtly. "In this satchel." He indicated a heavy woolen handbag, slung by its strap from the back of the wheelchair. "You might be interested in going through some of it. The majority are quite macabre, with a gruesome sort of horror-comic bent. More than a few appear to relate to events recent in the news. Disasters mostly. More evidence to support the theory of lucid intervals. Presumably he hears about these things on his radio, then creates his own comic-book versions." Bateman edged away. "If you'll excuse me," he said.

Then he was gone, gliding down the hall with an animated flourish that made Scott wonder—not for the first time—where the man's true sexual preference lay.

Still smirking, Scott moved closer to the wheelchair. "We'll go through some of these," he suggested, "then pack it in, agreed?" Noting the anxious nods, he reached into the satchel.

*"Owww!"* Scott cried, jerking his hand back. Blood welled from the pulp of his index finger, droplets of it spattering the armrest of the wheelchair. A few drops landed on the artist's bare arm, and the old man flinched as if slapped. Other drops speckled the floor at Scott's feet. No one noticed. All eyes were on his finger.

*"Son*ofa—" Scott breathed, catching a string of profanities in early stride. His gaze settled accusingly on the dark interior of the satchel. "What the . . . ?"

One of the students, an overweight girl with a runaway case of acne, produced a half-used packet of Kleenex and handed it over to Scott. Then, as if expecting something to spring out at her, she peered haltingly into the handbag. Once satisfied, she poked in a chubby hand. It came back holding a crisp sheet of paper, one edge streaked with fresh blood.

"Paper cut," she offered sagely. Then she withdrew a sheaf of drawings.

Unmindful of the commotion, the Cartoonist flipped to a fresh page and resumed his penciling.

Scott examined his cut finger. The wound was small but surprisingly deep. A few minutes' pressure and a bandage would control it—but it stung like hell. Looking down at the grubby old artist, Scott wondered when last he'd had a tetanus shot.

"Are you all right, Doctor?" the East Indian asked.

"Not fatal," Scott said. "Just sore." He shifted next to the overweight student, who had already begun leafing through the drawings. Despite himself, Scott's interest had been rekindled by Bateman's last suggestion: that some of the drawings related to events current in the news. He watched as the girl filed slowly through the sheaf.

Bateman had been right. Many of the sketches *were* quite macabre. Boneyard scenes with half-rotted ghouls clawing themselves free of the grave. Bloated sea creatures reaching up from weedy depths for the legs of unsuspecting bathers. Some dark, formless thing lurking beneath a sleeping child's bed.

This last one made Scott think of the nightfears Kath had suffered until just recently. Almost every night she would awaken at some ungodly hour, thrashing and screaming, insisting there was something under her bed, something with scaly wet skin that slithered and touched her toes.

"Here's one," Scott said, interrupting his own thoughts. He took up a sheet with his uninjured hand and displayed it. "I'm sure you recall the endless news coverage of the recent 747 disaster out at Uplands." Shown was a sleek, mammoth aircraft skidding out of control at the end of the runway, then nosing in jagged, flaming halves into a bordering cornfield. "Looks as if Dr. Bateman was right," he muttered, mostly to himself.

The students pored over the drawings with interest.

"You folks can scout through the rest of these if you like," Scott said after a moment. "I have to run." His mind had turned again to home.

Also anxious to leave, the students thanked Scott for his time, replaced the drawings in the satchel, then marched off down the hallway, chatting cheerily about the strange old man and the August weekend ahead.

Scott started away—but out of the corner of his eye he noticed a flutter of movement, and he paused, turning back in time to see a single sheet of drawings glide from the artist's withered hand. He bent and retrieved it, curiosity compelling him to study its contents.

There were four frames, again with a horror theme, depicting a lone figure in a decrepit, cobwebbed room. The figure was standing before an elaborate lion's-head fireplace, and using an ax to rip up the floorboards. In the last frame the figure discovered a mummified corpse underneath. The corpse had a knife in its heart, and something rectangular clutched to its chest.

*Great stuff,* Scott thought in amazement. *What a talent.*

Replacing the drawings in the satchel, he glanced again at the old man's work, intrigued by the almost mechanical persistence of his scribbling, by the uncanny ability that seemed to simply flow through him. He found it difficult to accept that the mind responsible for this talent could be entirely empty. From the first moment Scott had seen the old man, he'd been tempted to believe he could be reached, a channel of communication somehow established. His interest in this patient was only partly professional. It was mostly just plain old curiosity. It would be fascinating to learn more about the old man. Some of his comic-book styles rang faint bells in Scott's memory, taking him back across the years to that childhood fascination with comics. Maybe this old guy had been an illustrator for one of the classics: *Tales from the Crypt, The Vault of Horror,* or something like that. It was an interesting possibility—a senile celebrity.

A nurse appeared next to Scott. "Dr. Bowman," she said pleasantly.

Scott didn't answer. He hadn't even heard the woman's voice. He was staring at the drawing the artist was just then creating, a tingly sense of déjà vu coursing suddenly through him. He'd had a similar experience on one other occasion, several years back in a village in Bavaria, a place he knew he had never visited before. At the time he'd been examining some primitive instrument of torture in a dusty medieval museum. Krista had jived him about that, suggesting that in another life he had probably suffered public humiliation in a similar device for the unspeakable things he had done to a clergyman's daughter.

But what was this? The drawing hadn't even taken shape yet, just some ribbed, rounded objects, but geometrically arranged—

"Dr. Bowman?" the nurse repeated.

Abruptly the old artist began sketching more rapidly, adding texture and dimension, his pencil a hoarse whisper against the page. The rounded objects became cylinders . . . barrels. Four barrels. But that closely ribbed pattern—as if hoops had been wrapped around them at regular intervals—that was the familiar bit.

"Dr. Bowman."

Scott did a half-turn toward the nurse, then looked compulsively back at the drawing. With speed that was conjurer slick, the Cartoonist imprinted one of the barrels with a flower that looked like a rose. Then, equally quickly, he etched in a series of parallel slats— like boards but with abnormally wavy edges—joining the barrels from side to side.

*Where have I seen this before?* Scott wondered blankly. Had it been recently? Yes, there was a sense of newness to the recognition.

He felt a hand on his forearm and looked around at the nurse, whose face was flushed with exasperation. "Yes, sorry," he said, "but I . . ." Then he gazed again at the drawing, trying to place those shapes, their geometric relationship to one another, that big white rose.

". . . your wife is on extension one-one-three," the nurse was saying.

"Oh . . . okay," Scott mumbled, feeling oddly transplanted, as if awakening from a dream.

"There's a phone free in the interview room," the nurse said, shaking her head. Then she continued on her way.

As Scott turned reluctantly away from the wheelchair to pick up his call, the old man ceased his pencil scratching and shifted his gaze toward the doctor's receding figure. Down the hall Scott hesitated briefly, sensing those eyes on him. He did not turn. He walked on. But in that instant of hesitation his skin crawled avidly, as if someone had danced across his grave.

He took a bandage from a supply cupboard and put it on his finger, then let himself into the interview room to use the phone. His finger was throbbing like hell. He was thirsty, hungry, and he wanted to go home.

Krista's voice, cheerful and rich, made him forget the old man and that queer sensation of déjà vu.

For the time being, at least.

Alone in his wheelchair by the window in the hall, caught in the slanting light and sharpening shadow of late afternoon, the old man touched the droplets of congealing blood on his forearm with tentative, caressing fingertips. His dark eyes rolled. The corners of his seamed mouth twitched.

After a while he began to draw again.

# CHAPTER 3

"Hi, hon!"

Krista's voice sounded small and far away. Scott could hear the drone of a powerboat behind her, and knew that she was down by the lake, using the cordless phone.

"Hi to you, too," he replied, smiling. He knew she'd be getting ready for his party.

"Glad I caught you—" Her voice angled sharply away, then grew suddenly louder: *"Kathleen! There's poison ivy down there, pet!* . . . sorry, hon. Just wanted to let you know that we're out of beer. The Swains stopped by this afternoon and drank us all out . . . and I know you've been thinking more about the big Bud this hot afternoon than you have about your little wifey."

It was true.

"Okay, doll. Thanks. I'll pick some up and be along soon."

"Good. See ya." She hung up.

And suddenly Scott missed her. It was an ache.

He hung up the phone and left the hospital, heading for the parking lot in long, rapid strides.

The delay with the students—and stopping off at the Brewer's Retail to replenish his stock of Budweiser—wound up working in Scott's favor. By the time he got under way again the rush-hour traffic had thinned, and he was able to reach the city limits in record time. Once or twice during the drive out, his thoughts swung back to that ancient artist and his bizarre drawing, the curious subject of which Scott felt certain he had seen before. But the day was clear and his mood was fine, and eventually the car captured his full attention.

The Turbo Volvo was Scott's baby, the one totally outrageous luxury he had allowed himself after buying the new house in the Gatineaus, that long range of low green mountains on the Quebec side of the Ottawa river. Quick and responsive, the car gave Scott a wonderfully juvenile feeling. And on this particular August afternoon—his birthday—he was feeling perfectly juvenile.

A tune played over and over in his mind, competing discordantly with the music on the deck, André Gagnon's *La fin du jour.*

*Happy birthday to me, happy birthday to me, happy birthday, dear Scotty . . .*

Now he was on the home stretch, guiding the car fluidly along the twists and curves of the narrow Gatineau Road. Signaling, he turned left at a dusty road sign reading Sleepy Hollow and slowed to a crawl, protecting the car's undercarriage from the pits and pocks of the washboard side road. He stopped in front of a bank of green-painted mailboxes, fished out his mail—bills, journals, a few items of personal correspondence—then resumed the drive home. Soon the lake became visible through breaks in the birch trees hemming its banks. The water looked cool and inviting, its blue-green surface dancing with quicksilver.

The Bowmans' winding drive was all but hidden by the

dense summer overgrowth, and Scott had to watch carefully to avoid missing it. The gravel entryway was marked with a pine slab that read SANDY POINT HIDE-AWAY, a name coined by Krista after the tiny Atlantic village of her birth. Her mother lived there still, in a small ocean-side cottage.

As he rounded the last bend and swung into the drive, Scott saw his angular, cedar-sided house coming into view, and Kathleen, charging up the lane to greet him. He parked in front of the garage, killed the ignition, and powered open his side window. Afternoon heat rushed in like dragon's breath.

"Daddy!" Kath squealed.

"Hi, kid," Scott said, accepting her kiss through the open window. She was wearing a striped orange-and-white swimsuit, which clung damply to her skin. Kath was a pretty girl, with Krista's tall-and-tan figure and cornflower eyes. She was already in the breast-bud stage, a fact which Scott had remarked only recently, with surprise and a certain dismay. Her growth paralleled his own aging, her development reminding him of how Time, at least from his point of view, had managed to shift into overdrive. Right now, on the evening of his thirty-seventh birthday, his daughter looked like a grown woman in miniature. Scott gazed at her with something like awe.

After a moment Kath stepped back to allow her father out of the car. The cooling engine ticked quietly beneath the hood.

"Where's your mom?" Scott asked, tucking the mail and the triple six-pack under his arm.

"Round front, starting up the barbeque. Oh—" Kath held up the baby finger of her left hand for Scott's inspection. It was swollen and red. "Lookit where the wasp stung me."

"Oooh, the nasty beggar," Scott cooed dutifully. He could see the tiny red puncture-site surrounded by a paler wheal. *Thank God she's not allergic,* he thought. This was her first bee sting. "Sore?"

Kath shook her head and smiled. "Not now. Mom fixed it with baking soda."

Scott showed her his bandaged finger. "I got it today, too," he said, mimicking her pout. "Kiss it better?"

Eager to please, Kath pressed an overzealous kiss onto the tip of Scott's finger. Pain flared like sunlight on polished chrome. He smiled through clenched teeth. "Thanks, kid."

"Jody Loomis was here today," Kath launched cheerily. "You know, she's twelve, and she's got this icky white zit right here in the corner of her mouth. No wonder, she never brushes her teeth, and her brother, Tommy, told me that she actually kisses boys . . . *yuck!,* and . . ."

Scott hugged his daughter to his leg as they walked, and she filled him in on the highlights of her day. As usual, Kath had had more fun than her dad. Krista met them at the front door, wearing a pink ribbon in her hair and a bikini Scott had never seen before . . . and could scarcely see now.

He felt an ominous stirring in his briefs.

"Hi, Doc," Krista said brightly. "Look what I've got."

She held up a big freezer-frosted mug, just begging to be filled with beer. *There is a God,* Scott decided, and cupped Krista's cheek in his hand. She kissed him and then Scott followed her in, setting the mail on the newel post as he went by.

In less than a minute he was sipping that long-awaited brew. He stood by the window in the living room, guzzling heartily, watching his daughter as she skipped down the hill to rejoin her pals on the dock. He could hear Krista rummaging around upstairs, and his thoughts turned lustily back to that bikini. Feeling suddenly persuasive—and not just a little horny—he drained his glass and headed for the stairs.

But it appeared that Krista was on the same wavelength. Wearing only her bikini bottoms, she stood in front of the bathroom mirror, idly fingering the curls of her thick auburn hair. Her breasts seemed to wink with promise from inside the mirror.

Something about Krista's breasts—or, more exactly, Scott's slavering reaction to them—had long ago convinced him of the validity of Darwin's theory, and of his own descent from the orangutan.

"Want some?" she asked, smiling coyly.

"Does dogbane bend under the weight of the stinkbug?" Scott said, whipping off his pants as if they'd just met the business end of a skunk. In seconds he was standing there naked, semi-erect and grinning, with a sock in one hand and a pair of Fruit of the Loom jockies in the other.

But Krista was pulling on a wine-colored T-shirt. "Tough," she said, smirking. Then she was gone.

Scott growled, his excitement doubled. He knew her game: playful rejection now, *un*-believable later. That was one of the things about Krista that helped keep their relationship always fresh and new—Scott was never allowed to take anything for granted.

He hopped into the shower where he remained for a long time, letting the jets of hot water spear away the tensions of the work week behind him.

# CHAPTER 4

After showering, Scott sat in a fold-out chair on the deck, sipping his second beer and gazing out over Pike Lake. The surrounding hills brought dusk early up here; now, at seven-thirty, the light was already thinning . . . yet that hot, nearly palpable August haze persisted. It was as if a soft filter had been placed over the lens of the eye, lending a dreamy quality to the scene. Scott could see Bob Anderson out there, the dauntless fisherman, putt-putting along in his aluminum boat, a dim silhouette hunched over a trolling line and a beer. Anderson, a retired dairy farmer, lived with his wife in a refurbished cottage just five minutes' walk away on Cottage Road. It surprised Scott mildly to see Bob without his perpetual companion, Fred Mills, whose son ran the marina on the opposite side of the lake. As far as anyone knew, those two old boys had been fishing this lake together since the dawn of recorded history.

It had been this view of the lake, from the deck, which

for Scott had clinched the purchase of the house last December. A well-known artist had owned it previously, had in fact designed and constructed it, right down to backhoeing the hole for the foundation. She had used the room beneath the deck, presently the Bowman rec room, as a studio. If you aimed your nose the right way in that room, you could still catch a faint whiff of solvents and oils. Small but well lit, the room was Scott's favorite. He did his reading in there, his thinking, his relaxing.

Krista was standing across from him, poking at chops on the open grill. Kath was still down by the lake, laughing and squealing with her friends.

"So, what do you feel like doing tonight?" Scott said, fishing for hints of his party. So far no one had even mentioned his birthday, and he was getting the sinking feeling it had been forgotten.

"Oh, read, watch TV, feel sorry for myself." Crinkling her nose, Krista turned to look at him. "Got the curse."

"Rude," Scott said, believing now that she'd actually forgotten. "Not at all cute."

"What happened to your finger?" Krista asked absently, closing the lid on the barbeque.

"Paper cut," Scott answered—and for an instant the puzzle of the drawing flashed again in his mind.

On the subject of his finger Krista only grunted, and Scott's mind switched back to the problem at hand. He studied his wife for hints of a grin, a subtle twinkle in the eye, something to let him know that she was having him on. But there was nothing. She looked tired, even a little cross.

Suddenly he felt old, hurt, dejected.

Krista gave him a weary half-smile, then went back inside.

*Christ,* he thought gloomily, *she's really forgotten.*

He got up and fetched another beer, chugged it, poured out a fourth, then took that one down to the rec room, spilling some as he went. He scanned the channels, found nothing but news, and switched off the tube with a grunt.

He grabbed the evening paper and fingered listlessly through that, but he glimpsed only chaos between the lines and tossed it aside. He glanced at the antique rosewood fernstand he'd been refinishing for better than a year now, and almost slipped on the work gloves—but he decided he'd probably screw up if he tried working on it with a bellyful of beer.

Finally he picked up the phone and dialed Gerry's number in Ottawa. Gerry St. Georges was Scott's best buddy. He never forgot Scott's birthday. Scott had a twenty-years-running collection of gag Christmas and birthday gifts Gerry had given him: rubber dildos, clay dog shit, plastic puke, fake cracks-on-the-TV-screen, giant strap-on breasts, rude cards of every description. Gerry was six months older than Scott, a big man, powerful, protective. He worked as a provincial police-man.

No answer at Gerry's.

*"Dinner!"* It was Krista, calling from the top of the stairs.

Scott gulped down the dregs of his beer. When he stood, he realized he was high. He started up the stairs in an unsteady weave, giggling at his altered perceptions.

*She's just having me on . . . right?*

But dinner went by without mention of birthdays or parties. Even Kath betrayed no hint of a silent conspira-cy. She sat next to Scott, gnawing contentedly on the remains of a barbequed chop.

Still, he fished.

"What'cha doing tonight, big girl?"

What was that? A cryptic flicker of eyes? Some secret message passing deftly between mother and daughter?

"There's a sleepover at Lita's tonight," Kath replied, looking at Scott with pleading eyes. "Mom said I should ask you. . . . Can I go, Daddy? Please?"

"Wouldn't you rather stay home with your dear *old* dad tonight?"

Kath looked disappointed. "And do what?"

33

"Yeah," Scott said, finally accepting the truth. "You can go."

"Are you pouting?"

It was quarter of nine and almost full dark. Draped in a matronly looking shawl, Krista sat curled on the upstairs sofa, reading Blatty's *Legion*. Kath had been gone for about an hour.

He was pouting.

"No," he replied defensively. Seated in a chair across from her, he leafed distractedly through a medical journal. "Why should I be pouting?"

"Well, you're the shrink," Krista said, her eyes sparkling, "but I think you're pouting."

Was she baiting him?

"I'm going down to the rec room," Scott said, a childish "so-there" tone in his voice. He dropped the journal and stood. As he stalked away, he thought he saw Krista glance furtively at her watch. Then she was reading again. No signs of protest.

He stumped down the stairs—after pouring out a . . . what was it now? . . . fifth brew? Okay, so he *was* pouting. Being a psychiatrist didn't protect you from your own little hang-ups and insecurities. Remembering things like birthdays, embellishing them, was a sign of love. And in that department Scott was nowhere near above the need for reassurance. He'd always been insecure with Krista. Physically, she was a far more beautiful human being than he was, always had been. She outclassed him in the looks department by such a wide margin, in fact, that for years Scott had secretly cringed at parties or public get-togethers where Krista was exposed to other men. He knew he couldn't lock her up at home, and had never breathed a word to her about his fears. But men trailed after her like tail-wagging mongrels. He knew Krista loved him, knew she was happy, but still . . . it was scary sometimes. Scary how much he needed her.

At nine o'clock the telephone rang. Still hurt and

annoyed, Scott let it ring, waiting for Krista to pick it up. On the seventh ring he crossed the room to Kath's Mickey Mouse phone and grabbed the receiver. Mickey grinned up at him gleefully.

"Hello," he said a trifle too sharply. He could hear Krista padding across the floor above him.

"Scott! Happy birthday!"

It was Gerry.

Scott grinned back at Mickey. "Hi, man!" he said, instantly cheerful. "Thanks! I'm glad somebody remembered." *Juvenile,* he thought. But the words were already out. He was half in the bag now.

"What? Who forgot?"

"Just the entire Bowman harem, that's who."

"Oh, really?" Gerry said, chuckling. "I find that pretty hard to believe. Have you dropped any hints?"

Scott grunted.

"Well, you should. Anyway, what's new? Have you changed your mind about the trip?"

"No," he admitted. "As much as I'd like to, I still can't go."

The Boston trip had been a dinner table bone of contention between him and Krista for the past several days. Krista planned on leaving this Sunday, overnighting with her sister Klara on the Saint Lawrence, then driving on to Boston early Monday morning to spend a week with her half sister, Caroline. Krista wanted desperately for Scott to join them, but like most things, she had planned this jaunt on the spur of the moment. Next week was going to be a bad one for Scott. He would be up to his neck in a dozen or more things he simply could not walk away from.

"You sure it isn't because you can't win an argument with Caroline?"

Scott chuckled. "It's damned tough winning an argument with someone who's always right, this much is true."

Caroline, who was a few years older than Scott, had a Ph.D. in social anthropology and held a full professorship at Pine Manor College, a school for rich girls in Cambridge near Harvard. She had earned her degree at Berkeley during the sixties and was very much a product of that radicalized environment. She even had a framed photograph, proudly displayed on the mantel, showing herself giving the finger to riot police during a university uprising. Caroline was a hard-core feminist and, though good-natured and generous, took umbrage at some of Scott's more traditional views on boy-girl relationships. She was the sole offspring of their mother's first marriage, predating Krista by nearly nine years. She and Krista were very close indeed, and Scott had to mind what he said about her. But apart from what he viewed as her "opinionated nature," he cared a lot for Caroline.

"But, no, Caroline's not the reason," Scott said. "Not this time, anyway. I'm going to be up to my ass in all manner of administrative horseshit next week, stuff I just can't shirk. Sad but true."

If there was any single problem in his marriage, Scott reflected in the moment of silence that followed, it was this: in Krista's opinion he spent too much time at work, and not enough at home with his family. It was an old song, one which most physicians learned to live with— often as divorcés. The majority of the maybe half-dozen totally monstrous arguments he and Krista had had during their lives together had centered on this theme. And once or twice it had gotten quite ugly. The last major spat had occurred only recently, shortly following the purchase of the lake-front home.

They had made a killing on their house in Ottawa—its value had more than doubled in the eight years they'd owned it—and the deal on the lake-front property had been good. The artist-owner had been in a hurry, had needed cash quickly. Krista's argument was simple: Why should Scott continue to work so hard when in reality he could retire right now? (Not luxuriously, mind, but comfortably, and with enough left over to assure their child the best of educations.) Why, when he spent most of his time griping about committees and administrative time-wasting projects, should he continue to knock himself out? She didn't expect him to retire, of course not, but she failed to see why he couldn't at least keep his evenings and weekends free. He was a psychiatrist, for Christ's sake, not a goddamn heart surgeon.

Nastily, in his own defense, Scott had come around to the subject of Krista's expensive tastes. That was when things had turned ugly. At least no one could accuse him of dragging psychotherapeutic side steps into his marriage. When Scott argued, it was from the gut.

"I suppose you think I'm a boring old obsessive-compulsive, too," Scott said to his friend, breaking the silence.

Gerry chortled. "I think you're an asshole . . . but the nicest asshole I've ever met." Scott beamed. "Listen, I was over there this afternoon and left a present for you, but you've gotta go find it. I hid it behind a loose rock in the upstairs fireplace."

Scott's curiosity was instantly piqued. He loved surprises—pleasant ones, anyway. The fireplace was in the master bedroom, but Scott had never noticed any loose rocks.

He was beginning to smell a conspiracy.

"Gotta go," Gerry said before Scott could pump him. "Have a nice birthday. And drop a hint before it's too late."

"Thanks, pal. Bye for now." Gerry was giggling when Scott replaced the receiver in Mickey's hand.

*behind a loose rock in the fireplace . . .*

Half-lit and grinning, Scott thumped upstairs to the main floor. He padded quickly along the hallway to the next flight—pausing to peer into the living room and see that Krista had vanished—then started up. As he spun into the staircase, using the newel post as a pivot, his fingers nicked the letters he'd left there earlier and sent them scattering to the floor. Cursing softly, he bent to retrieve them, his gaze falling on one which had been postmarked in Winnipeg. There was a return address, but no name. The handwriting was distinctively female.

Feeling suddenly and inexplicably apprehensive, a gut-level sensation not unlike the one he had awakened with early that morning, Scott thumbed the letter open. And as he walked up the stairs, he read the single handwritten page it contained.

Dear Scott:

Even as I write this I cannot believe what I have to tell you. Brian is dead. We buried him three weeks ago, but only now am I finding the time and the courage to notify his more distant friends. It happened at the hospital, a freak accident. Brian was called to a cardiac arrest in the ER. He was about to give the patient countershock, but when he applied the paddles the apparatus backfired somehow and electrocuted him. They tried for more than an hour to resuscitate him, but they just couldn't get him back. Brian's heart was not all that good to begin with. All that extra weight, I guess. He loved his food.

It was a terrible, terrible tragedy. Our lawyers are going to sue, but that won't bring Brian back. He was a good husband, a good father, and a good friend.

Although you and I have never met, Scott, I feel that I know you. Brian thought highly of you, and spoke of you often. He told me what happened years ago, between you and him and that other man Jake. He swore me to secrecy, but I guess that no longer matters. It is mostly because of what he told me that I am writing to you now. It must have been terrible, especially for you. Still, I feel you did the right thing. Life goes on.

It was signed: Regretfully, Delia Horner.

Delia's letter, that last paragraph, summoned in Scott a memory so foul, so solidly encrusted beneath a years-long effort to eradicate it, that he had to steady himself against the shudder that curled up from his bowels. Lightheaded, he leaned against the door-frame to his bedroom and gazed up blankly from the letter.

As if in a dream, Scott saw his wife lying provocatively against a mound of pillows by the fireplace. A crisp yellow fire was burning, and Krista was wearing her most rude undies. In front of her, chunked down in a bucket of ice, leaned a bottle of vintage champagne. Beside her, gleaming in the firelight, stood two of their finest crystal goblets.

Now Krista was getting up, looking not sexy but frightened. Scott tried to smile, to pretend that every-thing was fine, that he loved the gag they'd played on him and that she looked delicious, and that if she gave him just a moment he would join her in a toast and then they would make love. . . .

But he couldn't. The memory prevented him.

Krista placed a hand in the crook of his elbow. "What is it, hon?" she said with concern. "You look dreadful." Then she noticed the letter in his hand, and apprehension wormed its way into her voice, making it waver, "Did someone die? Family?"

"No, Kris," Scott answered, his voice low. "Not fami-ly. Remember the guys I went through undergrad with? Jake Laking and Brian Horner?"

Krista nodded as the memory filtered back. Scott hadn't mentioned those two since before they were married.

"It's Brian Horner," Scott said. "The linebacker. He's the one dead."

"Oh, I'm sorry, hon. But you haven't been close to him in years. When I saw you there in the doorway, looking so lost and pale, I thought it might be . . . I don't know. You gave me a fright."

Scott balled the letter into his fist and flicked it into the fire. It went up in a bluish flare, then curled into black, diaphanous ash.

"I'm all right," he said, embracing his wife. "Had a few too many, that's all."

"You got room for one more?" Krista asked, popping the catch on her bra.

"You bet," Scott said, and lay with her there by the fire. As it turned out, his birthday present wasn't behind a rock after all.

Later, they fell asleep there.

And to Scott's relief, there were no dreams that night.

# CHAPTER 5

Scott awoke just before ten that Saturday morning, hung over and a little stiff from having slept on the rug. Beside him, an empty champagne bottle leaned coolly in a bucket of water. When he saw it, he smiled, remembering last night. . . .

But the smile vanished when he thought of Delia Horner's letter and the memories it had conjured. It surprised him that Brian had told his wife. Years ago, Scott had vowed he would never tell Krista.

He found a small, clumsily wrapped gift at the foot of the bed, and as he opened it, his smile returned. It was from Kath, some sort of unearthly creature she had fashioned from clay. He set it atop the highboy next to a framed photograph of his parents, then turned to the casement windows.

Outside, the lake was choppy, the sky the flat gray color of tin. In the east a thunderhead crouched like a dark colossus, only its crown and powerful torso visible above the jagged horizon. It was going to storm. Typical week-end weather.

As Scott turned away from the window, a shriek rose from outside, a high, startling sound that gripped him with its suddenness. Then he saw Kath and her friend Lita horsing around on the dock, pushing and squealing playfully. Relieved, he pulled on a pair of trunks, grabbed a towel, and ambled downstairs.

Krista was on the living room floor, twisted into some unladylike but fascinating aerobic contortion. Then she was shifting, spreading her legs to the limit, and Scott got an unlovely image of her splitting right up through the middle. She grinned, but it was more like a grimace. Scott blew her a kiss, then headed outside through the sliding screen doors.

Kath scurried up the path to meet him, and Scott bent to lift her as she thrust herself into him. She was soaking wet and cold against his skin. She kissed him heartily, enfolding his neck with her sturdy bronze arms.

"Didja get my present?"

"Yes, and it was lovely," Scott fibbed. What he had unwrapped was a multicolored blob-man—goggle-eyed, pig-snouted, with a punk-style haircut and a buck-toothed grin. Original, maybe, but lovely it wasn't. "But do you really think it looks like me?"

"Don't be a goof, Dad. I made him up. But now that you mention it . . ."

Kath laughed and Scott put her down.

"Going swimming?" she asked, pointing at the towel.

"Thinkin' about it," Scott said. "Know anyone who might like to join me?" He noticed that Kath's friend Lita had disappeared.

"Might," Kath said coyly.

Scott walked onto the dock to its far edge and bent to lay down his towel. As he straightened, two strong little hands buried themselves in the meat of his buttocks and pushed. Then he was tumbling into the cool blue enve-lope of the lake. When he bobbed up, suddenly wide awake, Kath cannonballed him. Scott pretended to chase her, and she scrambled spryly up the ladder, shrieking playfully and splashing him. He followed her up and sat beside her on the dock.

"Got a hangover?" she asked in an adult voice.

"Just a small one—" Scott admitted, stopping in midsentence when Kath gaped in horror at her wrist. "What is it, babe? What's the matter?" Visions of bloodsuckers flashed in his mind.

"My bracelet!" Kath squealed. "I lost my bracelet!" She angled her gaze to the water. "It musta fell off when I cannonballed you. Oh, Daddy, what am I gonna do?" She was suddenly close to tears.

In June Scott had given her a plain silver bracelet for her birthday, and Kath had worn it religiously ever since. Now there was only a fine white line where the bracelet had screened out the sun.

"Can you get it back for me, Daddy? Please?"

Scott squinted into the algae-clouded depths, shielding his eyes with his hands. He thought he could see a faint metallic glint down there, seven or eight feet out from the edge of the dock.

"We'll find it, kiddo," he promised. "Don't panic. Why don't you run up to the rec room and dig out Daddy's diving mask. It should be in that box of junk next to the workbench."

Kath was up the hill like a shot, her tanned legs pumping furiously. Breathless, she was back inside of a minute, Scott's black diving mask clutched in her hand.

"Here," she said, handing it over. "Can you see it?"

"I think so," Scott said as he fitted on the mask. "Not to worry."

He stood at the edge of the dock, hyperventilating, judging the trajectory of his dive. He could still see that faint silvery glint, like a star in a muddy sky. The lake got deep fast out here, dropping to twelve or fifteen feet just off the edge of the dock. It was one of the reasons he was glad that both of his girls were strong swimmers.

He took a last deep breath and dove in, submerging quickly, leaving a cyclone of bubbles in his wake. A dense bed of weeds sent undulant fingers up to greet him, broad, translucent strands that sent shivers skating through him. The water was cooler at this depth, almost cold.

After a quick scan Scott spotted the bracelet. It had landed atop a cluster of large, algae-mantled boulders. Eager for his daughter's praise, he snagged the silver loop and turned back toward the surface, shoving off with his feet.

He noticed it then, as he stroked up into warmer water, and the association made an almost audible click in his head.

The undersurface of the dock! That odd pencil drawing, the one which had triggered that pervading sense of déjà vu. The senile old artist had been sketching the undersurface of the dock!

The complete absurdity of this deduction struck Scott even before he surfaced from his dive . . . and yet, if memory served him, the similarities were undeniable. He had seen the underside of the dock only once, late last April, the day he and Gerry had lowered it into the thaw. Because she lived alone, the previous owner had constructed the dock with easy handling in mind. She had built the narrow walkway in three short sections, which rested on cast-iron stilts in the shallower water near shore, and the main section of the dock was a simple twelve-by-twelve square of cedar that floated on barrels, easily detached in winter and reattached in the spring. Scott had gotten only a brief glimpse of the dock's crusty undersurface on that cool day in April—but he had noticed those unusual barrels, with their closely knit ribs and rose-shaped decals. Now the memory was very clear.

He pulled himself out of the water and sat on the edge of the dock, perplexed and a little off balance. Kath plopped down beside him, her hopeful eyes searching his hands.

"Didja find it?" she asked expectantly.

Scott opened his right hand, where the small silver ringlet lay cupped. Kath uttered a squeal of delight. She grabbed the bracelet and pulled it on, kissing Scott full on the mouth. Just then Lita reappeared, and Kath scampered off to fill her in on the details of the near-catastrophe, her eyes as she hurried up the path admiring the bracelet like newfound treasure.

It was impossible, of course, just a coincidence. That was the only explanation for it. Clearly the old artist had been sketching something else, something which had triggered Scott's memory through some vague similarity to real life. That had to be it. How could he have seen the underside of the dock? Of *this* dock? He might have known the artist who lived here before, Scott reasoned lamely, but even if he had, how could he possibly know who lived here now?

*But what if he does?* Scott's mind countered with one of those crazy thoughts that crazy situations have a way of inducing. *What if the old guy* does *know that I live here? And if so, was he trying to communicate with me? Using the drawing as some sort of sign?*

But no, of course not. The old boy was out of it, not even a flicker of a mind left. And even if he *had* been trying to communicate, why choose something as obscure as the undersurface of the dock? If he knew where Scott lived, why not simply sketch the house itself? It was nuts.

Scott sat wet and shivering in the prestorm cool and wondered about that drawing, trying to recall the details of the few bizarre moments he had spent alone with the artist the previous afternoon. First had come that uncanny sense of having seen the objects before, then the nurse had come by with a message for Scott . . . and hadn't the old man hurried up just then? Started drawing more quickly? As if he feared Scott might leave without seeing the drawing? Without making the connection?

Shaking his head, Scott stood, his mind's eye conjuring an image of the drooling, demented old man whose talent seemed so drastically out of place. He tried shifting his thoughts to firmer ground, to write it all off as a trick of the mind.

But it was no good. He was unable to reconcile the association his mind had made and had fixed on despite his best efforts to explain it away. Glancing back into the depths, he decided there was only one way to settle this thing once and for all.

He turned and hurried up the hill in uneasy strides.

In the rec-room closet Scott rooted around in search of his waterproof Minolta. He found it still in its box behind a set of unused golf clubs. The compact, plastic-encased camera was a gift the girls had given him this Christmas past. He had used it on Christmas day, snapping off shots of the family around the tree, then had put it away. In fact, he hadn't had the film developed yet. The partially used roll was still in its cartridge. That was good. It would save him a trip into town for a new one.

He tested the flash and found it operational. Then, after a cursory glance at the instructions, he hurried back outside. Kath joined him partway down the path.

"What are you gonna do with that?" she asked, indicating the danger-yellow camera that dangled from his wrist.

"I have to check something under the dock," Scott said distractedly.

Kath frowned. "But you told me never to go under there, Dad. Isn't it dangerous?"

"Only for little girls."

Clutching the camera, Scott dove into the lake. After a few quick strokes toward bottom, he turned back to examine the dock. From this depth, suspended above the rocks, he could make out the four crusty barrels and, just evident in the poor illumination, their tightly cropped ribs. And there were the white-rose decals, faded but still visible—old White Rose oil drums. It all looked damned similar to what he could remember of the drawing. But his angle wasn't right for a photo. The point of view in the sketch had been from further out, and deeper.

Scott stroked back to the surface and filled his lungs

with air. Kath was standing by the ladder, looking down at him, her tiny face pinched with worry.

"Don't stay under so long, okay?"

"Okay, hon," Scott promised.

He climbed onto the dock and waved at an approaching motor boat. Bob Anderson and Fred Mills were just returning home from their early-morning trolling session. Grinning proudly, Bob held up a string of fat-looking pickerel. By now Scott knew their routine: fish from seven until eleven, back to Bob's for sandwiches and beer, then head out again until four.

Camera in hand, Scott plunged like a human spear, feet-first into the lake. As he descended, he could hear the pinging knock of Anderson's small outboard. In seconds he reached bottom, landing atop the same greasy cluster of boulders that Kath's bracelet had lit upon a half-hour earlier. Chest-high weeds surrounded him. He tried to ignore their creepy texture and peered back up at the dock.

Yes, by God, there it was, the same pattern that had triggered his memory when he'd glanced at the drawing the day before. The four ribbed barrels, the faded roses, the wavy lines that were actually the cedar slats of the dock's undersurface, distorted by the rippling lakewater.

Scott aimed the camera and shot. In the bright-white pulse of the flash, the dock flickered detail.

From behind him a freak undercurrent bore in a cold channel, sweeping several weedy tentacles onto his back. A long filament encircled his waist like a loose-fitting belt, and Scott shuddered, partly because of the icy undercurrent, but mostly because of the ghastly feel of those weeds on his skin. He crouched, preparing to thrust upward for the surface. . . .

And that was when he slipped. His right foot skidded off the algae-scummed rock he was standing on, and the rock rolled back along the steep incline of the lakebed. It came to rest against the boulders behind it, pinning Scott's lower leg.

Galvanized by a lightning bolt of panic, Scott gaped down at his leg. A precious portion of air escaped in an unheard shout and rose boiling to the surface.

He gave his leg a solid tug. Pain torched up through his ankle, but his leg did not move. He tried rolling the big rock away, first with his free foot, then with his hands, but the push was uphill and the rock was too heavy.

Scott froze in disbelief. Weeds wound his chest, his arms, his legs. The cold undercurrent grew even colder. He tugged again, still holding on to some kind of control, still unable to accept the gravity of his predicament. He tried planting his opposite foot, twisting and pulling, but it was no use. His leg wouldn't budge.

Horror dawned like a sunless morning.

*Jesus, I'm really stuck!*

His hand released the camera, and it bobbed end-over-end to the surface. Around him, tendrils of weed swayed like doomdancers in the undercurrent ... touching, brushing, coiling.

Scott's eyes widened behind his diving mask. *Sonofabitch!* his mind shrieked in pointless anger. *I'm stuck! God! Why didn't I have someone standing by?*

Airhunger tapped like an impatient finger at his throat. He went down on one knee, searching for leverage, wrapping his leg in his hands and heaving until his muscles cramped with the effort.

But he could not free his leg. It was rooted.

The rocks had him firm.

He wrenched his leg again, until the sustained effort burned like brand-iron in his tendons. And this time, at the expense of twin strips of skin, he gained five or six inches, freeing his leg to mid-calf.

Relief swept over him—he would be out and away in one more tug ...

But his next pull gained him nothing. Again the rock shifted, seating itself more firmly against the low wall of boulders.

The need for air was fast becoming a physical thing, an irresistible force, and Scott knew that soon he would unstopper his throat and draw in lakewater; he would be powerless to prevent it.

Darkness pressed in, fogging the rims of his vision. In the midst of that darkness, a terrible image crystallized —the gnawed-off limb of an animal twitching in a trap—and Scott lurched again, as much to escape that image as to liberate himself from the lakebed. He leaned back against the boulders, wedging his heel against the rock and pushing . . . but the rock was too slippery and his foot skidded off, goring the pulp of his heel. He tried again, and again his foot slipped away.

He hung there motionless, transfixed, terrified into momentary inaction. More air squeezed out and bubbled wasted to the surface.

*This can't be happening!* his mind screamed in the green-black silence. *How can I be stuck in the lake no this is insane no NO! come on pull pull!! PULL!!*

An inner dam lifted then and rage flooded hotly in. Scott began a wild dancing struggle—flailing, pin-wheeling, digging his foot into the grasping lakebed, creating blinding mud-swirls around him. In answer to his struggle, asphyxia spawned furiously in his chest. Every muscle demanded that he open his mouth, his lungs, suck in air! He looked up dizzily to the surface, to the light, the air . . . so damned close! And he fought, spending himself and his precious reserve of oxygen.

But it was pointless. He was stuck. And the rotations of his body as he thrashed frantically about were entangling him in weeds like a fish in a net.

Another gulp of air escaped the tightening vise of his chest.

*Why doesn't somebody come? Bob! Krista! Please! PLEASE!!*

Scott Bowman thought about dying. He was twelve feet below his own dock, and he was going to drown.

There was a greenstick *snap!* inside his head then, and his mind went white with something pure and primitive, beyond the simple images of fear. The need for air would no longer be denied. It was everything now, the center of a fading universe, and Scott's body obeyed its bellowed command. Helpless, he opened his mouth and inhaled. Water found passageways it had never been meant to find.

Scott's eyes bulged as suffocation roared like a brush fire through his brain. His chest clamped down furiously in an effort to expel the water from his lungs. Distantly he heard the mechanical clatter of Anderson's outboard— or maybe it was the rattling bones of the Reaper, he no longer cared, was no longer capable of rational thought. Wholly desperate animal now, he lunged with a fierceness that flayed tendons from their bony tethers.

But his leg would not move.

His brain started to swell. Myriad bright-colored images capered crazily in. Water replaced air.

He was drowning.

Through darkening mists Scott saw the anchor, cutting the water like some macabre sea creature, all silver scales and spearheaded fins. Beyond understanding, edging on some oddly seductive and deadly euphoria, he watched its approach with idiot awe.

Then he saw the yellow nylon rope.

Bob Anderson's boat was passing directly overhead. And it was dragging its anchor.

Spurred by that most compelling of instincts, Scott fixed an eye on the rope and lunged. And when he had it, when it grew taut in his grip, he planted his free foot against the pinning rock and pushed, one last time.

Topside, Anderson gunned the outboard.

And Scott's leg came free.

# CHAPTER 6

Releasing the rope, Scott thrashed blindly upward, seeking the light and the healing air. He surfaced beneath the dock, rapping his skull on a barrel, and thrust his face into the meager foot of air space. His fingers poked up between the cedar slats and dug in like gaffing hooks. Hacking and sputtering, he opened his mouth and sucked greedily at the air . . . the exquisite air, the living air. The sound of his daughter's voice—high, hectic, shrieking his name in a pitch of terror—filled him with a strange kind of exultation. Hearing it meant he was alive. He hadn't expected to be.

Now Kath was on her knees, squinting down between the dock slats, grasping Scott's fingers. Then Krista was there, her voice escalating hysterically, echoing her daughter's terror.

"Scott, Jesus Almighty, are you all right? Oh, sonofabitch, you scared me! Can you get out of there! Oh, God . . . oh, *God!*"

51

Then Bob Anderson and Fred Mills were above him, and Scott could see them all, peering down at him through the cracks with fish-eye-lens faces. Lunatic laughter bubbled up in his throat and he coughed it out. He spluttered out mouthfuls of lake water, stared up with burning eyes between the dock slats . . . and he breathed.

The panicky gallop of female voices was interrupted by Anderson's booming command: "That's enough! He's okay. We got to get him out from under there, that's all."

"Oh, Scott . . . I thought you were . . . I . . ."

"Fred, take the missus up to the house—"

"No!" Krista protested, clutching Anderson's jacket sleeve. "I'm okay. I want to help."

Bob went down on one knee and gazed at Scott with his calm brown eyes. "Can you get your ass out from under there, Scotty?"

Scott hacked violently as he tried to answer, the sound like an animal's bray. "I don't . . . can't move . . ."

He was shivering helplessly, his muscles already seizing from the immense strain they had suffered. Agonizing cramps racked his arms, his legs, his belly. So tight was his grip on the dock, he felt as if the individual pads of his fingers had been nailed there. He didn't think he could let go.

And, of course, there was the fear. The fear was still there, the terror, fresh as a bleeding wound. Getting out from under the dock meant that first he would have to submerge into that dark envelope of water again—and right now, he simply could not do that.

"No . . ." he sputtered, still gasping for air. "Stay here awhile . . ."

Dressed in her Danskin leotards, Krista dove into the lake. She came up under the dock and swam in next to her husband. She placed a hand on his forearm; the muscles were iron-stiff.

"Come on, honey," she said shakily. "Let's get you out from under here." There was a series of four partially submerged joists that had to be passed to reach the dock's outer edge. "We'll go one section at a time."

Krista clasped his wrist and tugged, gently but firmly. She could see the fear in his eyes, a dull, winking shine, like headlights in a shrieking blizzard.

Reluctantly Scott let go.

"Deep breath, babe, then let's do it, okay?"

Gasping in air, Scott slowly nodded. Then, with Krista at his side, he submerged.

In a flash they were up on the opposite side of the joist, Scott lunging out so violently he struck his head again, this time on the edge of a metal joiner.

"Careful, sweetheart," Krista coached him. "Everything's gonna be fine. Three more to go, just three . . . oh, God, Scott, I thought you were . . ." Tears burned in her eyes. "Come on, babe, just three more."

And one by one, they did it.

At the outer edge of the dock, Scott slapped up an arm and grabbed on. Utterly spent, he rested his cheek against the rough surface of the wood. Krista remained in the water beside him, stroking his hair, whispering. Bob and Fred crouched on the dock in front of him.

"Okay, chum," Bob said soothingly. "Let her go and we'll pull you up out of there." He gripped Scott's wrist. "C'mon, Doc. Leave her go. You're okay now. C'mon."

Slowly Scott's fingers peeled away. Aided by Krista, the two old gentlemen lifted Scott's stiff and shivering two hundred pounds out of the lake.

Scott flopped like a dead fish onto the water-slick surface of the dock. Shallow wounds like racing stripes branded his leg, but there were no obvious signs of a fracture. Krista knelt next to him, kissing his face, fingering his tangled hair. Temporarily forgotten, Kath stood on the shoreline away from the dock, two fingers poked into the curled-down corner of her mouth. After a while Scott noticed her there, and felt his heart ache along with the rest of him.

Gradually that raw, mind-abrading panic abated, and he extended an open hand. Slowly, almost shyly, Kath came forward and took it.

They stayed that way awhile, Scott and his girls, Bob

and Fred standing silently by. Then they all helped him to his feet and up the hill to the rec room, where you could still catch the faintest whiff of artist's oils.

"I want to thank you guys," Scott said, his face open and terribly vulnerable. He was still breathing too fast. "You saved my life out there. You really did."

A half-hour had gone by. Bob had suggested they call an ambulance, but Scott had vetoed the idea, insisting between sputters and coughs that he would be fine, he just needed to rest. Krista had dressed his injured leg with snug-fitting gauze, and Fred had gone upstairs to brew some tea. Scott had tried sipping his (he had needed Krista to hold the cup for him; his trembling fingers had still been useless), but he had vomited immediately, dry, gut-ripping heaves.

Outside, the sky had darkened to the color of slate, and now the first spits of rain dappled the patio flagstones. In the gathering squall the birches and spruce stirred restlessly, as if trying to flee their roots. In the hazy distance, thunder grumbled like an empty belly.

Scott lay on the hideaway bed in the rec room, cocooned in a comforter that reeked of mothballs and cedar. Krista sat next to him on one side, Kath on the other. Kath looked pale beneath her summer tan, and her eyes were too bright. She was in shock, Scott realized, and even through his own discomfort he was deeply disturbed by it. Bob and Fred stood between the hideaway and the color TV, decked out like *Field & Stream* centerfolds. The two old gents looked uncomfortable there, oddly out of place. Fred shuffled in his gum boots. Bob chewed nervously on his pipe.

Now Bob removed the pipe from his mouth, and as he spoke, he tamped a thumb into its empty bowl. "Our part was luck, Scott." He pointed at Kath with the stem of his pipe. "It was your girlie there. She's the one that saved you."

Scott touched Kath's waist, and she jumped, startling

back from some gloomy place in her mind. She tried a smile but couldn't quite manage it. After a moment her eyes went glassy again.

Frightened by Scott's first dive, Kath had stood breathless vigil following his second, waiting for him to resurface. When the camera bobbed up in a rush of air bubbles, she realized something was wrong and began yelling for help. The fishermen had already docked-in over at Bob's, and were just climbing out of the boat. In response to Kath's screams, they hopped back aboard and gunned the motor full throttle, cutting across the short stretch of open water between Anderson's place and the Bowmans'.

"If she hadn't piped up when she did . . ." Bob said, letting his words trail off. He clapped his partner on the back. "It was old Fred here thought of draggin' that anchor."

Grinning sheepishly, Fred looked down at his boots. "Did you get stuck down there, Scotty?" he asked. "On the bottom?"

Scott nodded and the nod turned to a brief convulsion. Feeling it, Krista hugged him closer. Even Kath came back from that dark place in her mind long enough to stroke Scott's quivering arm.

Between still-labored breaths, Scott did his best to describe to his rescuers the horror of his last dive. Then he fell silent.

Bob placed a hand on Fred's shoulder, indicating Scott with a thrust of his chin. Scott was still shivering, but his eyes were trying hard to close. He was physically exhausted, a condition Bob Anderson understood only too well. He had experienced it himself more than once in his lifetime, after sixteen hours of farm work under a punishing, mid-July sun.

"Let's get along," he said to his friend, and Fred nodded grimly.

"Thanks again," Scott mumbled as the two old-timers let themselves out.

Then his head was on the pillow, heavier than he had ever known it, and a welcome darkness was falling. As the first spreading web of electricity shattered the vexed summer sky, Scott slid willingly into that darkness. He slept fitfully through the storm that raged through the balance of that morning, then well into the afternoon.

He awakened with a muffled shout, feeling the clutch of the lake at his throat. But it was only a pillow he had dragged across his face while he slept, its feathery weight triggering the hideous dream-illusion of drowning. Hearing his cry, Krista came stomping down the carpeted staircase, calling his name in alarm.

"I'm all right," Scott said, his voice thick and low. "Scared myself, is all." He rolled over onto his side, then tried shifting to a sitting position.

It wasn't until then that he realized how much damage had been done during his brief underwater struggle. Sometime during the inactive hours of his sleep, gravel-laced cement had been mysteriously deposited inside his joints and had hardened there. Muscles everywhere shrieked in an almost audible chorus of agony. When he leaned over to push himself up off the bed, his abdominal muscles bunched into an exquisite cramp. To relieve it, he had to have Krista draw his legs out straight. Finally, with Krista's help, he perched on the edge of the bed, where he began a grim personal inventory.

The stiff and tender muscles proved to be much the least of it. The pain had worked its way right into his bones. With the slightest movement came the feeling that jagged metal filings had been packed into each moving part. His spine was a jouster's lance, driven down through the top of his head and out through his tail. His leg throbbed beneath Krista's snug dressing. His hip was a stiff and tender swelling: with his last effort to free himself, Scott had torn the joint capsule and some of the surrounding muscle fibers, an injury he knew would engage him in annoying, damp-weather conversation for some time to come. As well, the circulation had not yet returned to his limbs; they were still cadaverous and cold. His fingers hurt. His toes hurt. His teeth hurt . . . even his scalp hurt.

He moaned.

Krista became mothering, and he let her.

"Oh, you poor thing," she cooed. "That must have been *horrible.*" She stroked his stubbled cheek. "I didn't know what to think when I heard Kath screaming like that. I thought she had hurt herself or something. Her friend Lita ran off like a scared rabbit." She hugged him closer and he winced. "Thank heaven you're all right. Do you want anything? Something to eat or drink? How's your tummy feel?"

Scott smiled, discovering that those muscles hurt, too. Krista was in a low-grade state of panic, and Scott imagined that if someone were to slam a door behind her just now, she really would leap out of her skin.

"My throat hurts from coughing, hon," he said weakly. "I don't think I could swallow much yet. I'd like to get upstairs, though."

Krista helped him to his feet. His head spun and the room wowed a little, but then everything was all right again. His feebleness as he negotiated the steps, leaning hard against Krista on one side and the banister on the other, made him think again of the Cartoonist, of that old and wizened body.

And that made him think of the Minolta.

At the top of the steps, where the hallway gave an angled view of the living room, Scott saw Kath sitting on her haunches in front of the "Bugs Bunny-Road Runner Hour." He saw, too, that her eyes were not on the screen but on her hands, which lay in a slowly writhing knot in her lap. Startled by her parents' approach, she snapped her head around, giving a wan smile as they shifted cautiously into the room.

Professionally, Scott recognized his daughter's behavior as a manifestation of severe emotional trauma. During the three or four minutes of Scott's battle against drowning, Kath had for the first time in her life experienced terror, that purest of all emotions; and like a junkie after a fix, she was still coming down from it. Though Kath's reaction worried him, he believed he knew how she was feeling. Terror had pushed him to the very rim of sanity down there at the bottom of the lake.

"I'll lie here on the couch awhile," he said. "I want to visit with my girl." Kath helped her mother lower Scott to the couch.

"Sure I can't get you anything, hon?" Krista offered again, once Scott was stretched out and covered.

"I'm okay," he said. "Really." Then, trying inexpertly to sound casual, he added: "Did anyone pick up the camera?"

"What camera?" Krista asked, shaking her head.

"I forgot," Kath murmured, looking both guilty and forlorn.

"What were you doing down there, anyway?" Krista said.

Not wanting to explain the real reason, which seemed pretty far-out in the face of what had happened, Scott fibbed. "Nothing, really. I just took a notion to try out the Minolta. There were some sunfish down there, in around the weeds. I was trying to get off a few shots. Would you mind having a look for it? The camera, I mean?"

"Okay, Professor Cousteau," Krista chided. "Anything to please." She kissed him lightly on the forehead. "I'm just so glad you're all right." Smiling broadly, she left him alone with their daughter.

Scott patted the edge of the couch with his hand. "Come sit over here," he said with affection. Kath obeyed, but in a dazed, automatic way. He drew her close and kissed her on the cheek. Her skin felt feverish against his lips.

"I'm okay now, sweetheart," he said, and Kath's mouth quivered as she bit back tears. "I really am. And

Bob was right, you know. I've got you to thank for it."
The quiver became the beginnings of a smile . . .
but a lone tear appeared, coursed quickly down her
cheek, and then fell. It landed on the back of Scott's
hand.

"Are you really okay, Daddy?" Kath said, more tears
brimming now.

"Okay as ever."

Kath hugged him then, suddenly, viciously, painfully,
and let the tears come in great sobbing rushes. Still
shivering, Scott did his best to console her.

Wearing one of Scott's windbreakers like a cape, Krista
trod barefoot down the hill to the lake, being careful not
to slip on the rain-beaded grass. The sky, which had
cleared enough to allow the sun to wink briefly through,
was lowering again, and the air was beginning to stir. As
she stepped onto the dock, Krista heard the chop and
chuckle of water under her feet, and drew the jacket more
snuggly around her. The morning's insanity had temporarily short-circuited her capacity for thought, and it
took her a few blank moments to recall why she had come
back down here in the first place.

*The camera.*

Questions bobbed up in her mind as she toured the
outer edge of the dock, looking down, watching for a
bright yellow flash. *Sunfish?* a voice kept repeating. *Why
would he go down there after sunfish?* But there were no
answers, only the dry electric hum of relief, and the
phantom weight of her terror.

She had almost given up when she spotted it, snagged
in the half-submerged boughs of a willow at the west-
ern edge of their property, bobbing like the questions
in her mind. She had to wade in past her knees to retrieve it, soaking her jeans but not caring. She scooped
it up and shoved it directly into a pocket, disturbed
by its flat yellow glare in the light of the coming
squall.

When she got back from the lake, Krista found her daughter and husband asleep on the couch. They stayed that way for another hour. By then the morning storm had come full circle, returning more heavily armed than before, and a thunderclap brought the two of them awake with identical, startled cries.

# CHAPTER 7

"Who are you calling?"

It was ten-thirty and they were in bed, Scott propped against the headboard, Krista angled toward the phone with the receiver in her hand. Kath was asleep in her room. Scott had taken some Valium before crawling into bed. The drug would do nothing for the pain, he knew, but he thought it might help him nod off . . . and for what ailed him, rest was the only cure.

"I'm calling Caroline," Krista said in answer to his question. "I tried her this afternoon, but there was no answer. I want to warn her that Kath and I won't be coming to Boston this weekend."

"Why not?" Scott asked . . . but he knew.

"You know why not. I can't leave you alone like this."

"Listen, Kris," Scott said with quiet authority. "Hang up the phone and talk to me for a minute, will you?" She did. "There's no reason for you not to go. I'm fine now. I'm going to ache for a few days, but that'll be all. I'll have Steve Franklin take a look at my hip on Monday—"

"You're not going in to work on Monday!" Krista cut in, nearly shouting. "Cripes, Bowman, I can't believe you! Here you are nearly drowned, and already you're thinking about work!" There was some real anger flaring now. "I thought if anything you'd take the week off, maybe even fly down to Boston on Tuesday if you were feeling better."

So that was it.

"I didn't say anything about work," Scott said patiently. "If I feel even half this rough on Monday, I won't be going in to work. All I said was that I'd like to have Steve take a look at my hip." Steve Franklin, a friend of Scott's, was an orthopedic surgeon. "I can't take the week off, hon. We've already been through this. There's just too much going on."

He pulled her close against only a cursory resistance. "Wait until tomorrow before you decide, okay? Call Caroline now if you must, but tell her you'll be getting in on schedule. You can still have a great time together. All right?" Krista allowed him a begrudging nod. "I'll have Gerry over if I need any help, but I'm sure I'll be fine. It's only sore muscles." He grinned. "Anyway, I'll be giving myself a nice Budweiser anesthetic all day tomorrow . . . no need to fret over me."

Uncharmed but at least resigned, Krista turned and made her call. Afterward, she fell asleep that way, with her back to Scott.

By midnight the Valium Scott had taken was finally hitting home. He wasn't asleep, but a dull sort of mental and physical numbness had crept over him; under the circumstances, he supposed that it passed for relaxation. Krista lay snoozing beside him, restless, probably dreaming. From the hallway leading to Kath's room came only silence. The house was asleep again.

Outside, like a river, ran a low and choppy wind, the

dying exhalations of the storm. In those erratic last breaths, the sheers belled and twisted before the open north window. Every once in a while the metal dock joiners moaned lonesomely, and from somewhere out on the lake a loon gave an answering cry.

But Scott heard none of these sounds. The waves . . . he heard only the waves. Rolling, breaking, brushing the barrels, caressing the shoreline like practiced fingertips, strumming, reaching up . . . The sound made him think of the weeds, of their swaying death dance, and he listened compulsively to the rhythm, to its hypnotic symmetry.

Gradually, lulled by it, he dropped into sleep.

At the bottom of his descent was a pool of black water, and he entered it feet-first . . . but it wasn't water, it was quicksand, a foul and sucking quagmire, and he was in it up to the waist, sinking fast. Around him spread a formless green gray, a mist so thick it might have been liquid.

From out of the silence came the padding of tiny feet—unhurried footfalls, rhythmic, relaxed. Scott cried out pleadingly in the liquid mist, but no sound issued from his throat, only a great and wasted rush of air that bubbled up into the gloom.

The footfalls became a face . . . ghostly pale, disembodied in the dimness, with crimson eyes and an elfin, somehow familiar grin. It drifted closer, seeming to diffuse through some muddy membrane . . . then it was Kath's face, grinning her most playful grin.

But her eyes were still red . . . red and dull and hate-filled.

He blinked and now Kath was whole, blue-eyed and perfect, dressed in her orange and white swimsuit. She stepped in closer to the bog, leaned provocatively over, and smiled.

"Hi, Daddy," she said in a voice that was not her own. "You're going to die in there."

From the fingers of one hand dangled the yellow

Minolta. Smiling, Kath lifted the camera to her eye. The flash exploded light. Far, far above, the undersurface of the dock flickered detail.

"Help me, pet," Scott pleaded, pinpoints of light pulsing on his retinas. "For God's sake, *help me!*"

Kath only grinned and leaned out farther over the bog, offering the camera. "Here, Daddy," she murmured. "Now you take my picture."

Scott spat quicksand from his mouth. He could feel the stuff gritting between his teeth, and knew that soon it would cover him completely. . . .

But he took the camera and brought it up to his eye.

And as the flash cut the dimness he saw through the viewfinder that it wasn't Kath he was shooting, but someone else—some*thing* else, something with bloodless white skin, silver white hair . . . and those baleful red eyes, like the eyes of a road animal caught in the dazzling deathglare of headlights.

The quicksand sent cool tendrils up his nose. He dropped the camera and it bobbed away, into the green gray stuff overhead. Barely able to breathe, he lifted his chin from the ooze. It was seeping into his ears. . . .

Kath's face was disembodied again, and now it was blurring toward him through the gloom, distorting, coming apart, spattering blood . . .

But it couldn't get to him. No. Because now the quicksand was covering his eyes.

And he was drowning in it, drowning in it, drowning . . .

Scott's scream brought Krista awake with a frightened cry of her own. When she opened her eyes, she found him tangled in the sheets, struggling to his knees in bed.

"Scott!" she cried, grabbing the rigid column of his arm. "Scott! What is it?"

Wheezing like an engine, Scott opened his eyes and saw the billowing curtains, the familiar shapes of the bedroom furniture, Krista . . . then he slumped against the headboard in a sweat. Krista drew him down, kissed him, lay with her chest against his back, comforting, murmuring over the wind.

Before sleeping again, this time dreamlessly, Scott asked her to close the window. She did this without question. As she returned to bed, Scott noticed the sheers behind her, hanging dead against the wall.

It was better with the window closed. He couldn't hear the waves.

He slept.

And later, when dawn spilled bleach into the heavens and Krista hurried out to Kath's bedroom, to comfort the child in the wake of her own nightmares, Scott didn't notice she had gone.

# CHAPTER 8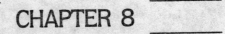

After getting Kath settled again, Krista returned to bed. She drowsed fitfully for another hour, then got up. In spite of her poor night of sleep, she could remain in bed no longer.

She stood naked in the gray morning light, looking down at her husband for what seemed like a long time. He lay on his side with his knees drawn up, one arm wrapped loosely around his pillow. His respirations were deep, and the corners of his mouth twitched like the muzzle of a skittish horse. Krista noticed his eyes darting crazily beneath their lids, and wondered what he was dreaming.

It dawned on her then, with the brute force of a hammerblow, that she might have awakened to an empty bed this morning . . . and every morning for the rest of her life. Another minute, maybe two, down there at the bottom of the lake, and they would have been dragging for her husband's body instead of wrenching it to the surface to gasp and grapple and live.

At this thought Krista shuddered, her skin bristling at every follicle. She grabbed her housecoat and pulled it on. . . .

And suddenly she wanted to waken him. Suddenly his stillness disturbed her to a degree that was as irrational as it was blackly terrifying. She recognized this irrationality immediately—but still, the urge to waken him, to hold him and to hear his voice, was almost overpowering.

She glanced at the bedside digital as she stooped forward to rouse him, hesitated, then decided to let him sleep. It was still only a quarter of six.

As if sensing Krista's unease from the dreamscape of his slumber, Scott moaned and then shifted onto his back, dragging his pillow along with him. Still shaky but somehow relieved, Krista turned and left him to his healing sleep.

She was unsurprised when she found Kath's comforter folded back and her bed empty. Stepping into the room, she touched the hollow where Kath's body had been and found it cool. Concerned, she hurried downstairs and ran a systematic search of the house.

But there were no signs of Kath anywhere. She hadn't even had her ritual bowl of Cocoa Puffs. More than a little frightened now, Krista stepped out onto the deck, her eyes cutting through the fine morning mist to the lake.

There, alone on the dock like some winsome figure in an oil painting, sat Kath.

Wrapping herself in her housecoat, Krista walked barefoot through the dew toward her musing daughter. She sat beside Kath on the dock . . . the Bowman harem, as Scott liked to call them. Kath's feet were dangling in the water, and she was watching a trio of loons.

"Neat the way they dive, eh, Mom?" she said as the loons submerged in silent sequence. Her voice was lifeless and flat.

Disturbed by her daughter's tone, Krista went momentarily blank. She simply could not think of how to answer. "Uh-huh," she said finally. "They sure can hold their breath. Let's see how long they—"

"What happened to Daddy yesterday, Mom?"

Krista turned to face her only child, who looked so small and vulnerable in the sketchy light of dawn.

"It was like he said in the rec room yesterday, hon," she began softly. "Your daddy got stuck in the rocks down there, and then couldn't get unstuck."

A deep cleft furrowed Kath's brow between her tired eyes. She kicked with one brown foot at the water, as if to punish it.

Then she looked squarely at her mom, fixing Krista's gaze as only a child's eyes can. Her next question seemed to quiver on her lips, a question she had been prodding and poking at since late the morning before.

"Could he have drowned, Mommy? Really drowned?"

There was only one answer to this question, and it was one Krista hated to give. For a cowardly moment she considered lying, telling Kath that her dad would have gotten out just fine on his own after another minute or two . . . but she choked off the idea as quickly as it raised its deceiving head. There was no room here for a lie. Later, it would not be forgiven.

The answer was a simple affirmative, a single syllable that cut the legs out from under every child's inbred belief that their parents go on forever, that their mommies and daddies are invulnerable.

"Yes, honey," she said gravely. "Your daddy could have drowned."

Kath fell silent then, her eyes resuming the same glassy blankness they'd acquired in the rec room the morning before. After a moment she stood.

"I want to go see if Daddy's okay," she said softly.

Krista took her hand. "Not now, sweety. He's sleeping. Let him sleep. He's all right. You can see him later."

Kath hesitated, looking up at the house and her parents' curtained window. Then she sat again. She kicked at the water, thoughtful. After a while she went in for a swim.

At about nine-thirty on that sunny Sunday morning, Scott cranked himself up into a sitting position on the side of the bed. His first thought was that he had never been so stiff . . . even yesterday had not been this bad. And now his head was in on it, too. He felt as if he'd just put the wraps on a giant, week-long booze fest.

*The Valium,* he thought as he rose unsteadily to his feet. The Valium had done its job. Wobbling like a wino, he took an uncertain step forward and had to prop a balancing hand on the night table. He waited for his head to clear, then shuffled carefully into the bathroom. More than anything he wanted a shower, but when he thought of standing there for the ten or so minutes it would take, he opted instead for a bath. Lounging in a tub of hot water would do more for his tender muscles anyway.

While he was sitting on the toilet and peeing forever, Krista raced in and drew up his bath. Just as abruptly she vanished again, only to promptly return with a tray of French toast and a pot of hot coffee. She helped him into the water, which was just this side of scalding, then rested the tray on the edge of the tub.

"Sore?" she asked, twining her fingers in his chest hair.

Scott nodded between gobbles of toast—suddenly he was voracious. "Understatement," he said after clearing the pipes with a mouthful of coffee.

Krista began kneeding the muscles of his right calf. In appreciation, Scott's eyelids drooped to half-mast. He finished his breakfast quickly and then stretched out, allowing the water to work its way up to his chin.

"You sure gave me a scare last night, mister," Krista said, donning an oversized sponge-glove and starting on the muscles of his thigh.

He regarded her quizzically. "What do you mean?"

"Don't tell me you don't remember! The nightmare you had? You sat up in bed—stood more like—then you asked me to close the window."

Scott shook his head. The last thing he remembered was Krista calling Caroline in Boston, and even that seemed curiously fragmented. *The Valium*, he thought again, searching his memory, trying to pick up an image of the events following the phone call.

"Can't recall," he said.

"I find that hard to believe," Krista said, temporarily suspending the massage. "I mean, you were right up on your knees, and you looked straight at me when you asked me to close the window."

Scott explained to her that one of the properties of Valium, particularly when used in conditions of stress, was the production of amnesia. He told her that this was the main reason the drug was so popular as an adjunct in anesthesia. Krista nodded with patient uninterest.

Then Scott asked her about her plans regarding Boston.

"I still don't know," she admitted, looking down at her folded knees. "I'd feel terrible if anything happened to you here all alone. You could fall, or . . . or . . ."

"Or what?" Scott said, not really expecting an answer. "Look, I'll make you a deal. If you go, you can take the Volvo."

Krista's face lit up like a child's on Christmas morning. Just as quickly, it clouded over again. "Are you trying to get rid of me, Scott Bowman? Are you having an affair or something?"

For a heartbeat Scott thought she was serious, and he was just getting ready to tell her how ridiculous a question that had been when Krista giggled and splashed him.

"Do you mean it?" she said, smiling sunnily.

"Would I kid about the Volvo? Anyway, I don't like the idea of you going all that way in the Chevette, new or not. If you ever got hit in that damned thing . . ." He leaned over and kissed her, dripping bathwater onto her slacks. "Okay? I want you to go."

This was a lie. He wasn't in the least looking forward to

being alone in the house; it would be his first time since they moved in. It wasn't that he was afraid or anything like that . . . it was just that he hated being alone. It was his personal neurosis.

He continued his sales pitch. "It'll do you both good. I'll call Gerry if I need anything, and Anderson's is only five minutes away. I feel a lot better today, anyway."

Krista arched a doubting brow.

"Deal?" Scott said gamely.

"Deal," Krista echoed after a considering pause. "I'll do it."

It was noon and they were standing by the idling Volvo, Scott in his bathrobe, Krista in shorts and a yellow tank top. The car was loaded (with, Scott was thinking in amused wonder, enough clothing and God knew what else to last his gals until sometime into the next century), and the day was clear and hot, ideally suited for a drive in an air-conditioned sports car.

"And don't forget," Scott said as Krista leaned into the back seat to secure the Coleman cooler. "When you stop for gas—"

"Use only unleaded high-test," Krista put in, finishing his sentence with noticeable exasperation. This was the third time he had gone through his twenty-point car-care instruction plan. When it came to the Volvo, Scott was the original "old woman."

"I'll take care of your baby," she said, returning his embarrassed grin. "Okay?"

Scott slapped her fanny. He was feeling much better now. The bath had loosened him up nicely, and afterward, he had taken a stroll along the private, tree-lined Cottage Road. The combination of hot water and gentle exercise had banished a lot of the stiffness. Now he felt only as if he had overdone it in a game of touch football or somesuch the day before. That was bad enough, but he felt nothing like the rusted hulk he had when he'd crawled out of bed this morning.

71

"Where's Kath?" he asked.

Krista's smile evaporated, her brow furrowing with the same deep line that Kath got when concerned.

"Down at the dock," she said hollowly. "She's still acting a little . . . funny. You know. I think your accident has affected her pretty deeply. I'll go call her—"

"No," Scott said gently. "Let me."

He found her sitting on the dock with her legs drawn up and her chin propped thoughtfully on her knees. She was wearing a cute tan outfit with short pants and short sleeves. And she was crying.

Scott felt something shift uncomfortably in his chest. He sat beside her, cradled her in his arms, and rocked her.

"What is it, Patch?" he whispered.

Kath looked up at him with wet eyes. She smiled weakly, then sputtered out a tears-and-spit giggle. She hadn't been called Patch since she was five.

"Do you remember why I used to call you that?"

She nodded. "'Cause I was always tearing my clothes and Mom was always patchin' 'em?"

"That's right." He hugged her. "So, what's up, Doc?"

After a moment of mute deliberation, as if fearing the question somehow inappropriate, Kath said: "Are you gonna be okay, Daddy? While we're away?"

"Of course, sweetheart!" Scott responded with assurance. "I'm fine now. It's all over, hon."

Kath grinned through renewed tears. "Promise you won't go swimming till I get back?"

Kath's caring words conjured something cold in Scott Bowman, deep inside, and the pause that followed was unintentional. He had meant to immediately reassure his daughter, to allay her childish fears. But suddenly the gentle sway of the dock was tilting his equilibrium, causing his stomach to flutter uncomfortably. When he looked out over the water, he thought he saw movement out there, just below the sun-dappled surface—

something dark, bulky, amorphous—and terror flared like a wooden match.

But it was only a stray rain cloud rafting slowly overhead, its dark face reflected in the mirror of the lake.

"No way, kiddo," he said finally. "No swimming for your old man. Not till his little lifeguard gets back." *Or maybe never again,* he thought morbidly. "Now. Let's get you up the hill. Mom's waiting . . . and I think she's gonna let you drive this trip."

A smile tugged at the corners of Kath's mouth. "I love you, Bud," she said, cuffing the tears from her cheeks.

"Me too you," Scott said.

He stepped off the dock and felt immediately better. Smiling, he took his daughter's hand, and together they made their way up the path, Scott limping, Kath doing her best to assist him.

"Are you sure you don't mind me taking the car?" Krista asked again, a vague guilt coloring her excitement —she loved the Volvo.

"Not at all," Scott fibbed, casting a glance into the shadows of the garage, at the dusty two-tone Chevette that would be his until Krista's return. "You'll call from your sister's?"

"That's the plan, man," Krista answered, rolling her eyes resignedly. Her older sister, Klara, lived with her husband on the north bank of the Saint Lawrence. From Klara's place it was only a ten-minute drive to the Canada-U.S. Customs crossing at Prescott. Stated mildly, the relationship between Krista and her only full sibling was strained. It would be a duty visit at best. Krista smiled wearily. "I hope she's not in one of her drinking moods."

"Does she have any others?" Scott said, a little ungenerously. He leaned on the sill and traded kisses with Krista, then stumped around to the opposite window and kissed his daughter. "Have fun, you two," he said, returning to Krista's side of the car. "And call me."

"I will," Krista promised.

Then, waving, she swung the car into the drive and motored up the hill. In less than a minute they had vanished from sight, only a gray-white dust plume visible over the crowns of the trees.

# CHAPTER 9

When the rumble of the engine had diminished to an insectile hum, Scott cut back through the house to the deck and lowered himself into a lawn chair. There were things he could do inside, but he didn't feel up to roaming the emptiness of the house just yet.

He missed his girls already.

Around him unfolded the perfect summer day, and he tried to think about that . . . hot, hazy, hypnotically tranquil, not even a power boat or a passing aircraft to mar the perfect quiet. The only sounds belonged to nature. The burring of a lone cicada, the lazy chuckle of songbirds, a faint whicker of breeze through the pines. Only the lake remained coolly silent, keeping its secrets hidden beneath its quicksilver surface.

As he knew they would, though, Scott's thoughts returned to the bottom of the lake. Thinking back on it now, he realized that his mind had begun to encapsulate the experience, and to bury it. When he tried to visualize the finer details of what had happened, the way he could readily picture Krista doing her aerobics or Kath charging up the lane to greet him, he found he was unable. The memory of his underwater struggle had already taken on the transparent consistency of a dream. As a psychiatrist, Scott recognized this phenomenon as a kind of built-in safety valve for the psyche. Any input the mind judged insupportable, it simply chucked back out, denied—or, in this case, softened to the point of unreality. Of course he hadn't forgotten that desperate sensation of suffocation, nor the brilliant, mind-bending terror that had seized him when he thought he was about to die. But the jagged-glass edges had been smoothed; the freshness of the experience had been dulled. It might have happened years ago, or he might only have dreamed it.

This clever mental safeguard made him think of Delia Horner's letter and the black, years-old memory it had unearthed. Operating here was another faculty of the mind, one that was anything but protective, one that Scott believed malign and powerful enough to dissolve the brain into so much functionless jelly. This faculty was instantaneous recall, the capacity of the mind to dredge up, abruptly and in hideously accurate detail, all the horrors it had so painstakingly buried. Reading Delia's letter the night before, Scott had reexperienced that long-ago summer's morning as if it were just then happening. Those few drawn-out seconds had flashed before his eyes in such crisp and staggering detail that for an instant he had feared his mind might suddenly snap, leaving him cold, vegetative, and empty.

He leaned back in his chair and let his mind work through it all again. He couldn't have stopped it had he tried.

After all these years—sixteen of them—the shame was the worst. The shame seemed immortal. And even as he sat there alone on the deck—muscles tensing, palms sweating, his mind bludgeoning downward through meticulously stacked layers of denial, transporting him back to the cramped Volkswagen and that dark, twisting roadway—the shame was on him like a disease, a wet, weeping, bubonic disease that he could almost smell.

*You ran,* a nearly forgotten voice reviled him. *You ran!*

The truth of those two words seared through him like a high-voltage backsurge. It had still been dark, and quiet . . . that ephemeral, almost mystical interlude between nighttime and day. Scott had been kneeling over the dead child, his mind skidding dangerously close to an inner precipice he hadn't realized existed, when he looked up into Jake's eyes and knew what his friend was thinking. There had been nothing supernatural about the insight, no ESP or mental telepathy. It had simply been a thought shared simultaneously by all three.

*We've got to run!*

They were lost, full of booze, miles off their home turf, Laking's bag of grass had spilled all over the back seat of the car when Scott slammed on the brakes . . . and the kid was dead; nothing could be done about that.

And inside of a breath they had known, without so much as a word passing between them, that to stay, to admit their guilt, would mean their utter ruin.

So they piled into the Beetle and ran, switching from road to road with a randomness born of shock and heart-clutching fear. They were running and it didn't matter where they were going as long as they were stacking up miles, widening the distance between themselves and the horror of that early morning, a horror lodged forever in the stuff of their memories.

In the lawn chair on the deck of his Gatineau Hills home, Scott Bowman shifted position, bracing himself like a man in a plane that was about to crash. His eyes were on the lake, but they were hazed and unseeing. He had never believed in God, not in the accepted sense— but he could feel the Eyes of Judgment on him now, as he had all those years ago.

Later that morning it had rained, a sudden, cleansing

downpour that had scrubbed away the bloody evidence from the car. The full tank of gas they had put in outside of Boston carried them all the way into Springfield, Vermont, where they stopped at a self-serve carwash and vacuumed up Jake's spilled marijuana. Afterward, they pooled their resources and bought a new windshield for the car. As fortune had it, the autoglass shop in Springfield had a matching windscreen in stock, and no other business but theirs. They were back on the road inside of an hour, sticking carefully to the speed limit, not a word passing between them.

It wasn't until some four hours later, when they crossed the border into Ontario (the Customs official, after mouthing the usual queries, had waved them through without even a hint of suspicion), that the sustained, fear-born energy started to wane, and the unspeakable ugliness of what had happened began to seep through. A mile or two north of the border, Scott pulled the car onto the shoulder, buried his face in his hands, and wept. Brian Horner, who had been mute since the accident, joined him, letting out wave after wave of shuddering sobs. Fidgeting nervously in the back, Jake stared out through the new windshield, wishing the three of them had never met.

They stayed there awhile, each entangled in his own breed of misery, then resumed the drive home, not even bothering to agree on a story to explain their return almost a month ahead of schedule. Scott's flesh still ran cold when he thought of the last words Jake had spoken to him. They had been parked in front of Jake's parents' house in Ottawa South, and a light rain had been falling.

"If you lose your nerve, Bowman," Jake had said without emotion, "if you lose your nerve and spill your guts about this thing . . . I'll kill you, man. I'll kill you dead. I mean that." Then he had gone.

Scott hadn't lost his nerve, no. . . . But he had nearly lost his mind. For the first two weeks sleep had been impossible. Each time he closed his eyes, there she was—slamming into the hood, shattering the windshield, lying in a spreading halo of her own blood. He became morose, lost his drive, his appetite, until finally he fell ill and had to be admitted to the hospital. At first they thought he had mononucleosis or an ulcer, then it was a brain tumor, and finally, cancer. When nothing could be found to support these diagnoses, psychiatry was called in. And Scott almost told the tall, soft-spoken man who became his shrink, and later one of his most respected teachers. He almost told it all.

But finally he kept it inside, where it festered and flared and visited his dreams.

Life seemed to come slowly apart during that first long year. Because of his hospitalization, he was late starting med school, a fact that nearly cost him his position. He withdrew from his parents and friends—Jake was at Harvard, Brian in Winnipeg—and immersed himself in his studies. Yet even with that his marks were only borderline, and more than once he was ostracized by his professors.

But gradually the sheer volume of the work began to act on him like a balm, and, aided perhaps by the rapid passage of those first four academic years, the memory of that tragic summer morning began to sink mercifully into the mud of his unconscious. But the experience changed him. Gone was the cocky, self-assured young man who come hell or high water was going to become an obstetrician. Gone was the bright-eyed boy who believed that life held nothing but good in store. How could he enter a specialty like obstetrics, become a bringer of life, when before he'd even started he had *taken* one, brutally and heedlessly? How could the future hold anything but guilt and shame?

The shame . . . the unutterable shame. The shame had outlived the horror, even the guilt. It had been there long after the nightmares had faded.

But then he met Krista, and even the shame began to subside. For a while after their marriage the dreams reared up again . . . but by then Scott had changed even more. Krista's love had changed him. And their child. By then, too, he had chosen his specialty. And as he studied it, as it helped him probe more deeply inside of himself, the old wounds finally started to heal.

Gradually, it was all buried. Not forgotten, but buried.

That night, before engaging in a hard-won battle with insomnia, Scott called Vince Bateman at his home. He told the department head about his near-drowning, and informed him that he would be taking Monday off. He promised, however, to show up for the department's annual business meeting Monday night, and for that Bateman was grateful. It was Scott's turn as chairman.

Krista called around eight-thirty to tell him they were fine, that Klara was in her usual drunk and disapproving form, and that Klara's husband, Joe, was, as always, henpecked and muttering. Avoiding mention of his hip, which throbbed something awful and caused him to limp like a cripple, Scott spent a long while reassuring Krista that he felt much better, just a little stiff was all. Then Kath came on the line, and Scott was relieved to find her sounding more like her usual self: cheerful, dauntless, excited about the trip. She said she loved him and gave him a sloppy kiss over the line, and Scott's heart ached a little when she hung up the phone. A part of him wished he could just chuck the whole week and sneak off to Boston to join them.

At some point during the course of that night, aided perhaps by the painkiller he had taken before lying down, Scott won the battle with sleep and dropped off into a dreamless slumber. Late the next morning, after a relaxing hot shower, he consumed a huge, artery-clogging breakfast, then got dressed. Before leaving the house, he removed the film cartridge from the Minolta and pocketed it. He did this almost without thinking. His heart sagged when he got to the garage and found Krista's

Chevette waiting for him. He'd forgotten she had taken the Volvo.

On his way to the city, in an effort to bury the Chevette's rattling road noise, Scott cranked the radio up to near full. Outside, the day was drab and overcast, and it looked as if it might stay that way forever.

# CHAPTER 10

The prints would be ready inside of an hour, the attendant at the photo booth told him, and if he wanted while he waited, Scott could find coffee and doughnuts at the nearby Dunkin' Donuts.

He wanted. The coffee went down like warm, sweet medicine.

A dark excitement stirred within him as he waited for the film to be developed. In the immediate aftermath of his near-drowning, he had all but forgotten the old artist and the oddball drawing that had twigged something deep in his memory. He hadn't altered his entirely reasonable expectation that it would all amount to nothing. But still . . .

He finished his coffee and left the doughnut shop. The prints were just starting down the narrow conveyor as he returned to the photo booth. He could see them through the clear Plexiglas sidewalls.

The first few made him smile. They were Christmas

pictures, their first in the new house. Leading the file was a shot of Kath on her haunches in front of the bauble-and tinsel-hung tree, smiling and showing off the best of the season's booty. Then came one of him and Krista, Kath's finger poking unprofessionally into the frame. Krista was embracing him, her eyes happy-wet, her new (and expensive) diamond earrings glinting lavishly in the glare of the flash. Here was another of Kath, modeling a new blue ski jacket over cotton Alf-print pj's. And there were others, good memories all.

Then, algae-green and underexposed, the shot he had taken under the dock came slowly down the conveyor.

Scott took a ragged breath. It was a crummy shot, but it would do. He could compare it to the drawing.

The last two prints came down blank.

His curiosity trebling with each passing minute, Scott paid the attendant and left promptly for the hospital.

He went directly to the old man's room, but found no sign of him there. The bed was neatly made up and his wheelchair was missing. He checked the lounge next and, finding it vacant, went to the nearby nursing station.

"Excuse me," he said to the nurse in charge. "Where's the patient in 209C?"

"The Cartoonist?" the nurse said, chuckling. "Out with his pals doing the Sunshine Bus tour. Mandatory crock airing, once a week whether they realize it or not." She folded beefy arms across an ample bosom. "Why, have you got students today?"

"No," Scott answered distractedly. "It's not important . . . thanks. I'll see him later."

Disappointed, he went to a phone to put in a page for Steve Franklin, the orthopedic surgeon . . . but as he lifted the receiver, an idea interrupted him. He replaced the handset and hurried back to the old man's room.

After a quick search he found the handbag portfolio tucked out of sight in the old man's closet. There was only one other patient and his two visitors in the room, and they paid Scott little heed as he fished carefully through the portfolio.

When Scott found what he was looking for, the blood drained from his face. The single drawing he had seen on Friday was now just the first of an incredible series of drawings covering two full pages. His hands shook like a drunk's as he studied them.

There could no longer be any doubt that the drawing represented his dock—he could see that plainly, without the need for comparison with the photo. The first sketch was as it had been before—the ribbed barrels, the white-rose decals, the distorted cedar slats—except that now the rippled reflection of a diver hung suspended over the water. In the second frame, which covered the middle third of the page, the cartoon diver dropped feet-first toward bottom. In the third, surrounded by head-high weeds, and with great rushes of air boiling out of his mouth, the figure gaped in horror at his rock-ensnared leg. . . .

Sweat beaded Scott's forehead as he flutter-flipped to the next page. The diver looked nothing like him; of course not, it was only a cartoon . . . but the circumstances were unmistakable.

The next frame showed the swimmer hopelessly entangled in weeds, doll eyes flipped back to reveal the whites, mouth a water-clogged clarion of terror. Above him loomed the hull and wake of a boat. In the foreground hung a rope and shiny anchor. In the background, leering up from a great and cloudy depth, were two red-stained, demon eyes. Poking up from between the rocks, a veined, reptilian claw clutched the diver's ankle.

The last frame, the one Scott viewed through a darkening tunnel, was a close-up of one groping, weed-entwined hand, reaching out for that rope . . .

And missing it.

"Mister?" a voice behind him said. "You all right?"

Scott tasted bile in his throat. Someone pressed a hand into the damp hollow of his back.

"Hey, fella, you'd better sit over here. You look sorta pasty."

Hands guiding him to the edge of the old man's bed.

"Betty," another voice murmured. "Go find a nurse."

Scott followed passively, his eyes still glued to that last frame.

Bateman sat hunched in his office chair, the drawings arranged on the desk in front of him, his quick hazel eyes moving with interest from frame to frame. Scott, feeling better now, sat on the opposite side of Bateman's imposing teak desk. He had come close to fainting back there in the old man's room.

In his office, surrounded by neatness and knowledge, Bateman was in his element. His desk, flanked on all sides by literal walls of textbooks and publications, supported a blotter, an extension lamp, and an empty in-out tray. The balance of its vast polished surface was vacant. A small chalkboard, spotless and black, stood like a henchman beside it. From behind that desk, Bateman presided over his department like a baron with a shiny new guillotine.

As much as Scott disliked Bateman's professional snobbery, his overbearing manner and his neatness neurosis, he had to concede the man's brilliance. A cum laude Harvard prodigy, Bateman was peerless in his knowledge of clinical psychiatry—in this respect he was a veritable phenomenon. In addition, Bateman had a special interest in the paranormal: in things, events, and individuals unusual. It was an avocation he had cleverly wangled into his research budget—and it was one of the main reasons his colleagues considered him somewhat of an oddity. On a shelf above his head, two books on the subject fronted a series of ten or twelve other leather-bound texts of Bateman's authorship. Scott had already related to the department head the incident in the lake, and how he had made the connection between himself and the Cartoonist's initial drawing.

"This is a real find!" Bateman said with genuine, almost boyish enthusiasm. "With your corroboration, Scott, this makes a nearly irrefutable case for precognition." He stroked thoughtfully at his reed-thin mustache.

Scott pushed another few sheets across the broad expanse of the desk. Bateman took these and spread them out on the blotter, his manicured fingers automatically adjusting their edges, lining them up perfectly as he studied them.

"Unless I'm mistaken," Scott said, indicating the first of the new series of sketches, "this represents the Air Canada jet that crashed at Uplands a few weeks ago. If you recall, the plane exploded at the end of the runway during takeoff."

"Yes," Bateman agreed. "Hell of a mess. More than three hundred dead. These are amazing!"

"And this one," Scott went on, pointing shakily to another sheet. "This is that restaurant on Sussex Drive . . . remember? The terrorist bombing last month?"

"Tremendous!" Bateman acknowledged with an exaggerated nod. "All along this old guy has been trying to tell us something."

"It sure looks that way," Scott agreed, frankly awed. "Here we've been assuming he'd heard about these things on his radio, *then* drawn the pictures. Pretty incredible to think that he's actually been foreseeing them. Jesus. I wish I'd known about this before I went swimming."

Scott paused thoughtfully. Like Krista, he was a realist. He'd always been skeptical of things like clairvoyance, ESP, telekinesis, and that whole mumbo-jumbo grab bag. But this . . . this was too fantastic to ignore. He recalled once again his Friday afternoon encounter with the artist, how he had seemed to speed up when the nurse arrived to tell Scott that Krista was waiting on the line. The old guy had actually been trying to warn him against diving in the lake.

Scott pointed to the second-last frame of the series

relating to his accident, to those sinister red eyes peering up from the depths, to that clutching reptilian claw.

"What about this?" he said. "Why do you think he's suggesting the existence of some aquatic monster in the lake?"

"My guess is that it relates to what you theorized earlier about this man. He probably *was* a professional artist at one time, and I'd bet dimes-to-doughnuts that he drew for a horror comic or magazine." Bateman's fingers stroked his mustache. "Assuming this to be true, then the suggestion that some monstrous force resides in your lake is merely an embellishment, comic-book icing left over from his career. The simple message that he's trying to relate—hey, Doc, you're going to drown down there —is dressed up in the man's inbred sense of dime-novel drama. You have only to look past the lurid gilding of the horror comic, however, to find that simple message."

Scott nodded. Given the old man's "wild talent," it seemed a sound interpretation. "Have you ever come across anything like this before?"

"The literature abounds," the older psychiatrist answered, indicating with a grand gesture the bookshelf behind him. "Countless claims and unproven examples of everything from precognition to phenomena as weird and wonderful as telepathetic mind control and pyrokinesis. But personally, no, I have never had the good fortune of witnessing something like this first-hand.

"In view of his apparent psychic ability," Bateman went on professorially, "the fact that your man is clinically senile makes this all the more interesting. Back in the seventies, the French did an experiment in which, based on a number selected randomly by a computer, they sacrificed rats, one each day, observing the survivors for signs of aberrant behavior. What they were able to demonstrate with statistically significant reproducibility was that small groups of the rats, five or six at a time, *did* develop erratic behavior—and, more often than not, the rat whose turn was up next was a member of that group.

"As well, also in the seventies, a team of Russian researchers studied rabbits whose offspring were sacrificed at a preappointed time and at some distance from the parent. Here, too, they were able to demonstrate some low-grade psychic perception, as many of the animals became noticeably agitated at or near the time their offspring were to be slain.

"My point is this: the human being, who seems to have the greatest difficulty getting in touch with that especially perceptive part of his mind, has this skeptical chunk of neocortex stuck right up here"—he tapped his forehead with a slender finger—"which refuses to buy into the messages it receives from its baser animal levels. But this cartoonist, with his shrunken, disconnected cortex . . . chances are he's functioning at roughly the same level as those French rats and Russian rabbits." Bateman grinned sagely.

His eyes still on the drawings, Scott nodded his agreement. But he wasn't interested in explanations. He had the evidence, and that was enough.

"What should we do with him?" Scott asked in awe.

"Study him!" Bateman spouted as if addressing a moron. "Isolate him! First thing tomorrow I'll arrange for a private room and assign a nurse to keep him under close observation." He grinned, and something flickered in his eyes that Scott didn't like. "We may have our own little fortune-teller here," Bateman said, his thin lips curling into a humorless grin. "And wouldn't *that* be something. If he bears out, he'll make an excellent case presentation for the annual parapsychology meeting in New Orleans this fall. Thanks for letting me in on this one, Scott. I owe you." He stood.

"Forget it," Scott said absently. "It just really struck me . . . these damned drawings." He hesitated, glancing again at those menacing red eyes. This was the only one of the artist's drawings in which Scott had seen color. He picked up the page and handed it back to Bateman. "What do you make of the pigment he used for the eyes?"

Bateman held the sheet up to the cone of his extension lamp, then scratched at the flaky red pigment with a thumbnail. Handing the sheet back, he shrugged.

"It looks like blood," he said. Then he answered his phone before the first ring was complete.

# CHAPTER 11

"Can you do it?"

The lab technician scratched his bearded chin. "I don't know, Dr. Bowman, it's an awfully small sample."

After leaving Bateman's office, Scott had gone directly to the hematology lab in the hospital's subbasement. Bateman's suggestion that the pigment might be blood had sent a chill trickling through him. He wanted to verify it now in case the old man was into some form of pathological self-mutilation, although there was no physical evidence to suggest that he was.

"Can't you dissolve it into solution or something?" Scott pressed. "It's important."

"I can try," the technician offered, scraping the pigment into a shallow glass dish. "But it'll take some time. Where can you be reached?"

"Have me paged," Scott said. "I'll be around the hospital most of the afternoon."

He went next to his office, where he informed his

secretary that he was technically unavailable, and locked himself inside. There, he sat with his feet on a chair and studied the drawings.

When he had first seen the sketches in the old man's room, it had been like living the experience all over again. Closing his eyes, he had actually been able to feel the weeds licking at his skin, the water clutching at his throat. It had taken several shocked seconds for the only remotely acceptable conclusion that existed to sift into his mind, the same conclusion he had reached on the morning of his mishap under the dock—that this was all just some bizarre and elaborate coincidence. His mind had lunged naturally for this safe old standby, an explanation still not unattractive, simply because of its sanity.

But what a huge and improbable coincidence it would have to be! The only major discrepancy between the drawings and reality—apart from the aquatic monster, of course—was the cartoon hand missing the rope.

Had the old man been incorrect on this point? Scott wondered now, believing in him despite his mind's desire to reject the whole crazy deal. Or had Scott somehow beaten his own fate?

He shook his head. He was wading into a sea of questions that defied logic. He released the drawings, allowing them to drift to the surface of his desk; and as he so often did during quiet moments in his office, he turned to look at the family photo on the bookcase behind him.

But the photo wasn't there.

Scott pushed to his feet too quickly, straining the muscles around his injured hip. After a moment's quiet cursing, he scanned the office for the photo. Then he buzzed his secretary.

Claire's voice drifted pleasantly out of the intercom. "Yes, Dr. Bowman?"

"Claire," Scott said, his irritation immediately obvious to his secretary of four years. "There's a photograph missing from in here, the one of my family. Is anything missing on your side?"

91

"Not that I'm aware of, Doctor, but I'll have a closer look."

"If you wouldn't mind. And Claire, find out who's been cleaning up in here. Maybe they just broke it and got scared. That picture was my favorite, and there's no negative around to make a new print."

"Will do," Claire said and clicked off.

Puzzled, Scott sat again, his hand moving unconsciously to his hip. In the recent past, the hospital had had some trouble with petty thefts: money lifted out of unattended purses, articles of clothing snatched from open racks. The pilfering had continued until two members of the cleaning staff were caught with some of the missing items in their lockers. What Scott couldn't understand was why anyone would want a photograph—although, he reminded himself, the brass frame was an expensive antique.

But why would nothing else be missing?

Giving them a final, incredulous glance, Scott slipped the drawings into a top drawer.

Then he made his call to Steve Franklin.

# CHAPTER 12

Later that afternoon, while Scott was dictating the last of a pile of past-due discharge summaries, his secretary buzzed him from the outer office.

"There's a call for you, Doctor. Hematology."

Before picking it up, Scott paused a moment, adjusting his legs into a more comfortable position. Earlier, Steve Franklin had X-rayed and examined his hip. He told Scott that he had done some structural damage to the joint capsule, nothing serious, but, as Scott had already judged for himself, he could expect it to grumble on and off for years—and possibly for the rest of his life. Steve gave him a prescription for an anti-inflammatory, which Scott filled at the hospital pharmacy, and a few potent analgesics. Afterward, Scott returned to his office and began clearing away some of the dry, uninteresting stuff he rarely got a chance to tackle during the course of a normal week, stuff he usually ended up doing on his own time.

Now, as he picked up the receiver and said hello, he fished out the drawings and spread them open on the desk in front of him. The underwater eyes were white and vacant where the technician had scraped away the coloring.

"Hi, Dr. Bowman. It's Mike from Hematology. It's blood all right."

"Human?"

"Human," the technician confirmed. "A-negative."

"Thanks," Scott said. "I appreciate it."

His heart loped uneasily as he hung up the phone. The old man's blood type was O-negative; he had checked it on his chart before meeting with Steve Franklin.

*If it isn't his own blood, then where did he get it?*

Scott touched the still-bandaged tip of his right index finger . . . and then he knew.

He groped in his hip pocket and dug out his wallet. Opening it, he fished clumsily through the plastic sleeves, letting the collection of cards contained there drop one by one to the desktop—medical license, CMPA membership, VISA, American Express—until he found the one he was looking for. A powder-blue card, slightly dog-eared. The Red Cross had given it to him the one time he had donated blood. On it were his name, address, and blood type: A-negative.

It was weird—almost too weird—but after a while Scott thought he had it figured out. He had done some reading on the paranormal (with the amused interest of the skeptic, granted, but he knew a few of the ground rules), and had seen a couple of the better-made motion pictures with talents like clairvoyance as their themes. Characteristically, some sort of physical contact had to be made between the psychic and his subject, often something as simple as the touching of hands. If this was true, then surely blood would work the same way. Evidently, after he had cut his finger on a sheet of the old man's paper, the artist had retrieved some of the blood—which had served as the physical connection between them—and had used it to stain the eyes in the sketch. The blood explained why the old man had tuned into Scott that day, and not one of the students.

Sitting at his desk, trying to reason this stuff through, it occurred to Scott with something like shock that he had become an instant believer in precognition. All of his thoughts regarding the old man were meaningless now without this phenomenon as a given. In the wake of this realization, he found himself quietly reexamining everything he had previously cherished as truth. Indeed, he began to question his entire concept of reality. If precognition was possible—and he was firmly convinced that it was—then what other wonders (and horrors) existed out there, just beyond the range of normal human perception? How many dozens of the other things he had laughed off during his life might actually be for real? The whole thing made him feel odd, offtrack somehow, as if he had stumbled off the globe and landed on a new planet, one identical to Earth in every detail . . . yet deeply and fundamentally different.

Scott felt a thick clot of panic massing in his throat. Some decrepit old crone using his blood to peer into his future—that was bad enough. But why the perverse use of the blood as a part of the drawing? That was the bit that crawled under his skin and festered there.

Over it all, though, one question continued to burn. Was he just a mindless old crone? Could he be as far gone as he appeared and still tap into whatever psychic stream he panned his visions from? Wasn't it entirely possible that if someone were to give it an honest try, perhaps using hypnotic suggestion, that the old man could be reached? As far as Scott knew, no one had yet made such an effort. It was a lamentable truth in medicine's dealings with those labeled as senile: the label was readily handed out—and once it was, no one paid its victims much further heed.

Suddenly darkly excited, Scott pocketed the drawings and hobbled out from behind his desk. He was going to try to get through to the weird old artist who could see where no man was meant to see. He was going to give it his best shot.

And if he succeeded . . . then by God, did he have some questions to ask.

He was alone in the ill-lit hospital room, strapped to his wheelchair by the curtained window, dressed as before in an undershirt and pale blue pajama bottoms, an old man's uniform that seemed to swallow him whole. His eyes were aimed at the radiator, the clipboard balanced on the slope of his folded knees.

And he was drawing. Scott could hear the pencil from the hallway.

*scratch,scratch . . . scratch,scratch,scratch . . .*

Scott took a step through the doorway—then stopped short. It hadn't been a conscious thing; he hadn't willed his body to stop. It just had. He remained there, framed in the doorway, allowing reign to whatever instinct or reflex had prevented his entering the room. His senses had keened, he realized. He could feel the adrenaline racing through him, making the blood bound in his neck and his breath steeply quicken.

Oddly, Scott's basic physiology came to mind. He was having a rather profound sympathetic reaction here, something the layman referred to as a "fight or flight" response. It was an automatic reaction to danger, or to fear, one that was common to all higher forms of life. And it was urging him to fight . . . or to flee.

But why? Where was the danger?

Lightheaded, Scott leaned against the doorframe, the nausea of unspent adrenaline having its way with him. He looked again at the elderly man in the wheelchair, sizing him up, weighing him in a rational light.

*O rationality,* he thought, feeling a suddenly lunatic surge, *that most deluding of all human faculties. He's a ninety-eight-pound weakling. You could snap his neck as easily as you could snap that pencil. . . .*

Now the pencil moved faster—as it had the last time Scott was nearby—the sound a harsh, erratic whisper against the page. Spurred by that sound, Scott took another step forward, then almost bolted into the room, his eyes scanning the page on the clipboard as he reached the wheelchair and leaned over it.

But it was nothing, just two or three macabre-looking graveyard scenes . . . weird but meaningless.

Scott's body went slack with relief. Sighing, he pulled up a chair and sat between the old man and the radiator, trying to intrude on the artist's sightline. Unmindful, the Cartoonist continued to draw, his radio droning raspily beside him.

"Hello," Scott said softly, endeavoring to keep his voice to a lulling monotone—but the hot, spitless flavor of fear was in his mouth, and it was gluing his words. "Can you hear me?"

In the dim evening light the old man's gaze shifted almost imperceptibly, and Scott shuddered. Again he found himself sizing the man up, as he might an adversary with whom a physical confrontation seemed inevitable.

Physically the old man was harmless. His precognition was an uncanny ability, but at best it was only a tenuous window onto the future, uncommon but not unknown. Uncontrollable, unmalicious.

*Then why this mindless fear? Why do I feel I'd be safer scaling the north face of the Eiger without a rope?*

Scott tried again.

"I want you to stop drawing and speak to me," he said as evenly as he was able. "I want you to talk to me. I know you can do it. Yes, I do. Won't you stop drawing for a moment and talk to me? I mean you no harm. You can trust me."

Scott spoke on in that same gently probing monotone, searching in the spare light of dusk for some sign of perception in that ancient face: a flicker of eyelashes, a betraying twitch at the corner of the mouth, some subtle admission of understanding.

*Or deception,* Scott thought, and the possibility jarred him. His mind cast back to the night of his birthday, to the dinner table at home and how he had been searching the faces of his girls in exactly this way . . . but for signs of deception, not understanding.

*Could he be malingering?* Scott wondered now. It was an attractive, if inexplicable possibility, one he could not too casually dismiss.

"There's nothing to be afraid of," he continued softly, although he sensed no fear in this eldritch little man— none at all. "I'm here to help you. We are all professionals here: doctors, nurses . . . to help you. But we need your cooperation. We need you to talk to us, to let us in."

Scott stopped then, sliding his chair back to the rad with a *thunk*. Twin blond girls of about fourteen had just appeared in the doorway, giggling and helping a bowlegged old gent with a walker into the room. One of them called the man Gramps. The other flicked on the light over his bedstead, and the thin yellow glow reached the Cartoonist's face.

In the improved light Scott looked again at the artist, who sat drawing and drooling, and wondered how he could ever have imagined him malingering. He supposed he'd gotten himself spooked, sitting here alone with him in the near dark. Looking at him now, he thought it might be easier to coax one of Kath's goldfish into talking.

The twins turned their backs on Scott to help their grandfather into bed. On an impulse Scott seized the steadily scratching pencil, hoping to catch the artist unawares, perhaps startle him into speaking—but the Cartoonist held on, and with surprising strength, his bandy fingers closing like a steel trap. Uncertain why, Scott persisted, tugging harder.

The old man's eyes, typically so aimless and empty, fixed Scott with sudden fury. His lips folded back and a dull lowing sound issued from deep in his chest, a savage animal sound that pitched steadily upward, until it became a menacing snarl in his throat.

As if releasing a hot ember, Scott's fingers sprang apart. He tried to swallow but couldn't. Now there was an odor about the old man, an acrid reek that sheared through the perpetual fecal and ammoniacal rancidness of the chronic ward. It was a smell Scott had encountered before, but only on brawling tomcats—wild, foul, primeval.

Scott rose to his feet, staggering slightly. The twins, flanking their grandfather, looked on with alarm and wonder. A nurse who had been passing by in the hall stood dumbstruck in the doorway.

The old man was gazing at that invisible point again, between his clipboard and the radiator. And he was drawing, as if Scott were not there. As if he had never been there.

"Hello, it's Dr. Bowman. Let me have Dr. Bateman, would you, please?"

He was calling the psychiatry conference room from the nursing station down the hall. The seven o'clock meeting was due to begin in ten minutes.

Bateman came on the line and said hello.

"Vince, it's Scott. Listen, something's come up. I'm not going to be able to make the meeting."

"What?" Bateman cried, his voice rising to a piqued, childish timbre. "Oh, come on, Scott! You're *chairing* the damned thing. Don't leave me hanging—"

Scott felt a small pang of guilt—as department head, Bateman would be expected to take over the chairmanship of the meeting—but he felt compelled to keep trying with the Cartoonist. The tug-of-war he'd had with the old man had made a stunning impression on him. He had been incredibly strong. Not so long ago Scott could bench-press more than two hundred pounds, yet he had not been able to pry the pencil from that knotted fist.

And that face, that twisted, hissing snarl.

*Those eyes . . .*

"Sorry, Vince. Sandra Dunphy from Admin will be doing most of the talking anyway. All I'd planned to do was review the minutes and then turn the meeting over to her."

Pause. Heavy sigh. "I hate being unprepared, Bowman. *Hate* it!"

The line went dead.

Still a little dazed, Scott returned to the old man's room. The twins were just leaving, and they regarded him warily as he passed them in the hallway.

The old spook was asleep in his wheelchair, the clipboard wedged between his skinny thighs. The pencil, which only minutes before he had fought for like a petulant child, leaned free in one slack hand. His eyes, deep-socketed in sleep, were only half-closed, the exposed crescents gleaming like pewter in the twilight. His breathing was a quiet, shifting wheeze. On the opposite side of the room Gramps lay motionless in his bed, snoring contentedly. The other two beds were vacant.

Scott walked into the room, undergoing no more gut-reaction this time than could be ascribed to simple curiosity. Watching the old man's face, he reached for the pencil, half-expecting that thin, cadaverous hand to clamp tightly around it again . . . but the artist didn't budge.

Scott took the pencil and examined it with a certain awe. But it was only a pencil—HB, with an eraser on one end and *Castell* inscribed in blue script along one hexagonal edge. He reached next for the clipboard—and this time the old man twitched, but that was all. He picked it up and took a hasty step back.

The artist had tucked his most recent illustrations beneath a sheath of blank pages. Scott removed these, then replaced the clipboard and pencil where he'd found them. He took the drawings into the hallway, where he began a careful inspection of each frame. At first, in the stuttering glare of the overhead fluorescents, the sketches seemed connected to nothing real . . .

Until the last few frames. Then, as it had at the bottom of the lake, the hand of terror rose from its bath of ice and gripped Scott's heart.

\* \* \*

The entire sequence was set at night.

The first frame was an overview of a tree-studded graveyard. The second showed a distinctive-looking tombstone, two truncated tiers supporting a pyramidal shaft crested by a crucifix. The crucifix was damaged, missing an arm and a small wedge of headpiece. The inscription, indecipherable save for three or four legible letters, appeared on the lower of the two marble tiers. In the foreground, hideous in the moonlight, a rotted, shaggy hand poked up like a claw through the cartoon earth. In the third frame, a decaying, cyclopic corpse shouldered its way up from the confines of the grave. It was a classic horror-comic scene, yet so chillingly rendered that for a moment Scott imagined he could almost smell the black earth and moldering decay.

In the next frame Scott was presented with the following: the tombstone leaning in the foreground; the corpse, shambling toward a low flagstone fence and the roadway beyond; a gnarled, leafless tree on a hilltop, silhouetted against an oversized moon; and at the extreme left of the frame, some distance away on the winding roadway, the twinkling eyes of a car.

The fifth illustration showed the corpse in the middle of the moonlit roadway, arms extended like Frankenstein's monster; and the car, just cresting the rise before the cemetery, only the haloglow of its headlights visible. In the following frame, the point of view was from the back seat. Shown were the backs of two heads—the driver's, a woman with curly hair; and a passenger's, a child, probably female. The driver had one arm angled across her face. Just beyond the windshield, stark in the glare of the high beams, the corpse stood weaving in the instant before impact.

The next and most dramatic scene was portrayed from just beside the driver, the angle of view including the passenger seat and the inner aspect of the windshield. In it the zombie burst through the safety glass, its jaw ripped partially away, its single dead eye dangling against a worm-ridden cheek. The child, now unmistakably a girl, cried out in perfect terror, her mouth torn open in a silent scream, her face just inches from the dead thing that came through the windshield in a blizzard of glittering shards.

The last frame, the one that tore into Scott like a spray of jagged shrapnel, showed the car in the foreground, crumpled nose-first against the flagstone fence; and the corpse, one arm unhinged and dangling at an impossible angle, dragging itself back into the depths of the boneyard. The interior of the car was pitch, neither of its occupants visible. Steam hissed almost audibly from beneath the hood.

The car was a Volvo.

*Jesus, no, not them! Please, not my girls!?*

Scott reached out and found the wall as Bateman's words came reverberating back to him: *You have only to look past the gilding of the horror comic to find that simple message. . . .*

"Wake up! Wake *up*, damn you!"

He was back in the artist's room, prodding him, shaking him, trying desperately to waken him. But the old man remained slack and unresponsive. Were it not for that scarcely audible wheeze of breath, Scott would have thought him dead.

"Come on!" he pleaded, his voice escalating from a controlled whisper to a hysterical shout. "Open your eyes!"

He shook the man harder, deliberately digging stiff fingers into his bony shoulders in an effort to rouse him with the pain. But the Cartoonist's head only lolled round and round, as if his neck had been broken.

"Talk to me!" Scott bellowed. "What does this shit mean? Is this my wife? My daughter? What is going to *happen?*"

A nurse raced into the room, her complexion flushed with surprise. "Dr. Bowman!" she shouted. "What are you *doing?*"

Scott ignored her, shaking the old man so hard now that his remaining teeth clacked brittlely together.

The nurse grabbed Scott's arm. "Dr. *Bowman!*" She wasn't shouting now. She was screaming.

Scott released the mute artist and staggered back— and it dawned on him then, in a wave of lightheadedness, that he might have killed the old man.

Behind him, Gramps moaned like a gutshot wolf. The nurse withdrew her hand from Scott's arm, and the two of them stood there in stricken silence, staring down at the Cartoonist. His bald, peeling head hung limply forward. Drool strung like a rope from the corner of his mouth, creating a dark spot where it pooled on the leg of his pajama bottoms.

The drawings balled in his fist, Scott turned and fled the room. He could still hear Grampa's lonesome moan as he pushed his way through the exit doors, heading for his office on the second floor.

# CHAPTER 13

The phone was on its sixth ring when Krista's sister Klara picked it up.

"Klara, it's Scott."

"Hi, Sco—"

"Listen, have Krista and Kath left yet?" He knew they had, but prayed that for some unforeseen reason they hadn't. The digital timepiece on his desk read 7:12 P.M.

"Yes, early this morning. Your wife was in her usual snarky mood, too. Little Miss Know-it-all . . . is anything wrong? You sound pretty strung out."

"I . . . I'm sorry, Klara, I can't talk now."

He thumbed the cut-off button and dialed Caroline's number in Boston. Caroline answered on the first ring.

"Scott? Hi!"

"Are they there yet?" Scott said, blurting the words. "Krista and Kath?"

"No," Caroline replied, responding to the urgency in Scott's voice. "Not yet . . . what's—?"

*"Damn!"* Scott breathed.

"Scott, what's wrong? Is everything okay?"

Scott remained silent for a moment, breathing rapidly, struggling to get a grip on himself. He couldn't tell Caroline about all of this—not yet, anyway. There was no sense in alarming her further. The whole thing might be totally unrelated to his girls. He might simply be overreacting. His wasn't the only Volvo in the country, not by a long shot. . . .

But he was spooked. The old man's drawings had become hard to ignore. After those underwater scenes, the cartoon Volvo struck yards too close to be dismissed as coincidence. The trouble was, there was no way of knowing without getting through to the Cartoonist . . . and so far that had proved impossible.

"I'm sorry," he said finally. "Yes, everything's fine. I'm just a bit edgy, is all. I wanted to talk to Krista. We had a spat before she left," he lied. "Just wanted to apologize."

"Are you worried about them out on the highway?"

"Yes . . . a little." This, too, was a lie. He was petrified.

"Well, don't be. Krista's a good driver. They probably spent the afternoon haunting all those New England antique shops. Busting your billfold. Anyway, it's too early to expect them even if they'd driven right through. I'm sure they'll be here soon enough."

"Yeah, you're probably right." Caroline's words sounded soothing and good, and he wanted to believe them . . . but he couldn't. "Thanks," he said quietly. "Have her call me as soon as she gets in, will you? I'll be at home."

"I will," Caroline said, sighing heavily. "And how are *you?* The way I hear it, you gave your gals quite a scare the other morning."

"Myself, too," Scott said distractedly. "I'm all right now, though . . . Good-bye, Caroline." Knowing it was rude but beyond caring, he hung up.

His gaze jerked back to the drawings; to the woman and child in the car, and the exaggerated mask of horror that was the little girl's face; to the rotting ghoul bursting through the windshield; to the crippled car and its secretive interior. He thought of the icy channel at the bottom of the lake, and the weeds entangling him like the cerements of Atlantis. . . .

Then he grabbed the telephone and dialed information in Massachusetts. The operator was male, his voice clipped and nasal.

"Information. For what city, please?"

"Boston. The police department."

"Emergency?"

"Yes."

A brief electrical hum. Then a recorded voice, this one female, recited the number, repeating it as Scott broke the connection.

He had the digits partially dialed when he jammed his thumb on the cut-off button and thought: *What in hell do I tell these guys?*

He felt suddenly giddy.

*Excuse me, Officer, but I'm a shrink up here in Canada, and I have it on good authority that my wife and daughter are in mortal danger. What authority? Well, actually, a thousand-year-old cartoonist drew these pictures, see, and, well . . . trust me, okay? They're driving a midnight-black Turbo Volvo—nice car, you'll like it (please find it), and they're somewhere in New England.*

Scott took a deep breath and tried to think rationally. Whatever he told the police, it had to sound convincing. It had to be something urgent enough to *make* them look for the car. He could tell them the car was stolen . . . but then how would he know where the thieves were headed? He could say that the woman driving it was a psychotic who had escaped from the hospital, abducted a child, and was headed off to murder a rich aunt in Boston. . . .

God, it was so hard to think! The crystal image of crumpled bodies and twisted metal was overloading the circuits, precluding all rational thought.

He flipped the drawings face down, closed his eyes, and leaned back in his chair. Then he thumped forward again, reaching once more for the phone.

"Gerry," he said aloud in the after-hours quiet of his office.

He dialed the number for the Ottawa Police Department. It rang twice.

"Ottawa police. Sergeant Gennings."

"This is Doctor Bowman," Scott said, his voice breaking. "Can you tell me if Gerry St. Georges is working tonight?"

"One moment, please."

Hope flooded him. Gerry was a friend, a good friend. If there was any way to engage the assistance of the police in the States, Gerry would know about it—and he wouldn't ask too many questions. At this point Scott didn't feel up to explaining his reasons to anyone, not even Gerry.

Gerry's voice was big and booming. "St. Georges."

"Gerry, it's Scott."

"Scott, you old bag-biter! Where've you been? I—"

"Gerry, listen. I need your help."

As Caroline had done earlier, Gerry responded to the edge in Scott's voice. "Sure, man. What's up?"

"Krista and Kath are in New England someplace, in the Volvo. It's urgent that I get in touch with them. I think they're in danger, Gerry . . . serious danger. I'm not sure exactly where they are, but they're headed for Boston, so by now they should be in Maine at the very least. Is there any way you can get the police down there to find the car and detain them?"

"*Wow!* That's a tall order, chum. What sort of danger are they in?"

"Please, Gerry. Don't ask. Just trust me, okay?"

After a pause Gerry said: "All right . . . all right, I'll see what I can do. I know a few of the lads down there. Still, I'll have to come up with something pretty outrageous. Any ideas which route they might follow?"

"I've been down there with Krista only once this year. We took Route three-oh-two over to Interstate ninety-five and followed that into Boston."

"Well, if she sticks to the major routes, it should be easy enough to find her. She a creature of habit?"

"No," Scott replied without hesitation.

"Call you at home?" Gerry said.

"Yes . . . I'm heading there now." There was nothing else he could do.

# CHAPTER 14

The Chevette hitched and sputtered along the final stretch of road before the house. Scott had driven it hard, burying the tachometer needle into the red with every shift, and now the temperature indicator glowed an angry crimson.

Before leaving the hospital, he had gone by the old man's room again; but the artist had still been asleep—a sleep that was more like unconsciousness—in his wheelchair by the window. As Scott left the ward, the nurses regarded him as they might a walking contagion, and Scott guessed they had already heard about his encounter with the old man. News traveled fast through the hospital grapevine.

He ground the car to a halt in front of the house and jumped out, slamming the door behind him. His leg complained at the strenuous activity, but Scott barely noticed. He started directly inside . . . but before the mocking eyes of the house he hesitated, feeling suddenly

109

cold and unmanned. Without his family in it, the house was simply a collection of bricks and boards, a cold and creaking tenement haunted with echoes . . . and suddenly, he couldn't bear the thought of going in there alone.

He paused on the path, tucked his hands into his armpits, and looked up at the turbulent sky. The clouds were alive up there, sailing in great warring fleets on a squalling ocean of wind. The moon was nearly full, and it seemed to be floundering against the tide. The breeze against Scott's face was damp with the promise of rain . . . and although he couldn't see it from where he stood, the lake was alive, too. He could hear it down there, deep and black and creeping . . .

Shivering, Scott hurried inside.

But in the dark of the foyer he hesitated again, trying to shrug off the alien feeling the house was giving him. The hallway ahead, now a low, tenebrous tunnel, opened onto the hunched and fuzzy shadows of the living room, which in the dark seemed to have been subtly rearranged, and Scott got the abrupt, frightening feeling that he was not alone.

He noticed it then, a small black shape, darker than its surroundings, leaning against the near wall, and it was all he could do to stop himself from bolting back out the door. He groped for the light switch and snapped it up, flooding the foyer in the 100-watt glare of the bulb—

And the shape against the wall became Jinnie, Kath's Cabbage Patch doll. Scott laughed, a little hysterically. To him Kath's doll—with its stubby hands and wattled moon face—looked like a deformed Lilliputian in the death throes of radiation poisoning. What attracted people to these dolls escaped him . . . yet for the past several years they'd been selling like hotcakes. Kath loved hers, pretended it was her own little child, even took it to bed with her. Scott guessed she'd leaned it here on Sunday morning and then forgotten it, though he couldn't remember having seen it here before now. He wondered if Kath was missing it.

He picked up the doll and tucked it under his arm.

Then, room by room, he roamed the entire house, turning on every light he could find. Tonight, the dark unsettled him.

Finally, Kath's doll in his lap, he sat in a chair by the Mickey Mouse phone in the rec room and started to wait, glancing every now and again through the sliding screen doors and out across the moon-spilled surface of the lake.

# CHAPTER 15

Kath had nodded off. That surprised Krista, because normally before Kath would even consider closing her eyes, she needed Jinnie tucked under her arm. Smiling, Krista glanced at her daughter's drowsing profile. The signs of Kath's growing up were coming fast and furious now, forgetting her doll at home being much the least of them. She was sprouting *breasts* for God's sake, and complaining of cramps that reminded Krista of her own early blossoming. She, at least, had been twelve before the action had started . . . but ten!

Krista's mood—which had gone from broody and smoldering at her sister's the night before to a fierce and flaming red earlier this afternoon when she realized they were lost somewhere in the timber trails of the White Mountains—seemed finally on the mend. She had promised herself this trip that she would not allow Klara to get her goat . . . but the promise proved a shabby one.

Klara, like their mother, disapproved of everything; it

was one big, overspreading blanket. And one of her pet peeves was Scott, whom she lustily tongue-lashed at every available opportunity. Though Krista recognized her sister's rantings as mostly alcohol-induced, Klara's cruel and unfounded attacks inevitably placed her on the defensive. Sunday night Krista had been trying to relate the details of Scott's near-catastrophe—mostly as a means of venting some of the pent-up tension the experience had generated—but Klara had cut in almost immediately with her caustic tongue.

"You mean to tell me your shrink husband went diving with a *hang*over? Jesus, what an irresponsible *shit* you married. What are you and your kid supposed to do while he's collecting barnacles at the bottom of the lake?" Klara had glared at Joe with dark, threatening eyes. "If *my* husband ever pulled a fool stunt like that, I'd kill him."

Krista, feeling tense, angry, and sorry for her invertebrate brother-in-law all at once, had begged off early and gone to bed. She tossed restlessly all night, and in the morning rose an hour ahead of the rooster—before Klara got a chance to start in on her again. She whispered her good-byes to Joe, left a note for her snoring sister, and whisked Kath away while the child was still eating her toast. The neatness of her escape and the promise of the clear blue sky gave her hope for the balance of their journey.

But, like a slowly brewing storm, things progressed inevitably from bad to worse. The Customs official at the border crossing was in a hassling mood, and he spent a good half-hour hunched over the Volvo's open trunk, rummaging through every scrap of luggage he could find and leaving it in wild disarray. Ten minutes into Vermont a cop nailed her for speeding, then dragged her back six miles to a small-town station to pay the fine. She ran out of gas outside of Montpelier, got the finger from an irate hitchhiker, and was dive-bombed by a homicidal sea gull on the patio fronting the McDonald's in Barre.

But the crunch, the real masterstroke of disaster, came just outside of Lincoln, New Hampshire.

"I guess we shoulda turned right instead of left back there, eh, Mom," Kath said. A statement, rife with undertones of "I told you so."

And Kath, who had been studying the AAA map, *had* told her so. But Krista had gone left. No real reason. It had just felt . . . right, more flowing somehow. It struck her later as rather odd personal behavior. She wasn't by nature impulsive, especially when she had someplace to get to. Sure, she'd noticed the abrupt change in the texture of the blacktop—it had become all sort of cracked and gray looking, making her think of the sunbaked mud flats she had played in as a child on her Uncle Albert's potato farm—and the narrower lanes. But the surroundings had been homey, the meticulous farms and cultivated fields reminding her of Newfoundland, the province of her birth.

But fifteen or twenty miles into it the asphalt had abruptly ended. Just like that. An edge of concrete, with society on one side and a dinosaur path on the other. After the first half-hour of dirt road, Kath had suggested a hasty retreat. But again Krista kept on, and for two reasons. First, the road had forked more than a dozen times and not once had there been a road sign—and *that* meant their chances of getting back to a town were pretty slim. And second, it just wasn't in her nature to go back. Never had been. Sometimes that was a good trait . . . and sometimes it wasn't.

Soon they were twenty-odd miles into no place—somewhere, Krista thought, to the south of Mount Hancock, a 4,430-foot mountain reduced to a microscopic triangle on the map—crawling along at fifteen miles per hour on a pocked and runneled goatpath through a cloistering tunnel of trees. Trees were everywhere: joining leafy hands overhead, filing away to infinity on either side, and in places threatening to block off the road entirely. Here and there bars of late afternoon sunlight broke through, but the overall mood was one of gloom.

They were lost.

As always, Kath was unruffled. Like her father, she saw the sunny side of almost any situation. She nudged a cassette into the deck and "Thriller" intruded on the silence. On the video screen in her head, Michael Jackson strutted prettily past a fog-wound graveyard, while Vincent Price prophesied doom in that famous basso profundo. Kath, a Jackson fan for life, began to break dance from the knees down.

They drove on, never exceeding twenty, in spots grinding to a near halt. Krista didn't mind the loud music—it dulled the metallic spangs and clunks from the Volvo's undercarriage.

The road was bad.

Alert for wildlife, Kath's gaze darted randomly from side to side. She had already spotted a few rabbits and one wobbly-legged fawn.

"Neat, huh, Mom?" she yelled over the music.

Krista nodded, thinking: *Yeah, real neat. Lost, tired, and knocking the shit out of your father's car. A lotta laughs, kid.*

After another five miles (and twenty minutes) Kath spotted a man in a sunlit clearing by the roadside. He was loading fresh-cut logs onto a wagon attached to a small red tractor. Resting on one fender, a chainsaw glinted sunlight.

Kath pointed. "Mom! Look! There's a guy in the trees over there!"

Krista, who felt as if she'd just stumbled onto the planet's last surviving human, stopped the car with a jerk. Straightening, the man in the clearing wiped his hands on the legs of his coveralls and turned toward the road. Krista bailed out and moved stiffly to the opposite side of the car. The paint job was gray with road dust.

"Excuse me," she called into the bush, waving her hands over her head. Returning her wave, the fellow began plodding toward her through the underbrush.

Krista felt suddenly intimidated by his enormous size.

"Yes, ma'am," he said almost deferentially, climbing

sure-footedly up the embankment. His grin was wholesome and friendly, and he was younger than Krista had originally estimated—up close he looked no more than eighteen or twenty. "What can I do for ya?" He pulled a blue bandanna out of his hip pocket, scrubbed his forehead with it, then tucked it away again. "Lost?"

"Yep," Krista said. "Took a wrong turn back near Lincoln."

The man's grin broadened knowingly. "Happens a lot. Where're ya headed?"

"Well, Boston eventually, but just now I'd be happy to get back to the main road." She glanced over her shoulder at the cow trail they'd been traveling. "*Any* road for that matter."

"Heck, that's easy enough." He angled his body into a half-turn and pointed, sighting along his extended arm like a gunbarrel. "Just keep goin' the way you're goin', 'cept stay right at the forks. That'll put you back on the pavement in nothing flat." Grinning, he took a half-step closer. "You folks from Canada?"

"Yes," Krista answered, edging back toward the driver's side of the car. "We are that."

She felt better with the solid width of the hood between them. He was grinning now at Kath, who was still bebopping in her seat behind the closed window. The guy seemed friendly enough . . . but he smelled bad, and he was a full head taller than Scott's six-one. And there was something wrong with his eyes. They shifted too much, and one of them was turned out, as if he were peering off sneakily behind you. Krista's imagination had a way of getting off on her. She had seen *The Texas Chainsaw Massacre.* There would be no struggling away from this guy if he took it into his head to drag them into the woods, aerobics or no aerobics.

"Thanks for your help," she said, sliding deftly into her seat. "And have a nice day." It was an expression she secretly loathed . . . it just seemed appropriate for the occasion.

He dug out the bandanna and gave his forehead

another swipe. "You too, ma'am. And remember, keep right at the forks."

As she motored away, Krista watched him in the rearview mirror. He stood for a moment, looking after them. Then, tucking the bandanna away, he trailed back into the woods.

The safari into the tree-choked reaches of the White Mountains wound up costing them three hours. To make up time they skipped their supper stop, nibbling instead on hoagies as they drove.

The dash clock read 10 P.M. Krista knew that by now Caroline would be expecting them, but they were still on Route 122, a good four hours from Boston. It had occurred to her to stop and find a phone . . . but she knew Caroline would understand. Like sister, like half sister.

As she drove through the deepening night, Kath snoring softly beside her, Krista's thoughts turned warmly to Scott. The scare he had given her on Saturday morning had made her acutely aware of how much he meant to her, of how pointless her life would have been, apart from her love for Kath, had he died. Scott knew almost all there was to know about Krista, and he loved her madly—there was no question in her mind about that. He had been a prince through ten years of marriage.

But sometimes Krista got the disquieting feeling there was something deep—and not entirely pleasant—that she didn't know about Scott. Some dark secret . . . something. She had sensed it less and less as the years crept by. But still, there were times . . .

Like Friday night, for instance, the night of his birthday. What had he been hiding about the content of the letter he'd received, the one informing him of his old classmate's death? The look on his face had been one of unalloyed horror, a look she'd've been surprised to see even if it had been Gerry who had died. What had made him pitch the letter into the fire as he might a wriggling snake?

117

Years ago, when they were first married, it had been the dreams, night-horrors that had wrenched him awake screaming and sheeted with sweat. Afterward, he always claimed he'd forgotten their content. And there had been other things: times when she was alone with him, nestled into the crook of his arm and watching TV perhaps, when Krista got the distinct (and spooky) feeling that he wasn't even aware she was there, so far had he lapsed from reality.

But those times had passed, she reminded herself. They had a wonderful family now, and a good future. They were going to grow old and fat together. Though she missed Scott when they were apart, she knew that separation was harder on him. After a few days he became sort of unstrung, drank too much, didn't eat properly or clean house. And yet, when Krista was home, he often cooked the meals and cleaned up, and seemed genuinely to enjoy doing it. He wasn't habitually sloppy or neglectful. He just needed his people close. They were the cement that kept him whole. This, too, was a comforting feeling for Krista . . . her man truly needed her. It was an obligation she openly treasured.

Beyond the horizon, heat lightning flared like silently exploding bombs. In the steady glow of the headlights, Krista noticed the leaves of the roadside trees, flipping over in the gusts to reveal their silvery underbellies. Her mother had always said that was a sign that a storm was coming.

Annoyed at the prospect of another delay, Krista nudged the accelerator a little harder, coaxing the needle up to seventy. In the Volvo it didn't seem fast at all, especially now, with traffic virtually nonexistent. The car hugged the roadway with ease, and Krista slowed only when passing through the smaller rural towns, which were far less frequent now.

Suddenly Krista jammed her foot hard on the brake pedal, grinding the car to a halt. Outside, shiny-amber eyes became a family of three raccoons, a mama and two little ones, waddling in sloppy single file across the blacktop. The coons glanced at the car with what appeared to be only mild interest, then vanished into the tall grass skirting the shoulder.

Kath snorted awake. "What happened?" she demanded, screwing a fist into one sleepy eye.

Resuming speed, Krista said, "Nothing, babe. Just a family of coons." Her heart had begun to triphammer in her chest.

Kath spun around in her seat and squinted through the back window. "Aw, I missed 'em."

"So did I," Krista quipped. "And lucky for them."

Kath smiled. Then, like a chameleon, she screwed her face into a pout. "Where's Jinnie?" she said, her tone suddenly childish and forlorn.

"In your room at home I guess," Krista said, thinking: *At least in her sleep she's still a little girl.*

"I forgot her . . . *oops!*" Kath broke wind, a small but definite *pop!* "I farted," she said, giggling.

Krista stifled a laugh. "Don't say 'fart.' It's unladylike."

"I didn't say 'fart,'" Kath countered. "I said 'farted.'"

"Kath!" Krista warned, her voice mock-stern.

"What do I say, then?"

"Say . . ." Krista began thoughtfully, taking a tight curve a little too quickly. "Don't say anything. When you fart, it's better to say nothing. Try to have it blamed on someone else."

Kath laughed. After a quiet interlude she asked, "Are we almost there?"

"Almost," Krista fibbed, hoping Kath would nod off again. "Tired?"

"Uh-huh." She brushed away a wet spot from the corner of one eye. "I hope Daddy's okay," she mumbled sleepily.

"He's fine, hon," Krista responded—but her mind jarred with an image of Scott lying limp and gasping on the dock. "You talked to him yourself last night on the phone."

The Volvo was just veering out of another tight curve,

over a hump and then sharply downhill. Krista angled the car into the bend, then glanced over at Kath.

"Yeah," Kath said, unconvinced. "But—*Mom!*"

Reacting out of sheer instinct, with time to do little more than glimpse the roadway in front of her, Krista jammed her foot on the brakes, and the car spun into a wild, angling skid.

# PART
# TWO

# CHAPTER 16

The breeze matured quickly, became a whining wind that seemed to run as if fleeing ahead of something else, something darker. In the distance, thunder boomed like leviathan footfalls. Offsetting this inconstant sound, an eerie calm-before-the-storm silence lay draped over everything. It was a maddening silence, more desolate than peaceful, the kind of lifeless quiet that set a mind to dark imaginings.

Scott sat alone in this silence, deriving little comfort from the cold cube of light that was the rec room around him. The night beyond seemed almost liquid, black water crowding in at the screens, waiting only for the lights to be unwittingly doused so that it might flood in and consume him. A draft found him where he sat by the Mickey Mouse phone, and he shivered in his short sleeves. He had been sitting here with Kath's Cabbage Patch doll in his lap for two hours.

Now he shifted in his chair, grateful for its squeaky

intrusion on the quiet that only moments before had seemed so inviolate. Feeling as stiff as he had on the day of his near-drowning, he climbed to his feet and crossed the room to the stereo. He chose something he'd listened to only once before: Bach, "The Goldberg Variations," performed by Glenn Gould. The rec-room stereo was an old one, its automatic cue function long since broken. Awkwardly, Scott dropped the needle onto the LP. There was a harsh grating noise . . . then cool, precise piano chords filled the room. He adjusted the volume to the just-audible range.

Then he went to the small basement refrigerator, dug out the last of the six-packs, and returned to his seat by the phone. He tabbed one of the cans and downed its contents in a single gratifying pull. A gentle dizziness danced immediately through him.

It wasn't too late for Krista to call. Any one of a hundred harmless delays might have befallen them, and he knew only too well how single-minded Krista could be if she got her sights set on something. If they were going to Boston, then they were by-God going to Boston, and nothing short of a hurricane or a nuclear holocaust had better interfere.

Thinking of Krista's sometimes mighty force of will made Scott smile in spite of his worry and fear. It had been Krista's strength during his years of specialty training that had on more than one occasion prevented him from chucking the whole damned thing. Krista was a force unto herself, an undeniable presence, even in her absence. The entire house glittered with her touch, her tastes, her invention.

Ripping the tab off a second beer, Scott found his mind drifting inevitably back to the day he first met her.

He had been in Sandy Point, Newfoundland, for exactly three weeks, and had just been getting the hang of Doctor Frith's family practice. Scott had taken over for Frith in the wake of the elderly practitioner's second heart attack. Like the first, this attack had been a mild one, but the old physician had seen it as a warning and had opted for a six-month leave. Scott, hoping to bank a small nest-egg before specializing, had found Frith's ad in the back of a CMA journal, and had applied. As it turned out, his had been the only application.

Frith's office ran on a simple system of two alternating examining rooms. His nurse, a Teutonic, no-nonsense type named Eva Underhoffer, kept the place humming like a well-oiled machine. Scott had only to shift from room to room and, waiting for him, he would find a new patient—weighed, urine-tested, and smiling.

That day, after weighing-in an elderly diabetic, Nurse Underhoffer had taken Scott aside and in her brazen, superior tone, warned him that he might find his next patient "a fraction unsavory," to quote the Frau's own discreet terminology. It was a young girl (a "heepy"), who had got herself into a family way and now wanted out of it. The Frau frowned on such requests with a burning righteousness.

Flanked by the barrel-calved nurse, Scott had strolled into room 2 and found Krista Draper, then still a teenager, seated on the examining table, sheet-draped and furiously blushing. Scott had been nervous enough in those early days, still only a fledgling physician, tottering about with a head full of rote facts and a black bag full of inexperience. But something about this girl had him immediately unstrung. Nothing he could identify at the time . . . something in those big, glacier-blue eyes perhaps, in their searching brightness. Whatever it was, he found himself suddenly dry-mouthed and stammering, nearly incapable of carrying off the doctor-patient cha-rade. Had he been more impulsive (and a lot less professional), he might have said, "Hey, how about you and I head downtown, buy a couple of sundaes, and wander out onto the jetty for a while, talk this whole abortion business over like sensible adults." But instead, he had asked all of the expected questions, made notes on her chart (which Frith had meticulously maintained throughout all of her eighteen and a half years), and then examined her.

And for once Scott had been glad to have Frith's fat, officious nurse present. The Frau's steely Aryan eyes had kept him keenly professional. But he had noticed this girl, her smooth olive skin, the thick mane of her womanhood, her warmth around his probing gloved fingers. And later he had felt disgusted with himself . . . yet oddly exhilarated.

When they met again, a few nights later, haunting the jetty for entirely different reasons—Scott, missing family and home, juggling around in his head the pros and cons of specialty training; and Krista, wavering unsteadily between thoughts of abortion and suicide—Scott had blushed with shame, imagining that Krista had been aware of his entirely inappropriate arousal in Frith's examining room. But Krista had been absorbed in her own turbulent musings, and had barely recognized him.

He found her sitting on the crumbling extremity of the jetty, her gaze directed dreamily outward, looking for all the world like some fanciful figure from centuries gone by, waiting for her lover's ship to appear on the swells. She had been in the midst of a painful transition that windswept night, graduating from girlhood to womanhood through the school of hard knocks, and Scott had ended up holding her comfortingly in his arms. And later, when the rain came in stinging sheets, he had kissed her and stroked her wet hair and whispered that everything would be fine. He'd been a goner before leaving the jetty. After walking her home that night and returning to his narrow cot in the clinic, he had lain awake for hours with a kind of phantom pain in his heart.

Seven months later, Krista's belly swollen like a concealed basketball, they were married. A month after that the child was born. They christened her Kathleen Marie.

This was something else Scott hadn't had a conscious thought about in years, the fact that Kath was not his by conception. That had gnawed at him at first, before Kath was born. But he'd realized even then that the gnawing was little more than his own oh-so-delicate ego. Someone else had been with the girl he loved, someone else had been inside of her. Sensing this, Krista assured him that it had been just a one-time thing, a boy she'd been infatuated with all through high school. "Just my luck," she'd moaned that night on the jetty. "The one time I try it, I get myself knocked up."

But once Kath was born and that precious round face began working its magic on him, Scott had been a goner all over again. Kath was his, and God help any man who challenged that fact.

At the trill of the rec-room phone Scott's body jerked convulsively. Kath's doll rolled from his lap to the floor, where it landed in a face-down heap. Lunging forward, he snatched the receiver from Mickey's hand.

"Hello?"

"Dr. Bowman."

It was Vince Bateman. Considering the hour and the circumstances, the call both surprised and annoyed Scott.

"I realize it's late," Bateman hurried on without waiting for Scott to reply, "but I've just—"

"Look," Scott cut in sharply, "I understand that you're pissed about the meeting, Vince. I'm sorry, but I can't talk about it right now. I've got to keep this line open. I'm expecting an important call."

"This has nothing to do with the meeting," Bateman persisted. "Which, I might add, went remarkably well in spite of your absence. I'm calling as department head, Scott. As I started to say, I've just been informed by the supervisor on Two Link that you created quite the scene with our psychic earlier tonight. Is this true?"

"Yes, but—"

"What in hell is going on, Scott?" Bateman's tone was openly reproachful. "According to the nurse, you might have done the old man some real harm. This sort of behavior does not look good, my friend. What's wrong? Are you under some sort of stress?"

Thinking it over now, Scott had to admit that it must have looked quite the scene. And it was true—he'd realized when the nurse prevented him from shaking the man any further—he *could* have done some serious damage. The old were frail.

But Scott found himself bristling at Bateman's patronizing overtones. Besides, he wanted off the phone.

"We'll talk about this another time, Vince, all right?"

"I wouldn't have called if I'd considered this unimportant—"

"It's the Cartoonist," Scott blurted desperately. "Some of his sketches . . . I'm afraid that Krista and Kath are in danger. A car accident. Please, I've got to keep this line open. . . . She should have called by now." Articulating his fears, Scott felt suddenly close to tears. "She might even be trying to reach me as we talk."

"Oh," Bateman said, his initial vehemence evaporating. "Well, perhaps it's nothing. These people aren't infallible, you know . . ." His voice trailed off.

"Good-bye, Vince."

"Good-bye," Bateman said, then quickly added: "Let me know if . . . good-bye, Scott."

Sighing despondently, Scott retrieved Kath's doll and set it on the counter. Its head drooped bonelessly forward. He glanced at his watch—and when he saw that it was pushing midnight, fear ran the peaks of his spine like a scorpion.

*She should have called by now.*

*Oh, God, she should have called. . . .*

A half-hour later the phone rang again. Uttering a cry of alarm, Scott scooped it up to his ear.

"Scott, it's Gerry."

Scott's heart sank. It should have been Krista. It should have been her, and then he could have forgotten this whole crazy deal. He could have told her that he loved her and then gone up to bed, written it off to an overactive imagination. But it was Gerry, and Scott fell suddenly mute. Afraid of the worst, a part of him didn't want to hear what his friend had to say.

But Gerry had called only to assure him that the Maine and Massachusetts police were cooperating fully. Gerry had told them they were after a kidnapper, but had cautioned them against using force, since it was suspected that the kidnapper was actually the child's estranged mother. To get around the reticence of law enforcement agencies to involve themselves in domestic disputes, Gerry threw in that the car they were driving was a stolen one.

Scott thanked his friend, apologized for his abruptness, then replaced the receiver in Mickey's hand.

He opened another beer and took a series of quick, thirsty gulps. He was tired, hungry, and getting rapidly drunk. His muscles ached, his hip ached, and now his head was aching, too.

Outside, thunder rumbled steadily closer, and from time to time sheet lightning flared in the south.

*She should have called by now,* his mind kept repeating. *She should have called. . . .*

At about one-thirty Scott reached for the six-pack beside him and found only empties. When he stood, he weaved. He crossed to the stereo and lifted the needle off the record—it had been bopping against the label for almost an hour—then returned to the phone and called Caroline in Boston. She had been asleep. The conversation was brief, the message clear.

There was still no word of them.

Scott apologized for waking her, and Caroline said that was okay. She told him not to worry. Scott said good-bye and hung up the phone. He tried to read—first a scientific journal, then a penny dreadful—but only stared uncomprehendingly at the same few lines. At around two o'clock the alcohol claimed him, and he slipped into a stuporous, image-ridden sleep. He kept seeing the cartoons, except that now the face in the drawings was Kath's.

What seemed like hours later (in fact it was only one), a clap of thunder brought him awake with a jerk. The power had gone off in the summer storm that was now raging, leaving the house steeped in darkness—but in the instant Scott opened his eyes, the room was dazzling with the flashbulb brilliance of lightning. In that fleeting glare he saw Kath's Cabbage Patch doll on the counter in front of him, its plump body knife-hacked, its stuffing protruding in ugly gray wads, a fresh red rivulet of blood coursing from the corner of its dimpled mouth.

Then darkness reasserted itself, lightning flickered, and the doll was whole again, just good ole Jinnie.

Eventually, dawn came.

At first light Scott called Caroline again.

"They probably just stayed overnight in a motel," she told him. But now Caroline's voice betrayed her own mounting anxiety. They both knew it was unlike Krista to miss calling. Again the conversation was brief.

After evacuating a tense bladder, Scott took the cordless phone down the path to the lake. The storm was taking a breather now, and only a light drizzle was falling. The air was clean and cool, redolent of rain-drenched greenery. Partway down the path Scott spotted a four-leaf clover, and instinctively bent to pick it. Instead, he marked the spot with a fallen branch, figuring he'd wait until Kath was with him, then pretend that he'd only just found it. . . .

Struggling to suspend his thoughts, Scott continued his descent to the lake. Around him, fat August blueberries dotted the green, many of them already falling away from the plant. Beyond the dock a gust roughened the surface, then whipped through the lakeside birches, rustling their papery leaves. To the west, masses of unspent thunderheads overlapped in an unruly regatta. Behind Scott, to the east, the rising sun fought for dominance, creating with its light a nearly fluorescent yellow green, an unearthly color that imbued the hills and made them glow against the gunmetal backdrop of the sky.

Scott walked out onto the dock and stood at its edge, gazing into the choppy water. He found himself trying to imagine diving in, stretching up onto his toes, arcing out . . . but he felt suddenly dizzy and had to step back onto solid ground.

*Jesus, I wish that phone would ring!* He could feel its silent weight inside his jacket. One way or the other, knowing would be so much better.

*Or would it?*

He sat on the picnic table with his feet on the bench and his face in his hands and rocked in silent anguish. The thought of harm coming to his wife or his daughter was unendurable. It filled him with a swooning kind of dread . . . no, it was stronger than that. Since discovering those drawings and their possible connection with his family, Scott had been terrified, jumping at shadows, imagining scenes of ruin that he was unable to sweep from his mind. He had even experienced what he supposed amounted to a fatigue- and stress-induced hallucination, seeing Kath's doll gored and bleeding in a flicker-flash of lightning. Every minute that passed without Krista's call doubled his certainty that the old man was right, that there *had* been an accident . . . and a bad one. He felt cold, husked-out, hollow, like the barrels beneath the dock.

At one point while he sat there in the strangely electric air, a gull mumbled plaintively behind him, making a sound that was disturbingly human. When Scott turned, imagining in his fatigue that it had been Kath sneaking playfully up on him, he saw the gray and white bird perched on a rock, disemboweling a minnow and watching him with wary yellow eyes. Furious at it for its unknowing deception, he flailed his arms and the gull lifted off, its call like a laugh as it winged away.

Tears welled in Scott's eyes. Through their blur he spotted something lying on the ground near the dock— twin, rose-colored irregularities. Looking closer, he realized they were a pair of Krista's barrettes. Then he remembered: she had taken them off before skinny-dipping with him a few weeks before and had later given them up for lost. As Scott picked them up, he smiled. He

131

took them with him to the table, where he reconstructed that night in all its warm and intimate detail.

It was a Saturday and Kath had been staying over with a friend, leaving him and Krista alone for the weekend. They had been down by the dock, getting tipsy, acting the fool, when Krista suggested a swim and began to disrobe. Scott remembered clearly the pale swells of her breasts, contrasting so erotically with the tan of her skin in the grainy half-light of the moon. Clear, too, was that vague, giddy fear of swimming at night, a sensation that had always heightened the thrill. *Until the other morning,* he thought grimly, *until that rocky bottom, those weeds.* They laughed and swam and splashed, and then Krista took him in her hand and made him hard. And they made love there, naked on the dock in the starlight. Good love. Afterward, incredibly, they fell asleep there, wrapped warmly around each other.

This memory lead to another—oddly, Kath swallowing an ice cube when she was five and nearly choking on it. Then, in a kind of cerebral chain reaction, memory lead to memory, until soon a brilliant cascade of them blurred through his mind.

After a block of time Scott would have been unable to define, the wind freshened up and it started to rain again. Adrift in that mosaic of memory, he missed the first warbling ring of the remote when it sounded inside his jacket. He heard its second ring and removed it from his jacket, but he did not answer it. He was unmindful of the rain. He was aware only of his dread, its weight, its crushing grip on his heart. It would be Gerry calling, and his big voice would say, *I'm sorry, Scott, but they're dead . . . they're both dead. . . .*

On the third ring he brought the phone to his ear. The voice on the other end—high, strained, familiar—cut in before Scott had a chance to speak.

"Scott?"

That single word was an anodyne. Pain and apprehension vanished in a quivering whisper of breath.

Scott started to giggle.

"Scott, listen . . . you're not going to believe the shit I'm into down here . . . are you laughing? I'm not kidding, Scott . . ."

It was Krista.

". . . will you listen?"

Before Scott could reply, he heard his wife's voice sharpen angrily, then muffle as she cupped a hand over the mouthpiece. She was addressing someone at her end—and none too politely.

"Could I have some privacy here, for Christ's sake? Jesus!" She came back on the line. "You would not *believe* these jackasses."

Scott found his voice. "Krista, what's going on?" He couldn't wipe the grin from his face. "Are you okay? What happened? When you didn't call, I—"

"I'm sorry about that, honey, I really am. But let me explain. Oh, it's a long story . . . I hit a goddam cow with the car last night—"

"A *cow?*" Scott blurted, starting to giggle again. *A cow,* he thought hysterically, *only a stupid bloody cow.*

"It's not funny, Scott. We could have been hurt . . . or killed! Anyway, that poor holstein is beef steaks by now. I busted its hind legs with the bumper. The farmer said he'd have to shoot it.

"You see, Kath and I got lost yesterday afternoon, and, well . . . you know how I am when I've got someplace to get to." He did. "It was dark and I was speeding on this windy road—that's one thing New England has plenty of, is windy roads."

Krista was genuinely upset; Scott could tell from her rambling dialogue. Still, he couldn't stop smiling . . . they were all right. Thank God, they were all right.

"We came around this sharp curve and there they were, cows, maybe sixty of them, all over the goddam road. And half a dozen farmers with flashlights and dogs. The cows had tramped down the fence and got out of the pasture.

"The car's okay . . . sort of. I mean, I can drive it. The grille's a bit crumpled. I swerved and took the ditch.

God, I felt like a criminal. Those farmers shot me some pretty dirty looks, too . . . and then they had to push the car back onto the road.

"Anyway, to make matters worse, it starts to rain, thunder and lightning, a real storm. And you know how Kath gets in a storm."

Sitting in the rain and grinning, Scott nodded to no one. Kath regressed five or six years in a bad thunderstorm. On one or two occasions the previous summer she had become nearly hysterical and had ended up bunking in with him and Krista until the storm had blown over.

"I was beat anyway," Krista was saying, sounding a trifle hysterical herself, "so I asked one of the farmers how far it was to the nearest motel. He looked as if he'd rather tell me to . . . well, use your imagination . . . but he told me anyways. So off we went, me shaking like a leaf after hitting that cow, Kath scared and carrying on like a three-year-old."

As he listened, Scott started back up the hill toward the house, aware only now that he had been sitting in an August downpour writing obituaries for the two people he cared for most in the world. Escaping his notice, the rain-soaked sole of his shoe crushed the four-leaf clover he had marked with a branch. Only the highlights of Krista's mile-a-minute account were reaching his higher centers for descrambling, but that didn't matter. Krista's voice mattered—feisty, exasperated, switching back in her excitement to the Newfie drawl of her childhood . . . alive. The car didn't matter. The cow didn't matter. The Cartoonist didn't matter.

"So finally I found this motel: Nomad's Notch." Krista uttered a short derisive laugh. "More like Nomad's Crotch if you ask me. What a dive." Her voice dropped to a whisper. "Oh, shit, that little bitch proprietor heard me. I was going to call you when I got here," she continued in a more normal tone. "It was late, after twelve, and I knew you'd be worried. But the lines were down with the storm, and the power, too.

"So Kath and I had to trek out into this muddy yard in

the rain, looking for room seventeen. Turns out the little frump gave us the shack at the far end of the row, with a leaky ceiling, no heat, and a musty old mattress. I woke up this morning with spring marks all over my ass!"

Krista was beginning to lose control, and Scott thought she might start to cry. In his relief, he hadn't appreciated the full degree of her upset. To him, Krista's tribulations seemed petty held next to the fate he had envisioned. But all things were relative.

". . . kept dreaming about that poor frigging cow. It shit itself when I hit it, Scott. Right onto the hood." Krista paused, her breath hitching noisily over the miles. "Then . . ." Now she *was* crying, and Scott could almost hear the teardrops. "Then *this!* At five-thirty this morning my motel room door is shoved open and these two brain-damaged *cops* come barging in!"

"Oh, Jesus," Scott breathed, finding the whole situation suddenly hilarious. Gerry . . . his detective work had paid off.

"Scott, what's going *on* here? They think I'm some kind of criminal. A kidnapper, if you can believe that. I've shown them my license and ownership and all that, and Kath told them I'm her mother, for Christ's sake, but they say they're waiting for some kind of clearance from Canada."

Immediately Scott saw a way to come out of all this smelling like a rose. Maybe even a hero. "Listen, sweetheart, don't cry. Give me the number there, and I'll call you right back. I'm going to get in touch with Gerry and see if he can't clear up this whole silly mess. There's obviously been a misunderstanding." He noticed the crumpled drawings by the phone and hesitated. Then, acting on an instinct he would only understand some several hours later, he added: "Then I'm going to book a flight and join you in Boston . . . meetings, job, psychiatry be damned."

"Okay, hon," Krista said, sniffling but sounding more in control. "You're a dear." She gave him the number. "Thanks. And I'm sorry about the car."

"Forget the car. My girls are all right, and that's all that matters. I was thinking of trading it for a Chevette, anyway."

Krista laughed and Scott felt like a millionaire.

"I love you, Scott."

"Me too you."

When they hung up Scott was still outside, standing on the deck in the cool, refreshing rain.

# CHAPTER 17

The phone rang again, and although it startled him, it no longer seemed fearsome. Just a phone ringing, a good sound, a sane sound. He stepped in off the deck and answered it cheerfully.

"Hello?"

"Scott." It was Gerry. "Listen, we found them and they're fine. Krista's madder than hell, though."

"Yeah, I know. She just called. Thanks, man. I owe you a big one." Scott chuckled. "Now, can you get me *out* of this? If she finds out I'm behind all of this, never mind the lunatic reason for it, I'll be a dead man."

"That's the easy part," Gerry said.

"Thanks, pal. You must think I've been out in the sun too long."

"Well, you know what they say about shrinks . . . no, really, I was moved by your concern for them. You're lucky to have someone you feel that way about."

"Yeah, I know," Scott said, feeling a small arrow of

pain for his friend. Gerry's wife, Steffie, had left him in the lurch two years ago—a ransacked apartment and a note on the kitchen table.

"Can you tell me about your 'loony reasons' now, or do I have to wait for the miniseries?"

"You deserve at least that much," Scott said. "But not right now. Next week over beer and pizza at the Hut, maybe. I want to get back to Krista. I'm going to join her in Boston tonight."

"Okay, José. But give me ten or fifteen to sort out the 'mix-up' in the States before calling . . . and stay out of the sun."

"Bye for now," Scott said through a laugh. "I'll give you a buzz."

He set the rain-beaded remote on the counter, then whipped spryly upstairs, taking the risers two at a go. In the bathroom, whistling tunelessly, he removed his soaked clothes and hopped into the shower. He felt great, better than he had in days. And yet, as the hot water worked its magic, he could feel the exhaustion creeping surely through him. He was headed for a major-league crash, and he knew it. He would probably sleep through his first two days in Boston.

*A cow,* he thought again. *No shambling zombies from the valley of the dead.* Not that he believed for one moment . . .

It occurred to him then that the Cartoonist had been right. Scott had been so distracted with relief, he had discounted this basic truth. His girls *did* have an accident, it *did* happen at night, and they *did* hit something in the road.

*So they're out of danger . . . right?*

He stepped out of the shower, toweled off briskly, then padded into the bedroom. Still a bit shaky, he picked up the phone and called the Air Canada reservations desk. The best they could do, they informed him, was a connecting flight from Montreal. He would be flying Air Canada out of Ottawa at eight, then Delta from Montreal an hour later, arriving in Boston at ten fifty-five. This suited him fine. The later flight would allow him time to straighten things up at the hospital.

Next he dialed the number Krista had given him. A woman answered in a Yankee drawl, which to Scott sounded contrived.

"Mornin', Nomad's Notch."

"This is Dr. Bowman," he intoned with as much authority as he could muster. "Give me Krista Bowman, please."

The receiver was clunked against something hard; Scott got an image of coffee-stained Formica. "It's fer you," he heard the woman say.

"Scott?"

"Hi, I reached Gerry—"

"Yes, I know!" Krista sounded cheerful and relieved. "They've gone, those mobsters. No apologies, no nothing. Just, 'Here's your license, lady, you can go.' Pigs. Well, we're going, all right. Kath thinks it's all a party. I called Caroline already. She laughed, but I know she was worried, too."

She paused a beat, thoughtful. Then: "I'm okay now, you know. You don't have to fly down here. I'd like it, but . . ."

Scott glanced again at the drawings, which he had tossed on the bed before showering. "Just have the harem assembled at the Delta off-ramp at eleven tonight."

Krista uttered a tiny squeal reserved for situations that delighted her.

"Krista?" Scott said in a voice that was almost a whisper.

"Yes, hon?"

"Do me a favor?" He saw the terror in the cartoon-child's face and realized that his hairline had beaded with sweat.

"Name it, Bud."

"Don't drive after dark tonight, okay?"

"What? Why not?"

"Please, babe. Just humor your schizoid husband for one night?"

"What about picking you up at the airport?"

"Bring Caroline along. Then I won't be worried, okay?"

"Okay," Krista echoed doubtfully. She was too tired to argue or to question him further. "See you tonight." She intentionally filled this last with erotic promise.

"Right," Scott said, recognizing the signal. "I'll be the man with the copy of *Pravda* under his arm and the unripened Chiquita banana taped to his inner thigh."

Krista laughed. "You're an idiot, Bowman . . . but I love you anyway. Bye."

"Bye."

The line went dead.


Before leaving for the hospital later that morning, Scott folded the drawings and tucked them neatly into his flight bag. He wanted to show them to Krista. He thought they could both have a good laugh over the whole ridiculous affair. Into another compartment, next to a pair of unused jeans, he stuffed Jinnie, Kath's Cabbage Patch doll.

On his way out he remembered the Christmas pictures he'd had developed, and he tucked those into the bag, too.

# CHAPTER 18

"You have *got* to be kidding!" Krista said in angry exasperation. She was standing in the blistering heat of midday, glaring at a grease-freckled mechanic. The man's eyes, an amazing bottle green, shone with faint amusement. Behind him, parked on the gravel shoulder, the Volvo hissed steam from beneath its dented hood. The motor of the nearby tow truck grumbled comfortably . . . almost mockingly, Krista thought.

She had gotten exactly twenty miles from Nomad's Notch when the car began to hitch and the heat indicator winked its accusing red eye. Predictably, she had been here, in the middle of no place, when it happened. And it had taken her more than an hour to flag a ride to the nearest town.

"No, ma'am. No joke. You've got a hole in your radiator as big around as that." He held up one beefy, oil-blackened finger for Krista's appraisal. "You must have took a branch through the sucker when you ran her off the road." Now his green eyes were smiling, flashing dollar signs.

Krista glowered at the crippled car. "Can you fix it?"

Rubbing his chin contemplatively, the mechanic shuffled back to his truck, where he propped an elbow on the sill and a boot on the muddy side-runner. In this pose his body partially framed the ad painted onto the door: ERNIE THURSTON TEXACO.

"I can fix her, all right," he said after a theatrical pause. "Need a rad, though. Likely have to call down to Boston to get—"

*"Boston!"* Krista cut in. They were still a good three and a half hours from Boston. "How long will that take?"

"Better part of the day, I expect. Maybe even into tomorrow. Have to send her up on the Greyhound. Might find one in Portland if our luck's in." He regarded the Volvo with open disdain. "These foreign jobs might be nice and all, but parts are a bitch." He spat, as if to emphasize this heart-felt conviction. "'Scuse me, ma'am."

Krista bit her lip. Unbidden, a favorite expression of her mother's came to mind in her mother's nattering voice: "Disasters always come in threes." Well, where should I start counting? Krista asked herself bitterly. First my busybody sister gets my goat, then Customs, then a speeding ticket, then I get lost in the mountains, kill a cow, sleep on a crab-infested mattress, and get arrested for kidnapping! Isn't that enough?

She looked at the hissing Volvo. A fat drop of sweat stung her eye. "All right," she said, giving in. "Let's get started."

The mechanic nodded and spat again. Then, green eyes gleaming, he climbed into the truck and backed it into position in front of the Volvo.

Meanwhile, Krista hailed Kath, who was down in the ditch hunting grasshoppers, and the two of them piled into the passenger side of Ernie Thurston's Ford. While they waited, Kath tugged absently at a tuft of stuffing that protruded from a crack in the vinyl upholstery.

# CHAPTER 19

The layover in Montreal consumed just over an hour, the bulk of which Scott spent in the concourse bar, drinking draft and ignoring the rather clumsy advances of a tipsy prostitute.

After speaking with Krista, he had spent the balance of the morning trying to catch up on his shut-eye. But his night of worry had worked on him like an amphetamine, and he found it impossible to wind down. He did manage about an hour, but awoke feeling flakier than he had before. He arrived at the hospital just after noon and sequestered himself in his office, where he spent a few hours dictating letters and rescheduling the week's meetings and appointments. Before leaving the hospital, he peeked in on the Cartoonist. The old man was asleep in his wheelchair. According to the nurse Bateman had assigned to watch over him, he had been that way since early morning. There were no new drawings.

Now, waiting in line at the boarding ramp, Scott was

feeling a tad more than tipsy himself—and unaccountably flattered by the hooker's persistence. She was still winking and waving from her stool in the nearby openfront bar.

*What a dog!* Scott thought, chuckling and returning her wave. By now he'd all but forgotten his wretched anxiety of the night before. And yet, even through the fatigue and the mild euphoria produced by the beer he'd consumed, something rattled bothersomely at the back of his mind, a detail lurking just out of reach. Something was wrong, didn't quite fit. It was in the drawings somewhere, an incongruity, ill-defined, but there.

As he waited, Scott became dimly aware of the old man's handiwork, folded in the pocket of his TWA flightbag. He fancied he could feel it in there, like a weight just heavy enough to make the straps dig uncomfortably into his shoulder.

"Boarding pass, please. Your boarding pass, sir?"

"Wha . . . ?"

Somehow Scott had graduated to the front of the line. Now he stood facing an irate Puerto Rican woman in a trim blue uniform. Her gloved hand was extended, palm up. The nearest passenger ahead of Scott was just turning the corner at the end of the on ramp, then vanishing. Grumbles of annoyance came from behind him.

He handed over his boarding pass.

"End of the ramp and then left," the attendant said. "Would you like some assistance, sir?"

"No fff-anks." Cripes, he wasn't that bad . . . was he?

Scott started carefully down the ramp. Through the long, semitransparent side window, he noticed the conical snout of the aircraft. A large red dot had been painted onto its tip. It made him think of a huge breast—the rolling, man-engulfing breast in Woody Allen's *Everything You Always Wanted to Know About Sex (But Were Afraid to Ask)*—then he thought of all that icy brew (how many had it been since the airport in Ottawa? Who knew?), and that pathetic, sagging whore in the lounge.

He smiled.

Faithful to instruction, Scott turned left at the end of the boarding ramp. Cool air, reeking of jet fuel, funneled in from over the tarmac. He could feel it riffling his hair, drying the sweat on his brow. He stepped on board, flashed his boarding pass at the flight attendant, then squeezed his way down the aisle to his seat.

"Would you like a drink, sir?"

Half-asleep, Scott lay slouched in a window seat near the tail of the aircraft. Lulled by the gentle vibration of the Rolls-Royce turbines, he had promptly and peacefully drifted off. Next to him, reading a thick paperback and smelling like a stale locker room, sat a woman so fat she spilled over into the aisle.

"No, thanks," Scott answered hoarsely. "I believe I've had enough."

The stewardess proceeded along the aisle, smiling and offering beverages from the clinking portable bar.

Angling her girth toward Scott, the fat woman dropped the paperback into her lap and smiled. Swiftly (and, he feared, a little rudely) Scott turned to face the porthole window. Glancing at his watch, it dawned on him that somehow they had managed to get airborne and halfway to Boston without his noticing.

Beyond the window a clear, nearly cloudless sky sloped away to the gentle arc of the horizon. A single cloud, black against the star-flecked heavens, raftered reposefully along in the middle distance. Its upper edge, screening the moon, glowed dully. Gazing dreamily at that edge, Scott was reminded of a boyhood fascination with the night sky . . . he and a chum used to scale the back fence, crawl up onto the garage roof, and gaze wonderingly into the heavens, pretending to be astronauts, always alert for shooting stars.

Gradually, as he watched it now, the moon drifted free of that screening cloud. First a jagged crescent, then the full pocked disk . . . bright, round, and perfect.

Scott's eyes widened as panic skidded into him. There it was, sailing the dome of night sky—the final piece in the irksome puzzle of the drawings, the source of the harping doubt he'd been juggling around in his mind since early that morning.

The moon.

God's midnight eye.

Like a junkie remembering where he'd hidden his stash, Scott grabbed his flightbag and dug out the drawings. His gaze scanned rapidly to the third frame, to the tombstone in the foreground and the shambling corpse, to the naked tree traced black against an oversized moon.

A full moon.

# CHAPTER 20

While Scott was sitting in the Outbound Lounge in the Montreal airport, ordering his second beer, Krista was finally pulling away from Thurston's Texaco in Fryeburg. Ernie had been right—the process had consumed the entire day. The bill had been an equally unpleasant surprise: four hundred and thirty-six dollars and eighty-eight cents—American! As she anteed up, Krista remembered her very first car, a 1965 Vauxhall Victor; she had paid less than half that amount for the whole damned car!

They were still about three hours out of Boston, two and a half if she booted it, then she'd have to find Logan International, a prospect inspiring little joy on the heels of the day she had already had. Earlier that afternoon she had telephoned Caroline and warned her not to expect them until after they'd recovered Scott from the airport, probably around midnight or so. Afterward, she and Kath had caught a matinee at Fryeburg's single cinema, the Magic Lantern. The feature was a rerun of Spielberg's *Gremlins*. Skeptical at first, Krista wound up enjoying herself. The theater's air-conditioning was a blessing after the sticky August heat, and the movie provided just the right blend of humor and gore to abate both the hysterical and urge-to-kill facets of her frustration.

By the time they reached I-95 southbound, dusk had already begun to settle. While Kath snoozed, Krista stuck like a squatter to the left-hand lane, cruising at a comfortable, if illegal, seventy-five. When dark did fall, and the irksome details of the past two days commenced a slow retreat from her mind, Krista recalled Scott's peculiar request, the one he had made over the phone that morning: "Don't drive after dark. . . ."

But what she remembered more clearly than the words was the tone Scott had used in saying them. He had been pleading with her—not manifestly, but she had sensed it nonetheless. Behind the slight break in his voice, behind his efforts to conceal it, Scott had been begging her.

*But why?* she puzzled now, as the center line unreeled ahead of her. She wanted to chalk it off to Scott's worry-wart nature, or to her own imagination, but none of that would cut.

Well, she had no choice now, did she. It was either drive till she got there or wind up in another Nomad's Notch. And there was no way she was going to suffer through *that* crap again, thank you very kindly.

She placed a hand on Kath's thigh, burrowed back in her seat, and nudged the needle up to eighty.

The temperature gauge started to glow again—dull and winking at first, then that same solid red—a mile or two from a service-exit sign reading BYFIELD. Too exhausted to muster even a vague pique, Krista slowed and exited. It was three miles to Byfield.

The grease monkey at the service station there looked suspiciously like Ernie Thurston, only younger. Something in the eyes, Krista thought as she related the tribulations of her day to the distracted mechanic. When she mentioned the radiator, his eyes seemed to shine, like Ernie's had.

"New rad today," the mechanic mused, one eye glued to the color portable on the desk in front of him. A Red Sox game was blaring. "Prob'ly just a loose clamp." He peeked out at the steaming Volvo. "Been bootin' 'er?"

"Yes," Krista admitted. "I'm in a bit of a hurry."

Following the man's gaze, she squinted through the bug-spattered front window. She could see Kath out there, her drowsing face angled toward the garage. Looking at her, Krista felt an unexpected, almost dizzying rush of love for her child.

"Yep," the mechanic said, pleased with himself. The diagnosis was made, and he wouldn't have to miss too much of the inning putting it right again. "Drive her up to the first bay there, ma'am, and we'll have us a look-see."

While the mechanic tinkered under the hood, Krista took a badly needed pee, then strolled out into the starlight. The August moon was full, a strange coppery color, like a shiny new penny. Mingled with the smells of grease and gasoline, Krista noticed the faintly putrescent odor of an unseen swamp. The air was filled with the chirring of its denizens.

Suddenly chilled—and oddly sickened by that faint odor of decay—Krista hurried back inside. Wrapped in her arms, she stood watching the mechanic and reflecting over the trials of the past twenty-four hours. Something about this whole sorry disaster bothered her in an obscure yet disquieting way. And that was the feeling— the absurd, gut-level feeling—that she had been led, and was *still* being led. It was a crock, of course, just the fatigue working on her mind.

But . . .

But what had taken her down the wrong road back there in New Hampshire?

Hadn't it been just an impulse?

Yes—a sudden and thoroughly uncharacteristic impulse.

149

Or had it been something more than that—
*(turn here)*
An inner voice? An inner command?
*(turn)*
And hadn't it sounded like someone *else's* voice?
*(here)*
Jesus, no, Krista reproached herself, shutting off this frankly lunatic train of thought. That's nuts, kiddo. It was nothing more than your basic snafu: situation normal . . . all fucked up.

The *crack!* of the closing hood jerked her back to the present, and the drab reality of the garage. Behind her, the baseball game droned hectically toward the top of the inning. In the car Kath startled awake. She gazed half-lidded around the dimly lit bay, then nestled comfortably back to sleep.

"Loose clamp, all right," the mechanic said as he hurried back inside, his quick eyes darting to the screen as the commentator's voice went wild over a play. "Needed some antifreeze, though."

"Anything," Krista said. "Just so long as I can drive."

Five minutes later they were back on the road, the temperature gauge a lifeless black square in the dash. Following the mechanic's instructions, Krista turned south instead of backtracking north and then east to I-95. He said she would find a link-up with the Interstate about three miles from the station . . . and there it was.

The left turn gave onto a little-used road reminiscent of the ones they had traveled in New Hampshire the day before. All at once the countryside was cloaked in an almost unearthly dark, the high beams reflecting back as if from a solid thing. Here and there, yellow oblongs of light glowed faintly in the pitch, farmhouses set well back from the road. There was no traffic.

"Are we there yet?"

Absorbed in her own musings, Krista jumped at the sound of Kath's voice. "Close, hon," she said softly. "Real close now. Why don't you sleep some more?"

"Not tired."

Kath had been a princess through it all, Krista thought now, through this whole botched-up odyssey. She could have fussed and complained and made things a whole lot worse than they were. But she hadn't. That precocity again, Krista decided. A small tantrum might even have been fun. They could have had one together.

"How ya doin', tiger?"

"Getting bored, Mommy dearest . . . *uggh!* Lookit!"

Krista followed Kath's pointing finger.

There was a groundhog dead in the road, near the ghostly center line. A large black bird, a crow or a raven, took a last quick tug at a rope of intestine before winging up out of the way. Krista hadn't thought birds did anything at night but sleep. The demolished groundhog glowed for a moment, then faded to black behind the car.

Doing a passable impersonation of Mr. Rogers, Kath said, "Poor Mister Groundhog," and craned her neck to watch it vanish into the night.

Krista glanced at the dash clock, then wedged her foot more firmly against the accelerator. Ahead of them the road banked hard to the left. The dark maw of the ditch opened briefly, then closed again as Krista corrected the car's trajectory.

"Grrr-reat green gobs of greasy grimy gopher guts . . ." Kath, in her worst singing voice.

"Kath!" Krista interrupted, laughing. "That's rude!" It was a song she had sung herself as a girl. Hearing it now brought back memories of campfires and late-night ghost stories.

"I know." Kath giggled. "Come on, Mom. Join in. Grrrrreat green gobs . . ."

Krista picked up the chorus:

> ". . . of greasy grimy gopher guts,
>     simulated monkey's feet,
>     constipated birdie's tweet . . . "

The car shot over one of those stomach-dropping humps in the road. *"Whoooh!"* Krista cried, accelerating

151

in time with the limerick. Inclining upward now, the road banked steeply to the left.

> ". . . all wrapped up in
> poison purple platypus
> and I forgot my spooooon . . ."

Beyond the incline the road jigged hard to the right, more sharply than Krista had anticipated. She was going much too fast to stop.

Only gradually understanding the change in her mother's face, Kath finished the song with a sort of vaudeville slide: "I'll—use—a—strawwww . . . *sluuuurp!*" Then she shifted her gaze out through the windshield.

There was someone standing in the middle of the road, weaving drunkenly.

In the span of milliseconds that passed before the inevitable collision, several thoughts surged through Krista's mind. None of them, however, had anything to do with her past life. During none of that brief, surreal interval did she imagine any harm might come to Kath or to herself. She wondered what a drunk was doing in the middle of the road in the middle of the night in the middle of no place. A part of her decided, quite coldly, that no way was she taking the ditch to avoid hitting this misfit (probably some retarded product of barnyard inbreeding), ruining the car—

*(is there something wrong with his face?)*

risking her daughter's life—

*(his clothes?)*

and her own. She realized fleetingly that Kath's seat belt was fastened and that her own was not. She wondered how much (more) damage would be done to the car and would the man be killed? and what was Scotty going to say?

*(is he grinning?)*

Instinct or reflex or simple humanity took control of Krista's hands then, and she jerked the wheel hard to the right, trying to avoid this doomed man—

(*is it a* child??)

in the road.

Like a dumb animal, the figure lurch-stumbled in the same direction as the car. Krista cranked the wheel hard to the right.

Kath screamed.

There followed a blunt metallic crunch—then the windshield shattered, became a swarm of angry, needling shards. The figure came through the glass headfirst, directly in front of Kath, and for a split second—the space of a discharging flashbulb—Krista saw its face in the dashlights. Most of one side of it had been torn away, and the jaw hung loosely agape, unhinged and drooling black blood.

Then something solid loomed up before them, brightened, and Krista was out of her seat, impacting the roof with her skull, grappling through numbness with the macabre idea—the wholly *insane* idea—that the face bursting through the windshield had already seen death, which followed her down an airless shaft into that most unforgiving darkness.

The car came abruptly to rest against a low fieldstone fence. Steam escaped the crumpled hood. The horn, jammed into life, bleat a constant, ululating note into the unheeding night.

Nothing moved.

# CHAPTER 21

Scott decided to have that drink after all. He told the stewardess to make it a stiff one. As he sipped it, he forced his mind into a more positive frame.

His girls would be there. Both of them. Standing at the top of the debarking ramp or huddled together near the baggage carousels, Bowman's harem in full regalia, all smiles and waiting hugs. Sure, tonight was the full moon—he had checked it against his wallet calendar—but that was merely a detail, part of the horror-comic veneer. Any good graveyard scene *had* to have a full moon. It was a given. Krista and Kath were in Boston, they had to be. They had probably arrived there in the forenoon. They would be at the airport and he would greet them, pull Krista close and hug her until he heard ribs snap. Kath would kiss him and then wrap his thumb in her hand, swinging his arm as they ambled out to the car. And Krista would tell him the whole sad tale all over again, her Newfie upbringing making it impossible for

154

her to skip the part about the cow shitting itself on the hood.

It would all be all right.

These thoughts followed him down into a restless stupor born of exhaustion, too much booze, and that gnawing, unappeasable fear.

The dream came instantly.

A tombstone like the stump of an amputated limb poked up through the ground mist of his imagination. In the stark realism of this dream Scott could see the stone's Gothic inscription, but was unable to spirit his dream-eye close enough to decipher the words. A sudden wet tearing sound issued from the soil fronting the marker, and then rot-blackened fingers groped into the frosty night air. An eyeless head followed, its black tongue hideously lolling, its yellow teeth glinting in the moon-light. Then came the hunched and creaking shoulders, slowly excavating themselves from the tomb with a sick sucking sound. . . .

Scott awoke in a lather of sweat. A stewardess was standing over him, one hand on his shoulder, the smile gone from her pretty face.

The seat beside him was vacant. The jet was on the tarmac in front of Logan International.

Gathering his things, Scott hurried down the aisle to the exit.

There was no one at the top of the debarking ramp. Not one of his girls. And no one at the baggage claim, either.

A weight like a dumbbell settled on Scott's shoulders. He called Caroline from a pay phone.

"No, not yet, Scott. Krista called this afternoon . . . said they had some trouble with the car. A hole in the radiator, I think. She said she'd pick you up at the airport before coming out here."

Fear, now a familiar companion, doubled the weight on Scott's shoulders. He stood there with his ear pressed to the receiver.

"Should I drive out and pick you up?" Caroline asked, filling the void of Scott's silence.

"No," Scott said, his voice nearly failing him. "You'd better stay there in case she calls or shows up. I'll wait here. I can see the Delta off-ramp from where I'm standing. Get a pencil, and I'll give you the number of this booth. Call me if you hear anything."

Scott read off the seven digits and hung up. Then he sat in a plastic contour seat by the phone and began to wait, powerless to block the horrible certainty that spawned in his heart. He spent the next forty minutes searching every face that passed by. Once, he was right out of his chair, jostling past glares of annoyance, lurching toward an auburn-haired woman in a blue windbreaker, and a child . . . but the woman was twenty, and the child was a boy.

When the telephone rang forty minutes later and Caroline's sobbing voice informed him that Krista was dead, Scott closed his eyes and collapsed into a dead faint on the concourse floor. The darkness came quickly, like a summer storm. His head struck the ceramic tiles like a flung melon, opening a half-inch gash in his scalp. Two things followed him down: one thought—

*(What about Kath?)*

and a voice, Caroline's voice, high, singsong and childlike, growing tauntingly louder and louder . . .

*Krista is deh-ed, Krista is deh-ed, Krista Is Dead . . . !! KRISTA IS DEAD!!*

# CHAPTER 22

Later, Scott would remember little of the hours that followed. He lay on the concourse floor for what seemed like a lifetime. When he opened his eyes, he saw the telephone receiver, dangling at the end of its coil. No one had seen him fall, and now people avoided him as they would a drunk. Fighting a fresh tide of vertigo, Scott gathered himself up, dropped heavily into the contour seat, and snared the receiver. He could feel warm blood braiding its way through the hair on the back of his head.

"Hello?" the receiver squawked repeatedly, the voice now a man's. "Hello?"

Hearing a man's voice, Scott clutched at the slim hope that this had all been some dreadful sort of prank . . . but when he replied, the voice said that it belonged to an officer of the state highway patrol.

"Are you all right, Dr. Bowman?" Scott could hear sobs in the background . . . Caroline.

"No," he breathed. "No, I'm not. Is it . . . ?"

"Yes, sir, I'm afraid it's true. I regret having to give you this news. I would have called personally, but Miss Patterson here went straight to the phone when I told her about the accident. At the time I had no idea of the circumstances or who she intended to call—"

"Where . . . wh . . ." Scott stammered. Then, nearly shouting: "What about Kath? What about my daughter?"

"Your daughter is in the hospital," the voice informed him—and Scott sensed a reticence in it that terrified him. "Her condition is listed as . . . critical. I'm sorry I can't tell you more. Can you get yourself to the General Hospital in Danvers? If not, I can have a cruiser by there in about twenty minutes—"

"No . . . I'll find a cab." He could hear himself mouthing the words, but had no idea what they meant. "How far?"

"A half-hour's drive, due north of the airport. The driver will know. Will you be all right?"

"How is Caroline going to get there? Caroline ought to be there. . . ."

"I'll take her in my car."

Scott hung up.

And when he did, he realized that none of it was real. It was a dream, and if it wasn't a dream, then it was a drunken hallucination. But it wasn't real.

No. Not real.

*It's a kind of shock,* he could hear himself telling an aggrieved patient only a few days earlier, an elderly gent who had just lost his wife of thirty years. Scott had kept his voice professionally controlled, professionally somber: *It's like a concussion, a sort of shell shock, if you will. It clouds the vision, distorts reality. It will pass,* he had assured the weeping old man. *It will pass and then you will grieve and then you will go on. . . .*

They were words he had read somewhere. Now they echoed in emptiness.

With the strap of his TWA flightbag wound tight in his grip, Scott moved away from the phone and shifted into the concourse, where he stood like a buoy in a river of people . . . determined people, smiling people, people with places to go . . . yes . . . he had someplace to go . . .

Forgetting his luggage, Scott left the airport concourse, with its brightly colored pennants and busily geometric ceiling, and stepped out under the portico. There, a black man in a burgundy uniform led him to a taxi and helped him inside.

"The hospital in Danvers," Scott said flatly.

The cabby hoisted the meter flag. "The General?"

Scott nodded and the cab lurched away. In the back seat he gazed out the window at the twinkling city lights. So many lights . . .

The Danvers General Hospital, squat and widely spread out, was a patchwork of new grafted into old. From the lobby a crusty old security officer led Scott along a series of antiseptic corridors to the Emergency Ward. Here he was met by a graying, tired-looking man in a vested suit who identified himself as Jim Holley, the county coroner. At first Scott expected the man to apologize, to tell him there had been a huge and unforgivable error, a regrettable case of mistaken identity. *We are sorry, sir, for whatever distress this blunder may have caused you.*

Instead, the hollow-eyed coroner asked him if he felt up to viewing the body for the purposes of identification.

*What body?* Scott's mind bellowed. But he only shook his head. "I want to see my daughter." He noticed the curtain drawn across a cubicle at the far end of the examining area, and wondered if Krista was behind it.

*No, not Krista, all a mistake . . .*

"I want to see my daughter."

Nodding, Holley placed a hand on Scott's shoulder. "I would, too," he said, the faces of his own three girls flashing in his mind. "Come on. I'll take you to her."

The Intensive Care Unit was located on the same floor as the ER. At the unit's entrance, Holley left Scott with the nurse who met them there. The nurse took Scott's hand and led him into the ICU, a twelve-bed facility arranged in a polygonal pattern around an L-shaped consul. At the consul itself, lights flashed, monitors beeped, feeble lifesigns were recorded. A young physician sat bent over a chart, a stethescope looped in his labcoat pocket. He glanced up briefly as Scott drifted by, then resumed his charting. Somewhere a ventilator hissed.

The nurse stopped outside a corner room, nodded, then turned silently away. Scott started to enter the room, then paused in the doorway. Beyond the edge of an encircling, rainbow-colored curtain he could see the foot of a single bed. And beyond that, Caroline, Krista's half sister.

Motionless, the middle-aged college professor sat hunched over the bed, her hands gathered in a despairing knot between her breasts. She had not yet twigged to Scott's presence, and for a dreadful instant Scott experienced a sensation of total nonexistence.

Then he inched forward into the room.

When he caught sight of one small arm lying limp on the bed, he stopped again, his mind reeling back to the night before, to another doorway in another hospital and a different kind of dread disconnecting his will.

He drew a loud, stuttering breath. Caroline heard it and turned toward the sound. When she saw Scott, her face collapsed in anguish.

"Oh, dear God," she murmured, pushing unsteadily to her feet. "Krista . . ." Her hands came up to her face and concealed it.

Still frozen in the doorway, Scott looked again at the arm on the bed. There was an intravenous taped to the back of the hand . . . Kath's hand?

Unbelieving, he dropped his flightbag and took another step forward.

Then he saw the silver bracelet.

Verging on tears, Scott folded his fingers around the edge of the curtain and drew it back.

Kath lay propped against a pillow, still as glass, pale beneath her summer tan. Her arms, limp and somehow diminished, flanked her sheet-covered body like rolls of half-baked dough. A gauze bandage similar to the one around Scott's leg covered the upper third of her right arm. Beneath the sheet her chest rose and fell. Apart from her arm, her body looked okay.

But her face . . . Scott would not soon forget the horrid mask of his little girl's face.

Kath's mouth was open, but not in the healthy, slumbering oval it had been when he'd peeked in on her the morning of his birthday. Her lips were drawn into down-curving lines, as if encircling a silent scream, and the tiny white pearls of her teeth were revealed. Her forehead, usually so shiny and smooth, was creased in the middle . . . Kath's worry-cleft, only deeper and badly twisted. Dried blood caked the flaring opening of one nostril, and two or three minor lacerations on her neck and right cheek were dressed with ordinary Band-Aids. Her eyes . . .

*Oh, God, her eyes . . .*

Suddenly woozy, Scott settled his weight on the edge of the bed. He took the hand with the IV into both of his and shuddered, partly because of the boneless cool of Kath's hand . . . but mostly because of her eyes.

Kath's eyes were open, so widely open it seemed that she was making a deliberate effort to force them from their sockets. Like doll's eyes, they focused on nothing.

Her expression was not one of shock or pain, Scott realized with black astonishment—it was an ivory sculpture of terror. His hand itched to reach out and close Kath's eyes . . . but a thought like a bullet entered his head and reminded him that that was reserved for the dead *(for Krista),* and the itch went away.

"Kath," he said in a whisper. "Kath, it's me . . . it's your daddy. Please . . ."

"Scott . . ."

It was Caroline. So small, so stricken. Scott willed his head to turn, but the command was ignored.

*Those eyes . . .*

"Dr. Bowman?"

Scott dropped Kath's hand and whirled toward the

source of the new voice—the young doctor who had been poring over a chart when Scott came into the unit. He gave the man a barely perceptible nod, then turned back to Kath.

"I'm Dr. Cunningham," the young man said, his accent thickly Irish. "I admitted your girl to the unit."

Scott's brain muttered "thank you," but his lips remained still.

Cunningham pressed on. "Apart from a nasty cut on her arm, which got sewn up in the ER, she's sustained no other injury we've been able to pinpoint. We CAT-scanned her the minute she arrived, but found nothing of significance. There's been no skull fracture or hematoma. Could be a concussion she's got, but I'm not so sure. She's lost a fair bit of blood from that cut arm, but not enough to require transfusion." He indicated the monitoring equipment mounted over the bed. Keeping silent time, a green blip squiggled out the electrical activity of Kath's heartbeat. "Her vital signs are stable."

*(all a mistake not really here not really happening)*

Scott's hand found the big tender goose egg on the back of his head. Deliberately, he pressed his fingers into the bogginess of it, causing pain to blossom brightly. That, at least, was real.

*It's like a concussion. . . .*

"A clear case of a life saved by a seat belt," the young doctor said, then paused reflectively. "Although, I suppose it was the fellow who found them that really saved her. He dressed that wound on her arm. Otherwise, I'm afraid she might have bled enough to do herself some real harm."

"What's wrong with her now?" Scott asked helplessly, his face twisted into a bewildered question mark. "Why is she . . . like this?"

"I think it's some kind of catatonic reaction. It would explain the dulled but normal neurological findings, and her present state of detachment." He indicated Caroline with an open palm. "Caroline here tells me that you're a psychiatrist. Does catatonia seem a reasonable diagnosis to you?"

And for the tiniest moment Scott *was* a psychiatrist again (although an instant later he would have been hard put to define the word, let alone make a diagnosis), and that part of him agreed with this bright-eyed intern. It was exactly the sort of explanation he would have offered for the child of a stranger. As a professional, he knew that traumatic situations quite commonly produced states of temporary detachment, and that these could vary in severity from a deliberate switching-off to a completely involuntary and far-reaching shutdown.

But then he wondered, and his wondering grew dark and fearful. Again his fingers itched. Why did her eyes have to stay open like that, blinking only half-shut over glassy orbs that were more like a taxidermist's props than living eyes? Why didn't they close so that he could pretend she was only sleeping?

"We'll be keeping her here for observation," Cunningham was saying in the somber tones of an undertaker. "At least overnight. Easier that way to rule out any hidden injury."

*Why is this guy talking to me as if I'm only a colleague? Why doesn't he leave us alone?*

As if the thought had reached him telepathically, the intern edged toward the open door. "I'll be right outside, Doctor . . . when you're ready to go back to the ER." Then he was gone, the tail of his labcoat belling out behind him.

Caroline's hand found Scott's and squeezed it. After a moment Scott stood and drew her into his arms. Shoulders hitching, Caroline pressed her face against Scott's chest and wept. In the emotionless void of disbelief, Scott's eyes remained dry. He tried to swallow but he had no spit. Something fluttered precariously in the pit of his stomach, and a terrible restlessness stirred inside of him.

# CHAPTER 23

He was with Dr. Holley again, the coroner, walking
beside and slightly behind like a heeling dog. Their
footfalls echoed in the late-night silence of the hospital
corridor. To Scott the sound seemed too loud, amplified
somehow. When they turned the corner into the Emergency Ward and Holley drew the cubicle curtain aside,
Scott remembered his first and only anesthetic, the way
sounds as he free-fell into limbo had seemed louder: the
voices of the staff, the clink and clatter of surgical
instruments, the hiss of condensed gases. This was like
that, an exaggeration of perceptions, real and yet not real.

Overhead shone a bar of fluorescent lights, one tube
fluttering on the brink of extinction. There was a BP cuff
mounted on the near wall, an adjustable stool in one
corner, and a stretcher in the middle of the rectangular
floor. A body, draped in a sheet, lay dead on the stretcher.
Only its feet, waxen and still, were visible.

Scott, or some primitive part of Scott, knew that the

body was Krista's. Who else would wear Sparkling Grape nail polish? He would know that slender shape anywhere, under a hundred blinding sheets. He had seen it so many times before, beneath a silk counterpane, waiting warmly for him to . . .

In fact, he thought, and the thought danced away, she was probably there right now, at home in bed, sleeping soundly beside him, peacefully unaware of this dark and terrible nightmare.

Scott approached the stretcher, fighting and barely suppressing the urge to flee. The floor was a cloud beneath his feet.

*That smell . . . what is that smell?*

Holley drew back the sheet. Beneath it lay Krista's fractured body.

*Death?*

Scott's eyes focused on an invisible point halfway between himself and the corpse on the stretcher. The sounds around him, still exaggerated, began to coalesce into a hum at the base of his skull, the pitch of high-tension wires in a high wind.

Slowly, like a mountaineer taking up slack in a rope, he pulled the image into focus. It came, blurred, then came again.

Scott Bowman looked down at his wife's dead body— forehead mortally dented; face swollen and raddled; nose and lidded eyes streaked with blood; teeth fractured; lips drawn thin in the death snarl of a roadside animal—but perceived only a specimen in a forensic pathology lab.

*Just like in med school,* he thought, and knew that the thought was insane.

Preventing Holley from covering her again, Scott took the sheet and drew it down farther.

There were her breasts, oddly deflated, reddened in an arc where the steering wheel had struck her. And the bruised, tense, melon-sized swelling of her belly. Her entire blood supply lay clotting in there, Scott knew. *Ruptured spleen.* Yes, it would have been her spleen.

But her hands . . . her hands were perfect.

Krista's hands.

And, oh, God, how pale they were.

Letting the sheet fall, Scott took Krista's left hand in his own *(with this ring I thee wed)* and kissed its icy knuckles.

*Why won't her elbow bend?*

He held her hand. Enfolded it. Tried to warm it. His blurring eyes found her rings. Here was the small diamond he had eased onto her finger that night on the jetty. And next to it, the gold band he had given her in the office of the justice of the peace.

"Is this her?" Holley's voice, a faraway whisper. "Is this your wife?"

But no . . . her hands were not perfect. Her fingers were swollen. Scott knew this because when he tried to remove the rings he was unable to get them over the first knuckle. As he tugged he became aware of a repetitive hissing sound, his own breathing, he realized. straining in and out between his clenched teeth. The cold of Krista's flesh seemed to be flowing into him, flooding toward his living core like ice water pumped into open veins.

When the rings came away, Scott dropped Krista's hand. He couldn't be sure, but he thought he heard a faint creak of tendons. He reached clumsily for the sheet to cover her again, but Dr. Holley took it and did it for him.

Like a rusted windup toy, Scott exited the cubicle and wandered off in the direction of an ER storage room. After a moment Holley caught up to him and led him away.

They were in a small dark office, Holley behind a paper-stacked desk, Scott sitting head-in-hand across from him. Holley lit his pipe, took a lingering pull, then exhaled a column of thick blue smoke. He leaned forward, his sharp face freakishly underlit by the low-wattage desk lamp, and uttered a comfortless condolence.

"I'm sorry, Dr. Bowman. It's a terrible shock. A terrible shock."

Scott didn't hear the coroner, or if he did, he gave no hint of comprehension. He was aware only of an ache inside his fist where Krista's rings dug into the flesh (there was hot moisture in there: sweat, or perhaps blood), and that maddening, unwavering hum inside his head. His mind was a series of crazily intersecting tracks, chaos in a busy railyard, thoughts like locomotives steaming furiously through, threatening to careen out of control. His mind was on that stretcher in the ER. It was on Kath's terror-stricken face. And it was on those drawings, and that creepy little man strapped to a wheelchair a thousand miles away.

His mind was on fire.

"How did it happen?" he whispered, clasping the rings.

Holley shifted back from the glow of the desk lamp and was nearly lost in shadow. He had left the room deliberately dark. He thought it eased the mind a little, helped to mute the shock of sudden loss. Regrettably, it was a scenario he had played out often before. Too often. He took another puff of Amphora before answering.

"The car was found against a stone fence about twenty miles north of the city," he said evenly. "A farmer called the accident in. As far as a cause is concerned, I can only speculate. Apparently, there were no other vehicles involved. My guess is that your wife lost control of the car for some reason. Maybe she was overtired, or speeding. Those rural roads are narrow and winding, and they're often poorly marked. It's quite possible that—"

"Rural road?" Scott interrupted, lifting his haggard face.

Holley dipped back into the pool of light above his desk. "Yes, one of several off-roads linking smaller settlements to the Interstate. The investigating officer reported finding a receipt above the visor from a service station near Byfield. Radiator trouble, I think he said. She was headed back to the highway when it happened."

The hum at the base of Scott's skull pitched up an octave. Invisible ants swarmed over his flesh. He sucked in a breath, but it lodged like a fishbone in his throat. Suddenly the reek of Holley's pipe threatened to turn his stomach. Fidgeting dizzily, he closed his eyes . . .

And there was the cartoon Volvo, crumpled against a low stone wall, steam hissing out of the grille, its interior dark and untelling.

"You mentioned a stone wall," Scott said, the words tasting like bile.

"Yes," Holley replied, shifting back into shadow so that now his voice seemed disembodied. "They hit the stone wall surrounding the Hampton Meadow Cemetery."

# CHAPTER 24

Once, when Scott was a boy of six or seven, another boy flung a basketball at him and it struck him dead-center, punching his wind out in a stunning explosion. His chest froze that way, with the air knocked out of it, and he was unable to take another breath for what seemed like several minutes. By then his mind had fogged over, tiny colored lights had begun to flash inside his eyes, and his fingers had begun to tingle.

He felt that way now. Breathless, punched out. It was as if some cerebral breaker switch had been kicked over by an unexpectedly violent electrical backsurge, and his ability to think, to abstract, had been fried in the process.

Again Caroline failed to notice him when he stepped into Kath's room in the ICU, and again Scott experienced that drifting sensation of unreality. It occurred to him that this was how a ghost must feel, able to observe and yet desperately unable to make contact, to involve itself in the cycle of life around it.

Then he noticed Caroline's face—waxy-pale, sweat-sheened, contorted in fear—and the way her fists were dragging at the corners of her mouth; and when she turned and her pallor deepened, when she told him between racking sobs that Kath had spoken only a moment before, Scott felt a vicious spasm in his chest. Because in the next instant he heard it, Kath's voice, welling up as if from a great and hollow depth.

"Dead" was the single word she uttered.

Then the convulsion seized her.

It began slowly, almost imperceptibly—a slackening of her stricken face; a vague ballooning of her neck; a fine tremor in her limbs—then it spread like a quake along a fault line until her back arched to the point of snapping and her limbs hammered out a driving tattoo against the mattress.

Before Scott moved, before his medical training leaped to the fore and spelled out the obvious diagnosis of grand mal seizure, he experienced a brief, irrational revulsion for his child. Watching her—jerking and hissing, eyes bugging, mouth foaming, urine staining the front of her gown—he was overwhelmed by a sudden, icy awareness. Something black and pure, potent and ageless, was seeping out of his child in oily beads that he could almost smell.

And that something was evil.

But the feeling passed, and in the instant before Caroline screamed and medical personnel began filing into the room, Scott's rational voice uttered the simple truth: *It's a convulsion, nothing more.* But now he thought he understood why, generations before, God-fearing people had believed that Satan himself had visited upon those afflicted with seizures. Apart from a shadowy physical resemblance, there was no sign of his daughter in that twitching thing on the bed.

Scott lurched forward to grab her, but the arm of an orderly restrained him, leading him away from the bed where Kath grunted and writhed and soiled herself. He caught a last glimpse of her twisted face before the hideously bright, rainbow-colored curtains were drawn, and the bed was lost behind them.

The image branded itself on his memory.

He knew exactly what they would do to arrest Kath's seizure: a mouth guard would be forced between her teeth; a nurse and perhaps an orderly would restrain her limbs beneath their combined weight; and the intern would inject a few milligrams of Valium into the IV tubing, stopping the convulsion and creating enough sedation to keep Kath quiet for the next several hours.

But that was only a fraction of what streaked through Scott's mind as he stood outside Kath's room in the ICU, Caroline grafted to his chest, the bank of monitors beeping chaotically behind him. There was a demon rearing up inside of him, a capering, cloven-hoofed thing with Dr. Holley's face, and it was claiming that the woman Scott had seen lying stiff and broken on the stretcher in the ER belonged to him. It was trying to convince him that the dead thing on that stretcher had only hours before been his wife, the warm island of flesh and blood he had married ten years before. But he would have none of its hectoring proclamations, and in his mind he clawed at the demon's throat, tore out its greasy workings and choked off its lies in a glut of cartilage and blood. He saw himself do this, and then he saw the three of them together, he and Krista and Kath, arm in arm and smiling, posing before a pair of umbrella-like floods for the family portrait he kept on the shelf behind his desk at work, the one that had gone missing a thousand years ago, when life was still something he thought he understood. His mind skittered next to the dock, to Krista and Kath kneeling over his heaving chest as he choked lake water from his lungs, to the comfort he had felt through his terror just knowing they were close and that they loved him. Full circle, it came back to

Holley *(they hit the old wall surrounding the Hampton Meadow Cemetery)* and the drawings which had told it all.

Gradually he became aware of Caroline, her sobs, her confused and desperate need, and he tightened his grip around her. Together, they waited for the curtains to be drawn aside.

The intern, looking dazed and weary, came out first. He told Scott that Kath's seizure had subsided and that now she was sleeping peacefully. He said he was going to call the senior physician in charge and that Kath would be seen by a neurologist first thing in the morning. Then he offered to show Scott and Caroline to a nearby family room, where they could lie down and perhaps sleep.

Scott declined, but urged Caroline to go ahead. She went reluctantly, looking hollow-eyed and beaten.

Scott returned to Kath's bedside. A nurse showed him how to fold out the large sleeper chair by the window, and after a while he stretched out on that. He tried to rest, but his eyes kept popping open, searching Kath's face for signs of awareness. Mercifully, because of the Valium, Scott guessed, her staring expression had softened and her eyes had finally closed. She did appear, as the intern had said, to be sleeping peacefully.

At some point Scott remembered Jinnie, and he got up off the chair to retrieve her. As he dug the doll out of his flight bag, his fingers snagged the drawings and pulled them out, too. He set the doll on Kath's pillow, then reclined again on the sleeper.

In the pale-orange glow of the exterior lamps, Scott unfolded the drawings and went over them frame by frame . . . until a chill crept into his heart and he could look at them no longer. Tears doubling his vision, he refolded the sketches and stuffed them into his shirt pocket.

And just when he thought he would never sleep again,

that he would lie awake with the images of his convulsing daughter and his ruined wife capering eternally
before his tired eyes, the accumulated shock and exhaustion of the preceding four days struck him like a bar-
biturate overdose, and he tumbled into a nightmare
slumber where dead men walked and pain was his only
companion.

# CHAPTER 25

When Dr. Holley came into the ICU on Wednesday morning, he found Scott curled on the fold-out chair, staring blankly at his unconscious child. It was apparent that he hadn't slept much at all. As gently as he was able, the coroner encouraged Scott to get on with the ugly business at hand.

"You'll have to make arrangements for the disposition of the body," he said in a tone Scott recognized, the one reserved by the profession for those sorry aliens known as "the Bereaved." "Customarily, the funeral home manages all of the details—pickup, transfer, all of that. You only have to call and let them know. There are a number of forms which require your attention, both for your wife and for your daughter. And your car has to be moved. As I understand it, there's been a fair bit of damage, but the car is far from being a write-off." Holley gave a sigh. "Have you called any of your relatives yet?"

Scott shook his head. It hadn't even occurred to him to

call. He would have to tell Klara first, then Krista's mother . . . or perhaps he could leave that to Klara . . . yes, that would be best. He should call Gerry, too, and a few of their other close friends, but that could wait.

Holley stood. "The nurses have the necessary forms," he said, indicating the computerized consul beyond the room's Plexiglas sidewall. "You can tackle those as soon as you feel up to it." He glanced at his wristwatch. "I have another hour or so of work to do around here, then I have to go into town. If you'd like, I can take you by the impound where your car is being stored. By now they should be able to tell us if there were any mechanical problems which might have caused the accident. And you'll be able to decide with them how best to deal with the car."

Scott shifted into a sitting position on the edge of the sleeper. Scrubbing his face with listless hands, he peeked through his fingers at Kath, whose eyes were half open and hopelessly blank. Dimly, Scott recognized what Holley was doing: gently but firmly, the coroner was attempting to keep Scott mindful of the realities, perhaps recognizing how easily he could be tipped over the edge.

"I don't know if I should leave her alone," Scott said thickly. His head had taken up a throbbing ache that seemed to be worsening now that he was upright. "Maybe I should stay here for a while." He rubbed his temples. His mouth was dry and tasted foul, and for a moment he thought his stomach might turn. But the feeling passed.

"Not to worry," Holley assured him, tapping the paper clipped to his belt. "I carry a long-range beeper. I'll make certain they call us if there's any change in your daughter's condition." Holley's urgings were taking on the texture of gentle commands. "Why don't you get cleaned up a little, take a shower, have some coffee maybe. I'll be back inside of an hour. Then you can start getting some of this stuff behind you. All right?"

Nodding uncertainly, Scott turned back to Kath.

"She'll be fine," Holley said, and for this he adopted

another of the Medical Man's repertoire of speech tones. "You'll see." Then he left.

Scott didn't bother getting cleaned up (though he hadn't shaved or bathed, and had been wearing the same clothes for more than twenty-four hours), and he refused the coffee one of the nurses offered him. Instead, he remained by Kath's small, motionless frame, his body disconnected and his brain on hold.

Before leaving with Holley an hour later, he checked in on Caroline. She was still asleep, muttering and tossing restlessly.

# CHAPTER 26

The police impound turned out to be a double-bay Texaco station in the city's south end. The Volvo, which from the back appeared undamaged, sat to one side of the station next to a wrecked Duster. Holley parked his silver Mercedes by the cluttered front entrance. As he climbed out, he hailed a mechanic who was working beneath a yellow Honda on a hoist. Scott waited in the car, deliberately avoiding the Volvo, looking instead at Holley and the mechanic. The mechanic squinted toward Scott, said something brief, then shrugged. Finally the two men moved deeper into the garage.

As if to do so was forbidden, Scott stole a glance at the Volvo. From this angle he could see that the front end was badly staved in, and he looked away again.

*How did this happen?* his mind demanded. *Had* there been some mechanical malfunction? Caroline had told him over the phone that Krista had had some kind of car trouble. Had the mechanic at the station Holley mentioned done something wrong? The Volvo was a foreign car, and with the turbo booster its engine would be Greek to all but a specially trained mechanic. Had that bastard tampered with something technically beyond him? Made some grievous mistake?

Scott started to get out of the car. He would ask these people himself if Holley was going to take all day. . . .

Then the coroner was stepping out of the garage again, moving briskly toward the Mercedes. He came to the passenger's side and opened the door. Scott climbed out and followed him to where the Volvo sat waiting.

As he approached the car, Scott became dimly aware of Holley's voice. He was telling Scott that although the mechanics had gone meticulously over the car, they had found no evidence of any causal malfunction. But the noise in Scott's head—the high-pitched hum that had begun in the ER cubicle and had since been slowly driving him mad—pitched suddenly higher, filling his mind with white noise as he moved reluctantly toward the Volvo.

Biting his lip, Scott urged himself to regard the evidence of his family's destruction. His eyes fought desperately to turn away, but he forced them to look. He began at the rear. There was no damage back here, and for the moment it was safe to pretend that none of this had happened.

Then he saw that the door on the driver's side had been punched in, and he hesitated, thinking: *This isn't so bad . . . a person could have survived this. . . .*

He took another step forward and stopped again, next to the undamaged side mirror. From here he could see that the hood was sprung, and that the windshield had been shattered. That explained the small cuts on Kath's face and neck.

Unconsciously, Scott rubbed the old scar on his chin.

Then he noticed a pool of congealed blood on the dash in front of the steering wheel, and that made him glance sharply away, his breath catching like an ice pick in his throat.

Stumbling on a loose chunk of asphalt, he trudged unsteadily toward the front of the car, where the bulk of the damage could be seen.

The Volvo's plastic grille had been reduced to splinters, the fenders accordioned back at least two feet. Through the yawning mouth of the hood, Scott saw that the engine had snapped its mounts and had dropped beneath the chassis. He remembered the salesman crowing about this special safety feature ("In a head-on collision the engine doesn't wind up in your lap.") and thinking: *Neat, but I'll never need that. Not me . . . not us.*

Still struggling to deny the whole thing, Scott grasped at the false hope that the car belonged to someone else . . . but then he leaned in through the open side window and spotted one of Kath's plastic shoes (Jellyshoes, she called them) lying on its side on the floor mat. And there was the V-shaped rip Krista had made in the upholstery with a shelving bracket she had bought at Canadian Tire. God, how she had fretted over that. . . .

It was his car, all right.

Like a sleepwalker, Scott returned to the driver's side of the car and tugged on the battered door. It screamed on ruined hinges. The spring adjustment groaned as he sat down, and the seat shifted back a notch, but then it locked.

He put his hands on the steering wheel and saw that it was bent.

Then he was sniffing the air, peering down beneath the dash, beside him, into the back seat. There was an odor in here, behind the still-new smells of the car—a musty, wet reek that reminded him of the time he had found a dead rat behind the washing machine in the basement at home. Rot or mold mingled with dampness and age. It was . . . was it? . . . the same smell he had noticed around the corpse on the stretcher in the Emergency Room? That whiff of death?

Then he saw the lid of the Coleman cooler, jolted loose in the impact of the crash, and reaching back, shifted it all the way open. Inside, a half-eaten submarine sandwich floated in a pool of milky water. It was rank.

Scott pressed the lid shut and climbed out of the car. The Volvo was repairable, but he knew he could never drive it again. After today this was the last he wanted to see of it. He would tell the mechanic to have it towed away, or let him sell it for parts or scrap.

He turned back toward Holley, who leaned patiently against his Mercedes. Then something occurred to him, and he leaned again through the open door to confirm it.

Yes, it was true . . . there were jewels of shattered glass in the back seat.

Scott bumped his head on the doorframe as he jerked it out of the car. How could there be glass in the back seat? Holley had said that the Volvo had spun out of control and struck a stone wall. If that was the case, then the windshield—*if it shattered at all,* Scott thought—would have shattered *out*ward, not inward.

*Unless they hit something movable,* he thought, and his fingers went to the scar on his chin again. *Unless something came through the windshield from the outside.*

Holley's pager sounded. The static-ridden voice was faint, but Scott was certain he heard a message to call the hospital. The coroner excused himself and hurried back into the garage.

A knot of fear constricted Scott's stomach. Was it about Kath? Had she taken a turn?

Nearly sick with anxiety, he stumbled into the garage after Holley. The gaunt physician was standing inside a small, ill-lit office using the phone. After a moment he handed the receiver to Scott.

"It's for you," he said.

Scott inched forward on rubber legs, unable to read a thing in Holley's eyes. Accepting the receiver, he beat back a pessimistic voice in his mind. But as he brought the receiver to his ear, that inner voice refused to be silenced.

*I'm sorry,* it said, *but she's convulsing again, and it's not so good . . . not so good at all.*

"Hello?"

Silence. A muffled sob.

"What is it?" Scott shouted, his scalp crawling. "What's happened?"

Again a pause, more brief this time, then Caroline was on the line. She was crying, and Scott felt his knees begin to buckle.

*she's convulsing again . . .*

"Scott?" Caroline said, her sobs turning to rich, hysterical laughter. "She's awake! She's awake and she's asking for you. Please come, Scott . . . quickly. I . . . I can't bear to tell her."

A relief so profound, so gigantic, welled in Scott that he turned to face Holley and let his own tears come without shame. "Give me ten minutes," he said. "Oh, God . . . she's awake?"

"Yes, and she seems okay . . . only a little groggy."

"Ten minutes," Scott repeated, and hung up. "Can you drive me back?" he said to Holley, almost shouting.

Understanding that this man, who stood a head taller than he and whose face at that moment bore all of the hallmarks of lunacy, would probably knock him to the pavement and steal his car if he refused, Holley agreed.

They climbed into the Mercedes and spun out of the lot at speed.

# CHAPTER 27

Ten minutes later the Mercedes screeched to a halt in the fire lane fronting the hospital. Scott jumped out, bounded up the steps, and jostled his way through the crowded front lobby. A Lady's Auxiliary volunteer started to ask if she could help, but Scott dashed by her unheeding. He swung left and ran along the hallway to the ICU, where he thrust open the doors and darted inside.

Approving smiles greeted him. Unmindful, he moved quickly past the bank of monitors to Kath's corner room. The bright-colored curtains were drawn, and Scott shouldered his way through them.

Caroline was sitting cross-legged on the window ledge. And Kath was propped against a mound of pillows, sipping water from a Styrofoam cup through one of those bent-elbow straws. She turned slowly toward Scott, her usually shiny eyes dull, and it seemed to take her a moment to recognize him, a moment which dragged painfully for Scott.

Then she moaned "Daddy?" and her little arms reached up for him.

Scott rushed forward, then slowed, sitting gingerly on the bed beside her. Kath wrapped her arms around his neck and squeezed weakly.

"You're scratchy," she said, drawing back, brushing a hand across one stubbled cheek. Caroline giggled.

"How do you feel, kiddo?" Scott said, trying in vain to hold back his tears. He kept her close so she couldn't see.

"Drunk, I guess," Kath said, smiling wanly at Caroline over Scott's hugging shoulder.

"Any sore spots?"

"No, just thirsty." She pulled back again, searching her father's eyes. "Caroline says we were in a wreck. Are you mad about the car?"

Scott thought of Krista worrying about the car over the phone the day before. She had been alive then. "Forget the dumb old car, okay?" He tried again to pull her close, but Kath resisted.

"When can I see Mom?"

He had known this was coming, had thought of nothing else during the endless drive in from the impound, but still the question crushed him like a bug beneath a stamping bootheel.

Caroline buried her face in her hands and burst into tears. Kath looked only at her father, searching his eyes, and it was all Scott could do to meet her gaze. His mind—the bit that reasoned, rationalized, and explained—was suddenly blank. Where were the words? *What* were the words? How did you tell a child who loved her Cabbage Patch doll, who believed in Santa Claus and Ronald McDonald, that her mother was dead? Had he really believed it himself before this moment? He thought not—because now the innocence, the very simplicity of Kath's question, brought that brutal fact home with all the destructive force of a cannon blast.

*Where are the words?*

But none were needed. Kath drew limply away and huddled against the pillows, shifting her somehow doomed eyes toward the window and the gray world beyond.

"She's dead," Kath said. A statement, flat and irrefutable. "I knew it. I dreamt it."

Caroline fled the room in a swell of tears. Scott buried his face in Kath's pillow and cried more bitterly than he ever had before. After a while Kath pulled him close, and they wept together for their lost Krista.

Sometime later Scott left the ICU, spent and blackly depressed. Kath had finally slipped off to sleep. Scott had been alarmed by this initially, afraid she'd relapsed into coma or catatonia or whatever it had been. But he found her easily rousable, and decided to let her sleep. For her, at least, there was that escape.

But then he remembered her saying that she'd dreamed her mother's fate, and realized there was no escape for any of them. Like one's own death, it had to be faced.

Yes, Krista was dead. He understood that now. And in the abandoned quiet of the ICU sitting room, he said it out loud: "Krista is dead." Kath's question had made that truth brutally clear. It had shattered the carapace of denial he'd encased himself in as violently as a ball-peen hammer striking glass. And the naked truth had come raining down in the shards—cutting, wounding, but not killing. Now there were things that had to be done, things requiring rational thought and meticulous planning, all the things Holley had been urging him to do earlier this morning.

The chores of death.

He had to bury his wife. God, yes. Bury her. He had to make arrangements with a funeral home in Ottawa, one that handled cremations. That had been Krista's wish, one she had expressed to him one late night several years ago, a week or two following his parents' funeral. Scott had awakened that night to the sounds of a violent summer storm and found Krista sitting in a chair by the window, staring out blankly into the squall. She told him then about a fear she'd carried with her since her father's death from cancer, when she was still just a little girl.

Kneeling before his casket during the wake, Krista had begun to wonder if her father's essence—his soul—might still be trapped inside his body. "How is it supposed to get out?" she'd asked Scott that night in the bedroom of their Frank Street apartment, as if she had not yet resolved that little-girl's dilemma. Her eight-year-old imagination had quite naturally decided that her daddy must still be locked inside, aware but unable to tell anyone because his body was dead. And as only a child is capable, she imagined him lying helpless inside his satin-lined coffin after the service was over, hearing the lid click into place as the mortician sealed it for the last time, seeing the pink undersides of his eyelids darken to eternal black. Then would come the jostling ride on the pallbearer's shoulders, the slow descent into the earth, the muffled intonations of the parish priest, the gradually fading *thud* of dirt tossed from the sexton's spade . . . and finally silence, pure and ceaseless, save for the scarcely audible slither of time and decay.

As a grown woman, Krista had decided she would rather have her soul (if such existed, a question she had never really gotten off the fence about) freed through the finite agony of fire than through the darker alternative—trusting its release to the slow oppressive weight of earth and decay. As disturbed as Scott had been by Krista's unexpected discussion of death—he, too, he realized now, had believed himself and his family invulnerable—he had agreed to her cremation, more to close the discussion than to form a pact. Now he would have to live up to that promise.

"Is there a phone I can use?" he asked one of the nurses at the console. "I have to make some long-distance calls."

The nurse nodded, her face brightening with something which to Scott looked like relief. At first the expression bewildered him, then he thought he understood. He realized from personal experience that his name had probably come up as a topic of concern during nursing rounds at change of shift. These girls were trained to monitor family members for signs of coping and were almost certainly aware that so far Scott had accomplished little in the way of Making the Necessary Arrangements. Phoning home was a good sign.

She led him to the family room where Caroline had slept the night before. It was like a miniature hotel room, with twin beds, a chest of drawers, and a TV set on a rotating pedestal.

The nurse, whose name tag identified her as Sharon McVee, indicated the ivory touch-tone on the night table between the beds. "Just dial zero," she said, "and tell the receptionist you're at local two-five-zero. She'll patch you through to an outside line, and you'll be able to dial direct. And don't worry . . . it's free of charge." She smiled a smile of sympathetic detachment.

"Thanks," Scott said, sitting on one of the beds and watching as Sharon McVee, someone he would never have met had his life not taken this violent skew, left the room, shutting the door behind her.

Suddenly alone, Scott wanted nothing more than to lie back and sleep. In the sane and unnoteworthy surroundings of this room, he realized how close his mind had come to cracking, how frayed reality had become since Caroline's phone call at the airport. Mingled with the raw horror he'd experienced just then, before folding into a boneless heap on the floor, had been a black and pervading kind of warmth, a dark desire to simply end it all, to disconnect the circuits and follow his wife into oblivion. How did that weepy C&W tune go? *There goes my reason for living . . .*

But there were other reasons for living, weren't there? There must be, because he was still here, still drawing breath, still feeling pain. Kath was one good reason, he thought, caught now in a macabre sort of inventory-taking. *What else? My professional life? Ha! Fifteen years and you can't even use your knowledge to help your family or yourself.* He regarded the phone as if it were some sort of alien device. *Don't forget your friends. . . .*

And then he knew, with a swell of relief that made his eyes water, who he was going to call first. His best friend, the guy he'd grown up with, the only guy in the world Scott knew would take a beating in his place. Gerry St. Georges.

*In a minute,* he thought, lying back and closing his eyes. *I'll call Gerry in just a minute.*

And not thinking he would, he slept.

Until two hours later, when a dream-image of Krista, cold and heavy in a refrigerated drawer in the morgue of the Danvers General Hospital, snapped him awake in a mantle of sweat.

He called Gerry's home, but there was no answer. When he tried the station, they told him that Gerry was off for the next few days. He called Klara next, and when she answered with a drunkenly slurred hello, Scott's initial impulse was to hang up and say to hell with her. But ginswill or not, she was Krista's sister, and she had a right to know what had happened.

"Klara, it's Scott." His voice quavered badly. "I'm afraid I have some terrible news."

Klara made no reply—but there was an abrupt cessation of her wheezy respirations. In the anticipatory silence that followed, Scott heard his own words reverberate as if in a tunnel, and a sick cackle crawled up inside of him at their utter absurdity. *Scott Benjamin Bowman,* he thought moronically, *new Baron of the Understatement.*

"There's been an accident," he said into the low hum of silence. "It's Krista. She's . . . dead."

There they were again, those words. The ones he had

mouthed to himself in the ICU sitting room. They got easier as you repeated them. Already their meaning seemed somehow diluted.

Klara resumed breathing. A sigh at first, then deep, hissing lungfuls as a bright disbelieving hysteria overswept her. At the phone by the well-used liquor cabinet in her living room at home, her mouth began to move, but only unintelligible grunts came out.

"Klara," Scott pleaded, "I need your help on this. I can't go through this alone."

Klara remained mute, but in the background Scott heard Joe's voice, asking what the trouble was.

"Give me the phone," Joe said, sounding closer now, and it struck Scott (oddly considering the circumstances) that this was the first time he'd heard Joe Harper assert himself with his wife. Then Joe was on the line, his voice anxious and high. "Who is this?" he demanded.

"It's Scott, Joe. Listen . . ."

Then he said the words again, and this time they came even more easily and sounded even more meaningless. Joe's shock was genuine, but more controlled than Klara's had been, and Scott was able to relate the essentials without having to bear the burden of another griever. Joe assured him that he would take care of informing their mother-in-law in Sandy Point, and asked Scott if he wouldn't mind chipping in on airfare for the old gal so she could attend Krista's funeral. Scott said that would be fine. To Scott's relief, Joe offered to arrange the business of Krista's transport from Danvers to a funeral home in Ottawa.

Finally, already past simple exhaustion, Scott called Dr. Bateman at the Health Sciences Centre in Ottawa.

"God, Scott, that's terrible," Bateman said, unable to give the sentiment anything more than a professional tone. "I'll inform everyone here. We won't expect you until we see you, so don't worry about a thing."

"Thanks, Vince," Scott said flatly. "Good-bye."

"Scott," the department head put in before Scott could break the connection. "Was it like in the drawings?"

Too weary to show his annoyance—had he thought about it before calling, Scott would have expected Bateman's academic interest to supersede his tact—he replied: "Yes, Vince. Right down to the time and place."

"What about the cause?"

*Yes,* Scott wondered bleakly, *what about the cause?*

"Good-bye, Vince," he said, and hung up.

# CHAPTER 28

The balance of that long and featureless day passed without incident—until darkfall, that is, when the horror flared briefly once more.

After speaking with Bateman, Scott stepped outside for some air. He found Caroline wandering the grounds, and he joined her for a while. Neither of them spoke very much. Later, he returned alone to Kath's room in the ICU. Kath slept soundly until a neurologist named Dr. Franklin came in to examine her at three that afternoon.

"Curious," the balding physician said to Scott after rousing Kath, shining a penlight into her eyes, and tapping her tendons. "The oddest course of concussion I've ever seen—if, in fact, that is what it was." Franklin's diagnosis was clearly at odds with Dr. Cunningham's, the intern who had admitted her. "Judging from her initial status, I would have anticipated a much more prolonged convalescence." Franklin said this last with what Scott recognized as professional embarrassment. "But your daughter seems completely recovered. In fact, I see no reason to keep her here in the unit much past tomorrow. A few more days in a nice quiet room on the Telemetry Ward, and—"

"Actually," Scott cut in, "I was hoping I could get her out of here and home. I appreciate everything you people have done, but we're pretty far from home, and . . . I've got a funeral to attend to."

The neurologist averted his eyes. "I see. Yes, you're quite right, of course." He glanced at Kath, who met his gaze expressionlessly. "Will you be flying back home?"

"Yes. As soon as we can," Scott said.

"Then perhaps that would be best. I'll arrange for your daughter's discharge and medications. I'll be leaving her on anticonvulsants to prevent any further seizuring . . . but of course!" Franklin said, suddenly remembering. "You're a physician yourself! Nothing to worry about, then." And with a nod he was gone.

An awkward silence ensued in Kath's undersized room. Scott was unable to think of anything to say to his daughter, only chatter and weak platitudes coming to mind. It was a foreign and dreadfully helpless feeling, and soon his gut twisted itself into anguished knots. Kath lay with her arm around Jinnie, fussing with the doll's dress, whispering softly into its cauliflower ear. Scott recognized the symptoms of regression in his daughter, but was undisturbed by them. It was a means of coping, one he thought he might employ himself before this nightmare faded into healing time.

It was Kath who broke the silence, sitting abruptly erect and fixing Scott with an expression of sheer bewilderment.

"Daddy," she murmured. "What are we going to do?"

Scott was quiet a moment, thoughtful. Then he said: "Go on, pet. We're going to go on."

"But I miss her," Kath cried helplessly. "I don't know what to do now, Daddy. What can I do?"

Scott leaned over and picked Kath up, dully surprised by her apparent weightlessness. Clutching Jinnie under one arm, Kath guided her IV tubing along with her. They sat together in the fold-out chair, and Scott rocked his little girl as he had done when she was still in diapers. They stayed that way until Caroline returned about an hour later, and a nurse came in with dinner trays.

All three ate ravenously. Caroline and Scott had not had a bite in twenty-four hours, and for Kath it had been even longer. Unlike typical hospital fare, the meal was quite good—a healthy slice of roast beef with gravy, mashed potatoes, a heaping helping of broccoli, and for dessert, the inevitable yellow Jell-O.

After they'd eaten, Scott led Caroline back to the family room. "Sleep," he said, and kissed her forehead, which felt feverish against his lips. Caroline was taking it hard, bottling it all up, making herself ill. Scott hoped he could help her soon. "We've got to get together on this," he said in a whisper. "Help each other through."

Caroline nodded, lay down in bed, and was asleep, just like that.

Night fell, transforming shape into shadow.

Kath lay on her side facing her dad, who sat slouched in a chair by the bed. Kath's blue eyes were cloudy with approaching sleep.

"Thanks for bringing Jinnie," she murmured dozily, stroking the doll's bloated cheek. Scott smiled a little. "But when I woke up in the car and she wasn't there, I didn't really mind." She hugged Jinnie to her chest. "I'm glad she's here now, though. Really glad."

Scott rubbed the old scar on his chin. For some reason it had begun to bother him, a dull sort of burning sensation.

"Can you remember the accident?" he said abruptly. The words were out before he'd considered their potential consequences. "Can you remember what happened?"

Kath's body jerked as if struck, and Scott knew immediately that he'd made a serious blunder. What little color she'd had drained from her face, and her mouth turned down at the corners. Her eyes, frightened and round, seemed to stare through Scott's chest, at some mental replay, perhaps, and her fingers gouged into Jinnie's torso, making Scott recall vividly the illusion he'd experienced at home during the storm—the doll on the counter in front of him, grinning in a lightning flash, its stuffing protruding in ugly gray wads.

"Try to remember," he heard himself saying when he knew he should drop it forever. "Try to think, hon. It's important."

Kath squeezed her eyes shut, forcing out a single glistening tear. "I can't," she whispered almost inaudibly. "I can't remember."

There was a dry popping sound, and Scott saw that Kath's clawed fingers had poked through the fabric of her doll's dress.

*Let it go, damn you!*

"Try."

"We were driving . . ." Kath murmured in a baby voice, "and singing . . .

*"Great green gobs of greasy grimy gopher guts,"* she half-spoke, half-chanted in a voice that was wistful and otherworldly, a voice that got inside Scott like something dead. Then her eyes rolled back and her hands curled into fists, and he wanted to stop her, but he wanted her to go on, too, to tell him what she had seen. He reached for Kath's hand, but she jerked it away.

"We were driving and singing, singing and driving, and . . . oh, so sorry, Mister Groundhog, you're dead! . . . and . . . and then . . . we hit him . . . he was dead and we hit him . . ."

"Who was dead? The groundhog?"

*"I can't remember!"* Kath shrieked.

Then her mouth drew down into that terrified bow again, and her face began to twitch, and the twitch spread, becoming a coarse trembling that curled through her body like a wave.

*Oh, Jesus she's going to seizure again!*

But he held her, clutched her, and the crisis passed. A

few moments later, when her face relaxed and then frowned with tears, the nurse who had rushed into the room at the sound of Kath's screams left Scott alone to comfort her.

"I can't remember, Daddy," Kath repeated over and over. "I can't remember."

And Scott rocked her and held her and told her it was all right, that it didn't matter. Sometime later he lay her back in bed and she slept, one arm wrapped lovingly around Jinnie.

# PART
# THREE

# CHAPTER 29

Scott pulled the rented Pinto to a stop at the mouth of the farmer's long gravel drive and gazed at the sagging gray clapboard that had once been white. Flanking the house on either side, weather-blackened outbuildings stood peacefully rotting. Beneath a huge old oak in an adjoining pasture, cattle clustered in groups against the drizzle that was falling.

The farm had been easy enough to find. Holley's directions had been clear, and the name on the mailbox, handpainted in large black letters, had been legible from a hundred yards away. The question was—and it struck Scott now, as he tried to imagine what he was going to say to Clayton Barr, the man whose timely intervention had saved Kath's life: What was he doing here in the first place?

The truth was, he had no idea. He hadn't a clue what he meant to say to Mr. Barr, apart from offering his thanks, and he didn't know what he expected to find later, when he planned to drive out to the scene of the accident. He knew only that he was here, that he had needed to get away from the hospital, from Holley and his forms that needed signing, and from the unseen presence of a corpse that belonged to Krista. He told Holley he wanted the farmer's address so that he could take a run out here and thank the man before leaving for Canada, and of course he was being sincere. . . .

*Come on,* an inner voice urged. *You know why you're here.*

Scott removed the drawings from the pocket of his shirt, the same shirt he'd been living and sleeping in for the past two days, and carefully unfolded them.

Yes, he supposed he did know why he was here and not back at the hospital, Making the Necessary Arrangements. It was these damned drawings, and the nagging questions their existence posed.

He glanced at the drawings and felt deeply cold.

Something had struck the Volvo's windshield, that much was certain. It was the only explanation for the glass inside the car. It might have been something as simple as a flying rock, or the jutting branch of a tree, but Scott had found no evidence of either in the car. The same was true of a large animal, another cow, maybe— no evidence. No hoof-scrapes on the hood, no tufts of fur hooked on to the jagged edges of the windshield, no dark gouts of animal blood.

But it was the cartoon tombstone that ate at Scott's mind like an ulcer. When he had first seen the drawings in Ottawa, he had discounted all but the obviously pertinent details: the car that was clearly a Volvo, and the woman and child inside. In the first few hours after speaking with Holley, he recalled only dimly the uncomprehending shock he had felt when the coroner told him that the Volvo had struck a fence surrounding a cemetery. Then, in the coroner's ill-lit office, the knowledge had struck him like a rabbit punch, but one dealt to a man already senseless and bleeding on the mat. Only later, sitting in Holley's Mercedes in front of the Texaco station, did the knowledge really begin to work on him, but even then the thought process had been suspended by Kath's abrupt recovery.

But last night, sitting awake in the ICU and watching his sleeping child, the whole thing had begun a sluggish distillation through his mind. That the Volvo had in reality struck a fence surrounding a cemetery brought up the blackly fascinating possibility that the cemetery in the drawing was the one at Hampton Meadow, the same one against whose boundary Krista had met her death. And that dragged Scott's attention almost obsessively to the tombstone, to the inscription which was indecipherable save for three or four enticingly legible letters.

Was there one like it at Hampton Meadow? And if so, then ... what? And how had the accident happened? Why were no answers forthcoming? Holley's proffered explanations—that Krista had fallen asleep at the wheel, or that she had simply lost control of the car while speeding—were patently inadequate in view of the fragments of glass inside the car. Scott knew that Krista liked to drive fast, but he couldn't believe she'd been negligent, not with Kath in the car. And the possibility of any significant mechanical malfunction had been dispelled by the police mechanics.

Now, even more than the crippling fact of Krista's death, not knowing how it had happened rattled with a vexing insistence in his mind. Was there a clue hidden in the drawings? As far as Scott was concerned, the Cartoonist's credibility was not to be doubted. The old man's grotesquely recorded predictions had been right on the money so far. And as long as there was a chance that the drawings could tell him more, Scott felt compelled to follow it up.

By dawn this morning, following another sleepless night, he had known exactly what he must do. He woke Kath briefly, just to be sure that he could, then made his way out to the lobby. After a little persuading, the switchboard operator loaned him a long-range beeper, and made a note of his instruction that he be notified of even the slightest change in his daughter's condition. He took a cab to a downtown Hertz outlet, rented the Pinto . . . and now he was here.

Scott replaced the drawings in his pocket, dropped the car into gear, and started up the puddled gravel drive.

The whole trip out here from the hospital had possessed a dreamy sort of quality. For a while as he drove Scott found himself grinning and imagining—no, actually believing—that he was twenty-five again and heading for Krista's place in Sandy Point, to pick her up and take her down to the beach, to their private spot, where he would hold her and kiss her and stroke her pregnant belly, and beg her to give him another chance. The past several hours seemed muddy, the product of some weird psychedelic drug. Yeah. Maybe that was it. A bad trip. Somebody, maybe the stew on the Montreal-Boston flight, had slipped a tab of acid into his drink.

As he crunched into the dooryard, an illusion of a similar clapboard in Newfoundland materialized before his eyes, and for a shimmering moment Scott expected to see Krista burst smiling through the doorway, arms flung wide in greeting. . . .

But a stooped, wary-eyed man appeared where Krista should have been, and the illusion misted into drab reality. A gaggle of geese, dirty white in the drizzle, scattered as the man strode across the unmowed lawn. He nodded, but the wariness in his eyes sharpened when he noticed Scott's haggard features. He stopped several paces back from the car, watching as Scott climbed out.

"Lost?" Clayton Barr said.

"I don't think so," Scott replied, curiously aware of his own voice. "I was hoping to talk to Mr. Clayton Barr."

"That'd be me," Clayton said, extending an open hand. Scott accepted the hand and shook it, aware at once of its callused strength. "What can I do for you, Mr. . . . ?"

"Bowman," Scott said, wishing for an irrational moment that he were someone else. "Scott."

Clayton's face emptied itself of expression, then grew somber, almost pained. He lifted an arm as if to encircle Scott's shoulders, then let it drop again. His eyes, sad, stripped of their former wariness, shifted to a point somewhere beyond the barn.

"Come on inside, Scott," he said quietly. "It ain't a day for standin' in the yard."

Remarking the man's bowlegged gait, and the darker green of his shoulders where the drizzle had soaked through his work shirt, Scott followed him onto the porch. Inside, a big old calico tomcat lay curled in the hollow of a sagging couch, and an assortment of mud-caked boots lay scattered about. A folded newspaper sat next to a half-drunk bottle of beer on the threadbare arm of an easy chair. Beyond the inner door a radio mur-mured a torchy country ballad, and, off-key, a girl's voice hummed along.

Clayton grabbed the beer. "Set right here," he said, indicating the chair. He shooed the cat and claimed its spot on the couch. Rusty springs chattered under his weight. "Helen," he called over the sound of the radio. "Fetch us a couple of cold ones, would you?"

Scott dropped heavily into the worn easy chair, which still had Clayton's warmth on it. The pager clipped to his belt dug annoyingly into his side. Smiling shyly, a homely girl of about eighteen brought the beers out onto the porch. Clayton waited for her to leave before speaking.

"Terrible tragedy, Scott," he said, leaning forward, picking at the label on his beer. "I know it don't help, but I believe I know how you feel. I lost my Sally years ago, givin' birth to Helen in there." He hooked a thumb toward the kitchen door. "She wasn't much more than Helen's age, neither. It hurts, hurts deep, and there's no words to soften it." He fell silent for a time, then said: "What brings you out here?"

Staring dreamily into his beer, Scott began: "I wanted to thank you . . ." But then, desperately, he said, "Can you tell me what happened? What happened to my girls?"

Clayton took a swig of his beer. "That I can't tell you, chum. Only what I heard and saw." He turned his dark eyes out to the yard. "Couldn't sleep last night, so I was sittin' out here, right where you are now, havin' a beer and . . . thinkin' about my Sally, I guess. Yeah, thinkin' about my girl.

"It was quiet—that's what struck me. I guess the quiet was what set me to thinkin' 'bout Sally." Clayton shifted, the couch springs griping rustily beneath him. "Quiet. I mean, there wasn't even a cricket singin'. Strange, now I think of it. Just dead silent, except for the odd semi roarin' by out on Ninety-Five.

"Then all at once I hear this horn blarin'. Some jackass, I'm thinkin', one of the Teevens boys out roddin' around. But this horn keeps right on goin', and its startin' to spook the cows.

"Well, I just ignored it for a while, you know. But it went on for ten or fifteen minutes, and I got to thinkin' maybe there's been an accident. So I lit out across the south field there and down to Route Five, the way you must've come in from the highway, except the other end.

"I found your car plowed up against the fence, down the hill from the cemetery." Clayton paused in uneasy reflection. "God's mercy, I took an awful chill standin' there in the road lookin' down at that car, nothin' movin', and that horn just a screamin'. I don't mean to sound like no pansy or nothin'. I mean, I wasn't afraid of what I'd see. It was a feelin', that's all I can say about it . . . but I wanted to turn tail and run. Somethin' in the air, I dunno. A smell. A dead smell, but old dead. Know what I mean?"

Scott said nothing—but he thought of the smell around Krista's corpse, and the similar stench in the car.

"Ended up talkin' to myself out there," the farmer continued with progressive unease. " 'Come on, Clay,' I said to myself. 'Get your ass down there. Suppose somebody's hurt?' "

"Was there anything around?" Scott interrupted.

"Anything they might have hit? A big animal . . . anything?"

"Well, I did see somethin', or I thought I did—a cloud took the moon just then—shiftin' around in the grave-yard."

"What was it?" Scott probed, his voice raised and a little menacing. "What did you see?"

"Can't say for sure. Every once in a while somebody's cows get out and they turn up in the boneyard, grazin' on the parish grass—"

"Well, what did it *look* like?" Scott pressed impatiently.

The wariness stole back into Clayton's eyes. "I can't say, chum. It might've been an animal, or a shadow, or just my beery imagination."

*Or a man,* Scott thought, remembering the drawings. *Could they have hit a man?* It seemed unlikely. If they had, where was he now? Surely no one could have survived such a collision.

Clayton took a long, gurgling pull on his beer, stalling to see if Scott had anything more to say. But Scott's eyes had gone glassy again, distant and reflective.

"Your wife was already gone," Clayton said. "God rest her soul. And your girlie, well, she was moanin' and . . ." He cut off in midsentence, dropping his gaze to the ratty-eared tom twining in and out between his legs.

"And what, Mr. Barr?"

"Well, she was moanin' and sort of starin'-like, with her mouth open and kind of twisted, as if she was screamin' but no sound was comin' out."

Scott knew the expression.

He started to push to his feet, but his elbow caught his untouched beer and sent it spinning to the floor. Beer boiled out and spread in bubbly-yellow fingerlets. Scott remained frozen in mid-motion, a Polaroid of a man getting out of a chair . . . or perhaps sitting down in it. He had no idea what he should do.

"Never mind that," Clayton said, getting to his feet. "Helen'll mop it up."

"Can you take me there?" Scott said. "To where it happened?"

"Now?" Clayton asked, glancing at his watch. "It's early for lunch, but we could offer you a bite . . . There's nothin' out there for you, chum."

Scott aimed for the door. "Thanks, no, Mr. Barr," he said, and started out through the drizzle. "I'll find it myself."

"Turn right at the end of the lane," Clayton called after him.

But the car was already rolling out of the yard.

# CHAPTER 30

Hampton Meadow Cemetery occupied an acre of hilly ground about a half-mile east of Clayton Barr's entryway. Finding it easily, Scott pulled off the road and parked in front of the wrought-iron gates. Before stepping out into the light caul of rain, he removed the drawings from his pocket and carefully unfolded them.

The westbound continuation of the road followed a sweeping curve for several hundred yards, then banked up sharply and out of sight beyond a low, hunchbacked hill. Keeping to the shoulder, Scott moved slowly toward that hill. Even from this distance he could see the deep gouges in the dirt where the Volvo had left the pavement. Skid marks like black ribbons curved into view from beyond the hill, overlapped, then opened again as they angled off to the shoulder. As he drew closer, Scott could see where the car had struck the wall; crumbled wafers of stone lay scattered about. There were no trees near the damaged section of fence, no low-slung branches to explain the Volvo's inwardly shattered windshield.

Skidding on the rain-slicked grass, Scott descended the steep embankment to the ditch. Something down there had caught his eye, a steely glint beneath a trough of stagnant water. Reaching in, he retrieved a section of molding that belonged to the Volvo. The water was foul, and his hand came away smelling as if he'd dipped it into a cesspool.

He dropped the molding and scaled the opposite bank. Then, breathing heavily, he stepped over the fieldstone fence and made his way into the graveyard.

As he ventured more deeply into it, the initially orderly cemetery became a mishmash of scattered memorials, a sizable proportion of which were little more than square granite plaques laid flat in the earth. It appeared that the grounds back here, with the exception of a few individually cared-for sites, were untended. Almost unconsciously, Scott avoided stepping on the actual burial plots. His mother had warned him against that when he was still quite young, and since then it had always bothered him in a vaguely superstitious way to do so.

Now he ascended an easy grade, pausing beneath a gnarled, leafless tree providing little shelter from the rain. Beyond the grade, in the contour of a shallow, monument-studded basin, a woman in black sat on her haunches before a sand-colored marker. She was rocking and weeping, making a wretched sound that reached Scott's ears in wavering bursts. A wreath of summer flowers lay rain-drenched atop the freshly sodded plot.

*Grief,* he thought. *Black grief.*

The precipitation tapered as he gazed at the woman's back, and suddenly the air seemed colder; Scott could see the vapor of his breath. Chilled, he eased down the opposite face of the incline, veering away from the mourner until he could no longer hear the loonlike quality of her wails. He was dragging his feet instead of lifting them . . . and yet he was possessed by an awful, badgering restlessness.

*Krista,* he thought despondently. *Dear Krista . . .*

In that instant Scott stopped short, the feeling of eyes on his back a physical thing. He wheeled around sharply, his legs now almost magically light, his muscles taut, ready to bolt—

But there was nothing there. Only that dead, wretched tree, cresting the rise, poking dragon fingers into the swirling slate of the sky. Nothing but a stupid tree. . . .

Something cold slipped beneath Scott's hide and spread like ripples on a pond. He clutched the drawings in both hands, tearing the page along a soggy fold-line, his gaze running giddily to the frame with the leafless tree stamped black against a cotton-white moon. When he looked up again, his eyes were round with disbelief.

The tree in the drawing was identical to the one in front of him. Every branch, every twist, every knot.

His balance betraying him, Scott scanned from landscape to drawing and back again, comparing, mentally photographing, shifting from side to side and then front to back, a surveyor lining up markers in proper perspective. Now he edged backwards at a gradual angle, squinting into the dreary geography before him, matching it to the sketch, to the frame with the tombstone a slanted silhouette in the foreground. The tree was shown from farther back . . . and there, off to the right, a partially ruined section of wall.

It wasn't just the tree. The drawing matched the whole dreary scene in every detail. It was as if the old man had been sitting right here when he drew this sequence, and not two-days' drive away in Ottawa.

The angle was still a touch off, though. . . .

*Back,* Scott's mind commanded him. *Back and to the right.*

*There. That's it. Perfect.*

Something hard met Scott's leading heel. Slowly, and with a dreadful certainty spawning in his heart, he turned to face it.

It was the same stone, just as he'd feared and at some deeper level had known it would be, and instinctively he shrank away from it, skittering off that sunken, six-by-three rectangle of turf like a child whose worst nightmare had suddenly come true.

Shaking his head to dislodge the gray, he read the weather-worn verse carved into the upper tier of the monument.

> *Time was I stood as you do now,*
> *And view the dead as thou dost me,*
> *E'er long you'll lay as low as I,*
> *And others stand and gaze on thee.*

Inclining his eyes, Scott read the name of the deceased: Marissa Rowe. And when he compared the two, he found that the letters legible in the drawing matched those on the monument in front of him, matched them exactly . . . the *M* and the *i,* the double *s* and the *R.*

But who was Marissa Rowe? The name meant nothing to him. . . .

Standing there hunched against the rain, puzzling over a meaningless name carved in stone, Scott's eyes ran almost absently to the dates.

And when he read them, when his mind made that final incredible cross-connection, a fear so elemental, so utterly unmanning blazed its way through him that he twisted around to flee, to run until continents folded in behind him. But his feet wouldn't let him, they were glued there, nailed there, and he only stood, gaping and making whimpering noises in his throat.

Because Marissa Rowe, who was ten years old when they buried her, had died on July 12, 1972. The same day that Scott and his two friends had struck down and killed a child with Scott's Volkswagen Beetle.

A little girl who couldn't have been much older than ten.

Kath's age.

*no*

Scott's legs dissolved and he sat down hard on Marissa Rowe's grave plot, his teeth digging painfully into the flesh of his lower lip as his chin struck one bent knee. He felt himself slipping, sliding closer to the stone as if dragged, and now there was something wet dripping from his chin, droplets of it splattering the back of one clammy hand . . . blood?

Yes, it was blood, and—

*glass was flying stinging like furious yellowjackets and the child was shattering the windshield with her face and when we got out of the car she was already dead but there was no one around and so much to lose our careers our futures we all knew that—*

*so we ran . . .*

Still on his backside on the ground, Scott scrabbled away from the plot on the heels of his hands and feet, trying to escape his own backlashing memory.

They had been lost that night, they could have been anywhere, even someplace close to here. . . .

*Someone must have seen us,* he thought wildly, bringing a finger to his slightly split lip. *Someone saw us and now they're getting even.*

Insane, the remaining flicker of his reasoning mind objected, utterly irrational . . . how could they (and who were *they?*) have enticed Krista into driving down *this* particular road? And why such an elaborate and long-delayed vendetta? How could such wild and disconnected events have been so artfully orchestrated?

Despite his reasoning, Scott's mind insisted on creating a most sinister scene. Maybe, he thought senselessly, someone had been following his girls since they left home, had kidnapped them when they stopped for gas or lunch, and then forced them to drive down here, releasing them without explanation at the other end of this sideroad. Maybe they had even been depraved enough to disinter Marissa Rowe's rotting corpse and prop it up in the road. In the dark it might have looked to Krista like a living person, especially if they stood it at the base of that sharp, humpbacked hill. Clayton had said he ignored the blare of the horn for ten or fifteen minutes before going out there, and the walk would have taken him another ten, plenty of time to remove the evidence. And they could have reburied the remains later on. . . .

*Was that what I smelled on Krista? In the car?*

Scott climbed unsteadily to his feet, his thoughts all aswirl. And in the rain that exploded into a bracing downpour as he stood there, he looked again at the drawings before a gust snatched them from his grip and bore them briskly away.

It had to be. Sixteen years ago someone had been crouched at the roadside and had seen them, had memorized the Volkswagen's license number, and then waited, waited long and with imperturbable patience, as Scott himself might have done had the same thing happened to Kath. . . .

Scott found his legs and started back to the car. If someone was after Kath, then she wasn't safe by herself, not even in the hospital. But then he turned and hurried back for the drawings, suddenly unable to imagine going on without them. They were his only tangible link with the lunacy he had uncovered, the only thing distinguishing it all from the workings of a demented mind.

He found them plastered against the stonework fence at the back of the cemetery, all tattered and soaked through. Beyond the fence, just visible through breaks in the overhanging trees, he noticed a road, paved but unused, probably for years. Sprays of milkweed and crabgrass poked up through fissures in the sun-bleached asphalt. There was a sign back there, leaning, faded, pocked by .22 shells. OLD BURWASH ROAD, that sign said . . .

And again his mind was reeling back across the years, braking at the rim of hell, where—

*they were in the car and peeling away, drunkenness vanished, weariness erased by a hideous shared alertness, and in the back seat Jake was fumbling with the map, tearing it in an effort to unfold it, his voice as he struggled crazed and high: Where are we? What road is this? Old*

*Burwash, Scott bellowed back at him . . . the Old*
*Burwash Road . . .*

Scott stumbled and nearly fell.

And all at once it was as if he had pitched through that
fragile membrane between sanity and its darker sister.
The hum in his head grew abruptly deafening, absorbing
into itself and amplifying the sounds around him: the
low-pitched moan of the wind; the beating pulse of the
rain; the hammering of his heart against the cage of his
chest. And when he bent to retrieve the drawings, the
frames seemed for an instant to come to life, moldering
corpses shouldering their way one by one through the
sleepless soil, he imagined he could hear them, smell
them . . . and in that instant of total unreality he whirled
to gape at the grave plots behind him. . . .

But the earth was undisturbed, its mortal weight
matted beneath dying grass and deepening rain puddles.

Scott leaned against the fieldstone fence, pressing his
temples with rigid fingers, waiting for the din in his head
to subside. When it had diminished to a tolerable roar, he
stepped over the fence and strode stiff with trepidation
along the Old Burwash Road, the late-summer rain
chilling him to the core.


*"Is she dead?"*

Scott stopped in the road about five hundred yards
west of where he'd stepped over the fence. He looked
down at his feet and thought he could make out a faint,
roughly circular stain in the asphalt.

Then Brian Horner was standing behind him, repeating over and over "Is she dead? Is she dead?" in a voice
that was shrill with terror.

*"Is she dead?"*


In the lambent haze of predawn they stood in horrified
tableau over the unmoving body of the child, watching as
the pool of red that haloed her head crept steadily wider
and wider. Dressed in white, all frilly-lace and summer-
pretty, she lay crumpled on her side, one leg wrenched

back at an angle it had never been meant to assume. Her arms lay slung out in front of her, as if she had tried to grab hold of something to stop her as she sailed dying through the damp morning air. On her feet were snow-white bobby socks, the one on the foot that was twisted behind her hanging half-on, half-off. The impact had knocked her clean out of her freshly polished Sunday-best shoes (it was Sunday, Scott had realized then, and she was already dressed for church).

*Is she dead?*

The kitten she'd been chasing came out of the shadows at a gallop, mewling like the tiniest lost soul in the universe. When the wind caught the child's silken hair, the kitten sprang jauntily forward, swiping playfully at the riffling, silver-white strands.

Feeling as though his head might explode, Scott knelt at her side and placed a finger over the carotid artery in her neck. He concentrated into the tip of that finger every ounce of sensitivity he had left, adding to that prayers he hadn't uttered in too many years. . . .

But his finger felt nothing, nothing but a soft ebbing warmth, and when he turned to look at his friends, still little more than faceless silhouettes behind him *(Ringwraiths,* he remembered thinking later, *they look like ringwraiths),* there were tears in his eyes.

He turned back to the child—an albino, he realized in a queerly detached, clinical way—and the world went abruptly aslant, its margins beginning to darken.

Then there were powerful fingers gouging into the flesh of his shoulder, and a lunatic voice spouting harsh, hissing words:

"Don't you pass out on me, you fucker! We've got to get *out* of here, man, and it's got to be now. You know that, don't you?" Jake Laking. "There's a light back there in the trees, a porch light, I bet, but I don't think anyone saw us." His eyes were a glowing amber, predatory and keen. "If we stay here, we've had it. Come on, get up. Get up *now!*"

"He's right, Scott." Brian's voice, a faltering echo. "Oh, dear Jesus, he's right . . . please . . ."

And he *was* right . . . wasn't he? To stay was to court unimaginable ruin. The kid was dead (Scott pressed a finger to her neck once again, just to be certain; maybe he'd missed that precious pulse of life the first time; after all, he wasn't a doctor, not yet, he'd only seen this on the goddam tube, they always did this on TV, even in the westerns . . . but there was nothing, no pulse, and even the warmth he'd felt there earlier had diminished), and there was nothing anyone could do for the dead. They had to think of themselves now.

They had to run.

The kitten was lapping, it was lapping at the slick creeping blood, its purr like a motor . . . a Volkswagen motor, and Scott realized that he was kneeling alone with his crime. The others had fled to the car, Jake rigid behind the wheel, Brian hunched low in the back.

Scott stood, weaving, unable to drag his eyes from the dead thing he had created in the road.

Then he ran, too.

He tripped in a sprawl over a tiny scuffed shoe, gathered himself up again, and piled into the car like a thief.

But not before he saw that twinkling yellow light in the trees.

Scott looked up from the ghostly stain in the road and into the rain-spattered woods.

There was a building back there. From where he stood he could see a section of its black-shingled roof.

Squat, swaybacked, with a single rotted gable and a screened-in porch, it was more a cottage than a house. And when Scott stepped soaked and shivering into the weed-infested clearing it occupied, he realized the place was abandoned. Once, years ago, the building had been jacked up onto stilts to avoid spring floods . . . but one of the stilts had long since shifted, and now, like a drunken cowboy, the house listed badly to the west.

Scott stood at the rim of what had once been the backyard. To his left, the rusted skeleton of a child's swing stood aslant in a puddle of water, and a staved-in doghouse hunched rotting beneath a droopy willow. On the stoop by the back door were an ancient ringer-type washing machine, an old wooden stool, and the corroded remains of a tricycle. The door itself, with a naked bulb miraculously intact in the ceiling above it, stood slightly ajar, its dark mouth crosshatched in cobwebs.

Had it really been the Old "Burwash" Road, Scott wondered now, soaking his shoes in a scum of rancid water. Couldn't it have been the Old "Anything" Road? Wasn't his imagination working on a strung-out sort of overtime right now?

*Is this the same place?*

Badly shaken, Scott crossed the balance of the yard in rapid strides, shifting his glance from side to side in the nervous jabs of a man who imagines himself watched. When he got to the door, he set his shoulder to it—and then stopped, his unease suddenly doubling.

What did he hope to find here? he asked himself. What possible good could any of this do? He should clear out of here right now, get back to Danvers, to the hospital and his only child.

Compelled, Scott looked again at the door. It had swollen over the years, and its frame had shifted in the direction of the overall list. It was meant to open inward, but when he tried it the foot uttered an abrasive shriek of wood against wood and then jammed. He had to suck in his belly to do it, but he managed to squeeze in through the gap.

He found himself in a dusty kitchen, dim, almost dark, the only light a diffuse gray cast from beyond the adjoining hallway. At one time the floor had been sur-faced in checkered linoleum, but now most of that was gone and planks showed baldly through. Empty whiskey bottles tented in dust-ridden webbing lay scattered about like extracted teeth. In a corner next to a wood-burning stove, a chrome-and-Formica table lay dead on its side. There was a single window, above the sink, but that had been boarded over.

*Leave,* his mind insisted. *Get out of here. Go.*

The narrow hallway was dark and festooned with cobwebs. Head down, Scott stepped unsteadily into it. The imperfect angles jarred his already muddled perspective, giving the place a bizarre, funhouse feel of unreality, and Scott moved with a hunted man's caution. Loose boards creaked beneath his feet. Broken glass gritted. Things skittered noisily behind cracked-plaster walls, perhaps fleeing, perhaps not. Partway along the hall Scott raked his hands out in front of him, and they came away clotted in webbing, each gray mass specked with the sucked-dry corpses of insects.

He edged toward the lazy square of light that lay ahead where the hallway widened into the staircase and the living room took its entrance. He swung left into the archway and his toe caught something rigid. There followed a brief but clamorous chain reaction: a warped plank that had swept across the archway like an aerial turnpike tumbled into a leaning beam, and both of them came crashing to the floor in a dusty clap of thunder.

Then there was only silence, save for the steady spit of rain against broken window panes.

The dust was slow to settle. Thick and ancient, it swirled like mist on a midnight moor. Gradually the light filtering in through the rank of multipaned windows began to penetrate, lending a blue-white cast to the objects in its radius. Beyond the swirls, nearly invisible in the center of the room's back wall, a low arch like the mouth of a Venetian bridge yawned blackly open. At first Scott figured it was just a fluky symmetrical defect in the wall.

But as he drew nearer, he saw that it wasn't just a chance defect. It *was* a mouth, but the mouth of a huge fireplace, which in turn was the maw of a stone-carved lion, King of Beasts, with massive, arching jaws that seemed frozen in the act of swallowing the room whole.

And Scott had seen it before.

The room, the lion, all of it.

*But where?*

Then, like a brutally thrust gunbutt, it struck him. The Cartoonist. The series of drawings the old man had let slip—almost deliberately, it had seemed at the time—to the floor on Friday afternoon, the first time Scott had laid eyes on him.

*That fireplace, this room, and . . .*

The floorboards. In that sequence of drawings there had been a man ripping up floorboards.

And discovering . . .

Slippery with dread, Scott stumbled back through the slanted hallway, lacy patches of cobwebbing teasing away and clinging to his arms and face. As he rounded the corner into the kitchen, his elbow clipped a shelf stocked with Mason jars and sent the whole lot shattering to the floor. Squinting in the dim, he searched the cluttered room from corner to corner, knocking things over, pitching things aside. By the woodbox next to the stove he found what he was after.

An ax.

Scott raced back to the front room and hoisted the ax on high, a compelling sort of fever suffusing him as he commenced his first violent swing.

And when the floorboards splintered beneath the force of that blow, he felt the final fragments of his coherent mind slip easily away. With his next swing a primitive roar escaped him.

As he bent to his wild work, dust rose in choking motes, smearing into the bars of light from the windows like blood in cold water. The floor became his anguish, his loss, his rage, and he pummeled it with the corroded wedge of steel. His breathing took on a harsh, machine-like whistle, and his throat became so parched with dust it was painful.

Old and tired, the boards came away.

At one point Scott stumbled, and the ax *thunked* into the tomblike rent in the floor. When he bent to retrieve it, a bat, disturbed from its slumber, whickered out and wheeled past him, stitching through the dust like a malign darning needle. Unheeding, Scott pummeled the boards, tears tracking his face in dusty streams.

When the air had cleared and dim light found the room again, half the floor had been torn away. Now, with his toes wedged against something brittle and dry, Scott remembered the last few frames of that macabre cartoon sequence.

The figure had discovered a mummified corpse, with a butcher knife through its heart and something flat clutched to its breast . . .

And there it was at his feet.

Scott reached down and loosened away the bundle from the dry, enfolding arms. The corpse, its gaunt skull-eyes like ice cream scoops out of bone, put Scott in mind of Dr. Holley, the county coroner.

*Is this her? Is this your wife?*

The bundle was a blanket enshrouding a book, a big soft scrapbook of the type Scott had used to paste in projects in public school. As he unraveled the fabric it crumbled in his hands, leaving moldy fragments that reeked of mildew and decay.

He shifted his body so that his back faced the windows, and sat on the rim of the hole. As he settled, his eye caught a faint metallic glint in the depths of the eviscerated chest cavity. When he leaned closer he saw the stainless-steel butcher knife, lodged in the corpse's spine. Impaled on its blade was a prunelike knot of tissue that had once been a human heart.

With the scrapbook open across his knees, Scott squinted in the ill light at the photograph glued to the first page. It was a time-faded Polaroid taken in the yard out back, the swing and hunched willow acting as backdrops. A pale, silver-haired girl stood at the hip of a tall, grinning man who was easily in his seventies, a man with the most striking dark eyes, eyes that were more like buttons. . . .

The words scribbled below in blue fountain ink were barely legible, as if time and putrescence had suspended their business just long enough for this corpse-guarded bundle to be found. The carefully written caption read: "Grandpa and Marissa Rowe. Missy's tenth, July 11, 1972."

The Cartoonist . . . the old man was the child's grandfather.

Feeling as if his skin had begun to tease lightly away from his body, Scott turned the page and tried to decipher the faded letter he found glued there. It was dated January 3, 1970. The script was scrawled and unsteady, created by a tremulous hand, and the text was riddled with errors, most of the words spelled out phonetically. To Scott, it translated into something like this. . . .

Dear Daddy:

I'm all better now. The doctors at the san say I'm ready to take up a normal life again. I haven't had nothing to drink in two years, and for the drugs it's been even longer. I want my Marissa back. I know you are the father, and I told the doctors at the san, but she needs her mama now, so please don't give me no trouble on this. The doctors say she is still legally mine. It's been nine long years. I don't want you doing the same things to her that you done to me. I'll be up there in a week. Please have my little girl ready. Tell her we're going to live in Boston, in a nice apartment near the water.

Your daughter,
Marietta

*Not her grandfather . . . her father . . .*
Scott turned the page. Glued there he found a child's crayon drawing. In it, a crude stick-child cowered behind

218

the leg of a tall stick-man with a knife in his hand. Standing before them was an ugly stick-witch, with a long warty nose and a bottle in her hand. The caption below, in childish script with some of the letters flipped backwards, read: *Please don't let her take me.*

On the next page was an old newspaper article, dated January 30, 1970.

> Reported missing by her father is Marietta Rowe, thirty-six, mother of Marissa Rowe. Miss Rowe had recently been released from a Boston rehab center and had been on her way home to reclaim her child when she vanished. Her father, Nicholas Rowe, has had custody of the child since shortly following its birth. No leads . . .

Along with the clipping was a photograph, also badly faded. A plain pallid face, hardened by alcohol and pain, peered out at Scott like a ghost.

Marissa's mother. Sullen, mean, cheated-looking. Around her neck hung a garish medallion, a peace sign looped in a silver oval.

Scott struck a match and tipped it into the hole. The yellow teardrop of light quivered, creating depthless black shadows.

Coiled in the area of the skeleton's throat were the chain and corroded medallion.

The old man had murdered his own daughter in order to keep Marissa with him. What a strange and terrible love. . . .

Barely breathing, Scott turned the page.

And found drawings.

Once again unreality washed silkily over him.

The drawings depicted that long ago accident . . . but from the child's point of view.

In the first frame a small white hand reached out for the playfully fleeing kitten. The kitten's tail stood straight up, its tiny legs taking quick, bounding strides. In the next frame the tall grass parted as the chase wore on, the kitten always one reach ahead, ducking, feinting, darting away.

Then came the road and the glare of the headlights, and that still, endless moment. Slopes of metal, glints of chrome, a wall of glass, a demon face that was his own . . .

And a white-haired child in a halo of blood.

*How does he know? How is he doing this to me?*

Embracing madness, Scott turned the page.

And found drawings . . .

A house on fire. A mansion. Tall and proud, like his father had been. Dancing, licking flames. A long shot from the mouth of the sweeping entryway, down by the pillared gates. The number forty-seven fashioned in brass, inlaid and polished to a gleam.

It was the house Scott had grown up in.

The house his parents had fried in.

Shaking so violently he could barely breathe, Scott turned to the last rotting page. There, he found a message in neat Gothic script. It said simply: *An Eye for an Eye.*

Fury slipped into Scott's horror, a streak of red in a funnel of blinding white.

Droplets of blood spattered the page in small beaded circlets. Scott lifted a hand to his chin and found that the old, pea-sized scar there had opened and started to bleed.

Now the book's cover seemed to move, to squirm against his supporting hand. . . .

A clot of slugs and shiny-black beetles oozed from the cover and slithered over Scott's bare forearm. Screaming like a banshee, Scott flung the book to the floor and swiped at his arm in wild, scything arcs. He clambered to his feet and took to his heel, but in the dark he tripped on a bottle and fell. Something sharp buried itself into the meat of his thigh. Ignoring the pain he rose again, moving quickly but more carefully now.

He had to get out of here. Had to get back to Kath. She would never be safe alone again.

# CHAPTER 31

As he burst into the lobby and heard the Code Blue call for the ICU, a single overmastering thought broke through: *Got to reach Kath. Got to reach my little girl.* It was this thought, more than any deliberate pattern of command, that carried him forward. He had no recollection of the drive in from the cemetery, nor would he ever have. He had become a creature of pure reflex, functioning on autopilot, drawing unconsciously on the previously learned skills of walking, running, and driving. The voice calling the Code over the PA boosted his run to a precarious sprint. Wide, unbelieving eyes recorded his progress through the lobby and down the hall to the unit.

*Not Kath, please don't let it be Kath. . . .*

The unit's heavy doors yielded to Scott's straight-arm, the racket they made barely contributing to the controlled frenzy of movement already converging on Kath's corner room. A nurse with harried blue eyes thrust a stainless steel crash cart ahead of her. A bearded technol-

ogist burst through a narrow back door, dragging a
robotic ventilator behind him. A squat, fat intern dashed
with surprising agility from her chair before the console,
nipping into Kath's room just ahead of the nurse with the
cart.

And they were all in on it. Every last one of them.

Scott flew across the gray-tiled floor, catching the nurse
by the elbow as she aimed the cart into the room, shoving
past her with enough force to almost topple the cart. He
flung the curtains aside . . . and froze in fearful bewilderment.

It wasn't Kath in the bed but an elderly woman with
tubes running out of every visible orifice. A nurse was
kneeling on the edge of the bed and administering CPR,
counting the rhythm out loud, her words rising above the
clangor of equipment and voices like some weird, ancient
incantation:

"One one-thousand, two one-thousand, three one-
thousand . . ."

The chubby intern touched Scott's elbow, and he
whirled to face her. "Your daughter has been transferred
to the Telemetry Unit," she said in a high, carrying voice.
"We needed her bed. Telemetry's through that door."
She pointed to the far wall, at the back of the ICU.
"Please, Dr. Bowman, we need all the room we can get."

"Is she . . . ?"

The intern flicked a glance at the resuscitation in
progress, then nodded. "Your daughter is fine. Now,
please . . ."

Grinning despite the chaos of suspended death around
him, Scott dashed out of the room and into the Telemetry
Unit, relief glowing in his face like the radiance of a stone
hearth.

Terry Deans, the nurse in charge of the Telemetry
Unit, glanced up from her charting and smiled. But the
smile faltered when her eyes met Scott's. Whoever this
guy was, she didn't want him in her unit. She knew that

immediately. And unless he had a legitimate reason for being here, she would usher him right back out again. He was unshaven and bloodied, his clothes were a mess, and there was something . . . maniacal in his eyes.

She got to her feet and said stiffly, "Can I help you?"

"I'm looking for my daughter," Scott replied eagerly, his bloodshot gaze darting from room to room.

"Her name?" Terry queried, finding it hard to believe that a man in this condition could have a daughter. She wondered if he was the father of the child-abuse case in 2C.

"Kath . . . Kathleen Bowman. She's ten. She was in the ICU until earlier this morning."

Terry felt something loosen in her chest. This was the poor sot whose wife had been killed in that MVA the other night. Still, it didn't explain why he looked as if he'd been out brawling in the rain.

"Your daughter's in 2F, Mr. Bowman. Down this hall, third door on your right."

"Is anyone with her? Her aunt . . . ?"

Terry shook her head. "No. Her aunt left a few minutes ago. Said she was going to scout up some magazines—"

Scott spun away. He didn't want Kath left alone for another minute. It had already occurred to him to call the police . . . but what would he tell them? That somebody was trying to even the score for a hit-and-run murder Scott had committed sixteen years ago?

God, that infernal noise in his head! It had changed subtly in quality. Now it sounded like rats foraging behind plaster, or . . . or . . .

*(or what?)*

2F.

Kath was asleep, lying on her back, Jinnie on the pillow beside her. The doll, its eyes perpetually open, grinned at Scott with benign imbecility.

Scott stepped into the room—this one even smaller than the one in the ICU, but unencumbered by all of that bulky equipment—and sat gingerly on the foot of the bed. Heaving a sigh, he placed a hand on Kath's ankle, which felt warm and vital to his touch. Without startling, Kath opened her eyes and looked at him.

But she wasn't really looking *at* him, Scott realized. No. She wasn't really looking at anything. Her eyes were open and aimed at her father, but they were as unseeing as the eyes of her doll.

Alarmed, Scott whispered Kath's name. Now there was a light in her eyes that had never been there before, a luster that was more like incandescence than reflection, and for a moment it seemed to intensify to an unnatural brightness, making Scott think of the evil offspring in *Village of the Damned*—and of Jake Laking's eyes on that night years ago.

Then it went out, leaving Kath's eyes as vacant and black as a shark's.

Scott stopped breathing and listened.

That noise! What was that Christless noise? It wasn't inside his head anymore, it was right in this room, all around him . . .

*scratch,scratch,scratch . . . scratch . . .*

Kath sat up in bed, *sprang* up, like a tin target in a carnival shooting gallery. Her hands clutched fiercely at her neck, and she began making grotesque gurgling noises in her throat, as if trying to dislodge an inhaled chunk of food. Her face, now almost totally bleached of its high summer color, darkened to the hue of a stormcloud. Her eyes remained dark and wide—and suddenly Scott understood why. Her pupils were dilated, so widely dilated that the blue of her irises was completely swallowed up.

*Brain damage,* he thought in sudden, icy panic. *She's been lying here alone in this fucking Telemetry Unit and convulsing herself into permanent brain damage!*

Scott opened his mouth to scream.

"Daddy . . ." Kath gurgled, striking him mute. "Make it stop . . . Daddy . . ." She raked at her throat, spittle flying from the twisted slit of her mouth. "He's . . . trying to kill me . . . Daddeeeeeee . . ."

*scratch,scratch,scratch,scratch* . . .

Scott looked on in paralyzed horror, the clamor in his head threatening to blow him apart. He watched as his baby strangled and choked, and couldn't lift a finger to help her.

"Oh my God . . ." It was Caroline, standing in the doorway, her face the color of old wax. An armload of magazines fell to the floor with a *thwap!* "Help!" she screamed at the top of her lungs. "For God's sake, somebody, *help!*"

Kath's hands left her throat and reached out for her father. "Daaaa . . ." she croaked, her eyes doing a hideous backroll. "Make it sssss . . ."

Scott clapped his hands to his ears.

*scratchscratchscratchscratchscratchscra*

"No," he roared, slamming his eyes shut. "No-no-NO!"

And then it stopped. All of it. Kath's strangling, Scott's shocky paralysis, the noise in his head . . . a noise that was so much like—

Kath flung her arms around her father's neck and held on like a drowning child. He could hear her breathing next to his ear, short, fitful gasps, and was reminded of his own choking horror beneath the dock.

Thudding footfalls materialized into Terry Deans, the unit's head nurse. "What is it? What's happening?"

"Make it stop it, Daddy," Kath pleaded breathlessly. "Make him go away . . ."

"Who, baby," Scott cajoled her. "Make *who* go away?"

Noticing Kath's labored breathing and the angry red marks on her neck, Terry Deans stepped closer, her expression drawn with concern. "Let me look," she said, and then pulled back as if stung when Scott jerked Kath away.

*"No!"* Scott shrieked, all control gone now. "You stay away!"

A lanky orderly appeared in the doorway.

"Ken!" Terry shouted. "Go get help. *Hurry!*"

The orderly vanished at a run.

"Caroline," Scott said shakily, clutching Kath to his chest. "Find Kath's clothes. We're getting out of here. Someone's trying to hurt my baby—"

"No," Kath choked. "He's . . . Daddeeeee!"

The hackles rising on his neck, Scott pushed back from Kath and stared at her face. It was purpling again, and her eyes . . .

*scratchscratchscratch . . .*

A tall black physician burst into the room, his stethescope bouncing at his neck like a jaunty scarf. When he saw Kath's condition, he lurched to her side, barking orders as he moved.

"Get a crash cart in here, and a ventilator, and get some help from the ICU. I want an IV of—"

"Is that him, baby?" Scott beseeched her. "Is he the one you mean?"

"Please, sir," the doctor appealed. "Clear the way. If this is your child then she's in grave danger. I must treat her now."

*"Get away!"* Scott roared.

Then an orderly was on him, dragging him back, and Kath was choking, mauling her throat, gaping at Scott with those soulless black eyes. People began filling the room—the fat intern, the round-eyed nurse with the clattering cart, the bearded technician with the mechanical lung. Another nurse tried to restrain Kath's arms while the doctor administered oxygen. Kath thrashed savagely, her throat bloating like a toad's, each effort to breathe diminished to a feeble, crowing stridor.

"Get *away* from her!" Scott bellowed, throwing off the orderly as if he possessed no more substance than a pillow. "Leave my daughter alone! It wasn't her fault, can't you see that?"

Hands clamped like manacles around his wrists. A powerful forearm encircled his chest. Scott thrust back an elbow and felt it hammer someone's jaw.

"Get him *out!*" the doctor commanded. Then, to the

nurse with the cart: "Give me a number six E-tube. I'm going to have to intubate her."

The room was tilting, spinning, bleeding darkness. Hands and arms were all over him, forcing him back through the doorway.

*That damned noise!*

And once again Scott was standing in the doorway to another room in another hospital, frozen with a bellyful of cold adrenaline, needing every ounce of control he could muster to avoid fleeing a harmless old man in a wheelchair. A harmless old man and his ceaselessly scratching pencil.

And then he knew, in a dark and ancient part of his soul, what that noise in his head really was.

Kath's struggling had ceased. Now she lay utterly still. The doctor was attempting to insert a tube in her throat. At the foot of the bed, a nurse was unwrapping a sterile surgical tray. Sharp, stainless-steel instruments winked in the cold fluorescent glare. Hopeless resignation dulled all the eyes in the room.

The curtains were drawn.

And the noise in Scott's head abated.

In one clean motion he twisted his body free—and in a dozen quick strides he was out of the unit, down the main hall, and bolting into the family room. He stopped by the bed and grabbed the phone, his breath coming in sharp, shallow rushes.

"I'm at extension two-five-zero," he shouted, recalling the instructions the nurse had given him the day before. "Give me an outside line."

In the pause that followed, Scott removed a tiny telephone directory from his wallet. He flipped it open to *L* and scanned to the middle of the page. It was a number he had recorded years ago, but never used.

There was the chatter of shifting circuits, then a dial tone.

He pressed out eleven musical digits. It rang three times.

"Yes." It was a woman's voice, dull, congested, drugged-sounding.

"This is Scott Bowman. I'm an old friend of Jake's, and it's urgent that I speak with him. Is—"

A bitter chuckle arrested Scott's words. "Is this some kind of joke?"

"What—"

"This is Jake's sister. Jake killed himself, Mr. Bowman. Himself, his wife, and his two sweet babies. We buried the lot of them four days ago."

*Oh, God.* "How did he—" But the dialtone cut him short.

Numb, he fingered a new set of digits, this time from memory, fumbling once and starting again.

"Eastern Ontario Health Sciences Centre."

"Two Link. It's Dr. Bowman. Hurry, please."

A series of clicks. Ringing.

"Two Link, Mavis MacDonald, RN."

"Mavis," Scott breathed, feeling something like relief. He knew this crusty old Grad and liked her. "I need a favor—"

"Dr. Bowman?" the nurse interrupted. "Is that you?"

"Yes. Listen, Mavis, this is terribly important." As he spoke he felt a shred of self-control returning. However incredible, the madness had a focus now. It no longer possessed that awful, free-floating quality. "I want you to run down to the old man's room, the Cartoonist, and I want you to take his clipboard and bring it back to the phone." He remembered trying to pry the pencil from that arthritic claw. "If he gives you a fight, have someone help you. Do it quickly!"

There was an uncertain pause. Then, as if to dismiss the ravings of a grief-stricken man, Mavis said: "I was very sorry to hear about your family, Doctor. We all—"

"Do it *now*, Mavis. Please!"

The distant *thunk* of the hold button cast Scott's waiting ear into a sea of hissing interference, a sound somehow more maddening than the vanished scratching.

Now Caroline was standing beside him, clutching his

arm, shaking him. "Scott? What's happening? Who are you calling?"

Scott raised a staying hand, startling when Mavis came back on the line. "Did you get it?" he blurted before the nurse had an opportunity to speak.

"Yes. No trouble at all. He was sleeping like a baby. What's—"

"Tell me what you see. What has he drawn?"

"Nothing. There's just a blank sheet—"

"Look underneath."

Paper being shuffled. "Weird," Mavis said into the phone. "It looks like some sort of ghoulish cartoon creature strangling the life out of a child . . . a girl, I think, in her bed."

"Oh, dear Jesus," Scott murmured, his body suddenly clammy and slack. "How can it be . . . how can . . . ?"

But he had known. Deep down he had known since the abandoned cottage, when he'd seen that musty old Polaroid, those loathsome, bullet-hole eyes.

"Doctor? Dr. Bowman, are you still there?"

Scott pressed the receiver to his ear. "Mavis," he said shakily. "I want you to take down an order. I'll countersign it when I get there tonight. I want you to give him seventy-five milligrams of chlorpromazine IM every three hours, without fail. I want—"

"Seventy-five milligrams!" Mavis repeated incredulously. "I don't mean to tell you your business, Doctor, but seventy-five milligrams will knock that old boy right on his ass. He's already asleep, for goodness' sake, why—"

"Just do it, Mavis. You don't want to ignore this order. I mean it. I want him flat out, unconscious. He's dangerous, Mavis, he's—" Scott cut off his words. He had said too much already. "Just do it. Please. It's important . . . more important than you can know."

"All right, Doctor," Mavis replied placatingly, already knowing what she would do. "You'll sign that order tonight?"

"I guarantee it. Do it now, Mavis." He hung up.

"Stay right here," he told Caroline, ignoring her questions. Then he rushed back to the unit.

As Scott hurried in, the physician who had been working on Kath rose from behind the desk, his grim expression confirming Scott's darkest expectations.

"She's had some sort of catastrophic respiratory embarrassment," he told Scott, his coffee-colored eyes defeated but unwavering. "I've never seen anything like it before. There was no foreign body there, but when I tried to admit the tube, it was as if the tissues were being compressed from the outside . . . I just couldn't get it past. I had to do a tracheostomy—"

"You mean she's *alive?*" Scott blurted, and a grin that was perilously close to mad creased his face.

For the first time the older doctor's eyes fell away from Scott's. "She's alive, Dr. Bowman . . ." Words seemed momentarily to escape him. "But I'm afraid there's a strong chance she's sustained some damage to her brain. It's impossible at this early stage to determine exactly how much. . . ."

Still grinning, Scott brushed past the doctor as he might an inanimate obstruction and headed for room 2F.

But as he stepped inside, the glimmer of self-control he'd recovered while on the phone extinguished like a dying star. How many times as an intern had he witnessed a similar scene? A hundred . . . two hundred times? A respiratory tech, fiddling with the dials on a ventilator like a kid glued body-and-soul to a video game. A nurse, grimly gathering the bloodstained utensils employed in the emergency tracheostomy, hunched over her tray like a waitress wearily approaching the end of a double shift. And a patient, motionless in a clean white bed, each breath fed into her lungs by a relentless rubber bellows.

But this time the patient was his own little girl.

This time the patient was Kath.

The respirator was connected to a plastic adapter at her throat. A drop of blood, thinned to a wash-pink by disrupted tissue fluids, leaked out of the incision and coursed down her neck like a bloody tear.

Swaying like a drunk, Scott imagined all the life-support apparatus away—and was left with an image of Kath in a mahogany casket. The lid was open, and the cloying reek of flowers was sickening, unendurable; he could feel his stomach doing a slow, deliberate rollover . . .

He closed his eyes and the image vanished. When he opened them again he was alone in the room with his daughter.

He noticed Jinnie on the floor beneath the bed. The doll had been knocked over during the save-a-life frenzy that had taken place in this room only minutes before. The doll's bloated face was all that was showing, and its unblinking eyes seemed to accuse him. He picked it up and set it back on Kath's pillow.

Kath's eyes were closed.

*Sleeping,* he thought, finding comfort in the self-delusion. *Just having a nap.* He placed a hand on her forehead.

Then, in a reflex action learned in medical school, he lifted her eyelids and examined the globes underneath.

Nothing. Blackness. Dark pools of stagnant, cold water.

Scott's first instinct was to try to waken her, to reach inside and scoop her up from the drowning pools of her eyes. It was the doctor in him that spared him the horror of attempting to do so.

He backed away.

And then an idea so utterly implausible and yet so irresistible struck him that he began to tremble at its very possibility. Whatever it was he was dealing with, he had no sane idea . . . but none of this was sane, was it? Had he come nose to nose with Satan himself, personified in that wretched old man? Or was it some bitter, avenging Angel of God? Four days ago (was it really only four days?), had someone told him that within a matter of hours he would believe unquestioningly in psychic phenomena, he would have uttered a hearty laugh. Had the same individual suggested that within a week he would be contemplating a deal with the devil, he would have had the fellow forcibly incarcerated.

But if the old man could make these things happen simply by drawing them—and wasn't that exactly what he was doing?—then maybe he could *un*do them, too. Maybe he could be persuaded to restore Kath to her normal self, retrieve her soul and spill it back into those vacant eyes.

At that moment the possibility that he had gone totally insane flickered through Scott's mind and was summarily dismissed.

He went to a phone and called the airport. They could have him on a direct flight at three o'clock, which would put him in Ottawa at ten past four. It was now two-twenty.

Returning to the room and grabbing his flight bag, Scott took a last look at Kath before whirling away.

He collided with Caroline in the doorway.

"Scott! Where are you going?"

He seized her arm, causing pain. "Stay with her," he said with maniacal intensity. "Protect her."

"Sco—"

As he brushed past her, his flight bag snagged on the door latch and jerked from his grip. Clothes spilled out, a toothbrush, and the envelope filled with Christmas photos. The pictures skidded free, fanning in an arc like a gambler's deck. Scott scooped up the bag and stuffed his clothing back inside. Bewildered, Caroline bent to retrieve the photographs.

When she looked up again Scott was gone.

The pictures of Krista were the hardest . . . yet she fingered through them compulsively, her expression switching from anguish to pleasure back to anguish again.

Her baby sister, dead. It was inconceivable . . .

Tears filming her eyes, Caroline came upon the underwater photo of the dock. She gazed at it wonderingly, feeling suddenly cold, then shuffled it to the bottom of the pile.

The next print was blank . . .

Or was it?

Caroline watched in disbelief as the quality of the unexposed print changed, ever so subtly. At first she thought it was just her imagination, conjuring illusions in her overwrought mind.

But no . . . the thing was changing, developing, like a Polaroid, only slower. There was a face beginning to appear, or part of a face . . . and a pair of hands, reaching up.

*My God,* Caroline thought in fearful astonishment, *that expression* . . .

The face in the photo, appearing now as if a wreath of dirty smoke were being slowly sucked away, was hideously contorted, as if screaming its last. And it seemed mired in something . . . below the chin, around the ears, framing the forehead . . .

*Quicksand?*

Yes, it was the face of a man sinking in quicksand.

But not just *a* man . . .

*Scott?*

The nerves fled Caroline's fingers and the picture twirled to the floor. The same gradual unmisting occurred in the next print, also a blank. Baleful red eyes appeared, snaggle teeth, huge sprays of blood . . .

Caroline screamed, and this time all of the pictures fell, scattering over the floor like the fragments of a shattered dream.

233

# CHAPTER 32

"Where is he?"

Janet Brown, the ward clerk on Two Link, took an involuntary step backward, quietly thanking God there was a desk between her and the man on the opposite side. She had been chatting on the phone with her boyfriend when Scott came up behind her and began digging frantically through the chart rack.

"Where is who?" Janet asked nervously. She had never seen a doctor look such a mess. Drunks or accident victims maybe, but never a doctor. And there was something wrong with his eyes. Red-rimmed and too shiny, they shifted almost constantly, as if he feared the building might suddenly collapse, or that some savage beast might pounce out and devour him. *Hunted.* That was the word she wanted. The guy looked hunted.

Scott planted his fists on the desktop and leaned toward her. "The old man. The Cartoonist. Where *is* he?"

Janet took another step backward and stumbled into her chair. She realized that her boyfriend was still on hold. She glanced along the hallway in both directions, damning its dinner-hour emptiness, then looked back at Scott.

"Transferred," she said, almost shouting the word. "They moved him down to Psychiatry about an hour ago. Is there anything I can do . . . ?"

But Scott had already turned away, heading at a run for the stairwell. The clerk waited until he had slipped through the doorway, then dialed zero and had the nursing supervisor paged from her supper.

*Bateman,* Scott thought as he flew down the stairs to the main floor. He had forgotten about the department head's interest in the old man. Of course Mavis MacDonald would have called Bateman to verify Scott's wholly inappropriate order, and of course Bateman would have vetoed it.

He pushed through to the main floor and darted into the nursing station, which at the moment was abandoned. He went to the desktop Rolodex and began flipping hurriedly through it, scanning for the old man's new room number.

"Can I help you?" a wary voice asked from behind him.

Scott ignored it and kept fingering through the files, cursing his trembling clumsiness.

"Dr. Bowman?" the voice said uncertainly. "Is that you?"

"What room is the Cartoonist in?" Scott demanded, turning his crazed green eyes on the nurse.

The woman flinched back, as the clerk on Two Link had done. She answered by snatching a chart from the rack and thrusting it at Scott. He flung the chart open and scanned to the telephone order he had given to Mavis MacDonald. Following protocol, Mavis had written in Scott's order and signed it. But in the section below was another order, this one inscribed in neat, fountain-ink script: *Cancel above,* it read simply. *Transfer patient to psychiatry.* It was signed *V. Bateman, MD.*

The Cartoonist was in 117, a private room at the end of the hall.

Scott moved quickly into the corridor—then fear ran its finger down his belly, and he slowed, overcome once again by that drifting sensation of unreality. Breathing deeply, he fought to reorient himself. The corridor was familiar. He had walked it almost daily since the hospital opened more than eight years ago. His office was at the end of a similar corridor just one flight down. He made his living in this building. It was a good place, a safe place, a sane place.

But was it real? Was any of it *real?* The flight up from Boston, even the drive into the city from the airport, had already faded from concrete recall, now seeming more dreamlike than real . . . except that he remembered climbing into Krista's Chevette in the airport parking lot. That he remembered with awful clarity. The lingering scent of her perfume. The objects, now meaningless, that had once lived through her personality: the punky, rhinestone-studded sunglasses she'd forgotten to take with her to Boston; the unopened packet of Trident bubble gum on the dash; the pair of sheer nylon pantyhose still in its package on the seat . . .

*scratch,scratch . . . scratch,scratch,scratch . . .*

Scott started forward, then froze outside the doorway to 117, his flesh going cold with apprehension. He took the last few steps with his back pressed firmly to the wall.

The artist was in his wheelchair by the shaded window. His back was to Scott, and he was drawing, the sound of the pencil seeming to fill the room.

And suddenly Scott knew he couldn't face the old man. Maybe he really *was* an agent of an angered God . . . because Scott really was guilty. He had slaughtered a helpless child and then fled like a sniveling coward.

*He's killing me, Daddy . . .*

No. It had to end. It had to end now. God or demon or one-eyed alien. He would have to face it.

Breathless, Scott bolted into the room and seized the clipboard from those murdering hands. The Cartoonist —Nicholas Rowe—didn't move, didn't even flinch. He only drooled, his black eyes aimed unblinking into space. Scott's gaze ran furiously to the two completed frames— but, as the graveyard sequence had at first glance, these sketches seemed connected to nothing real, nothing meaningful to Scott. Shown was a grim-visaged judge hearing the pleas of a man clad in old-style prison fatigues. In the second frame two guards restrained the prisoner while the judge, delivering his verdict, brought the gavel down with a crash. The next few frames, though neatly squared off, remained ominously blank.

Scott wadded the unfinished sequence into a ball and tossed it to the floor. He flipped the clipboard onto the bed and stepped in behind the wheelchair.

Then, abruptly, he took hold of the hand grips and swung the wheelchair around. A rope of drool whipped back from the old man's chin and plastered itself to his cheek.

"You can cut the act, Rowe," Scott said, unable to disguise the raw fear in his voice. "I know all about you now."

The old man didn't respond—but now that odor was on him again, the alleycat reek Scott had smelled when he'd tried to pry the pencil from that knotted fist four days before.

Scott took hold of Rowe's seamed yellow face and twisted it up toward his own, trying to see something— *anything*—in the pits of those eyes, eyes that were so much like Kath's had been the last time Scott had seen her.

"Please," he murmured, verging on tears at the wan, empty image of Kath his mind had thrown up. "Please stop this." His grip tightened on the slack flesh of the old man's face, puckering his lips like the mouth of a carp. "It wasn't her fault . . . it . . ."

The old man leaned away, freeing himself from Scott's grip, and reached for the clipboard on the bed. Scott grabbed the arm of the wheelchair, preventing him by bare inches from reaching his target. The artist persisted, stretching, grunting, his deformed fingers clutching at the air like the fingers of a drowning man, oh, yes, a drowning man, Scott knew *that* feeling . . . and suddenly the terror beneath the dock came flooding back with the abrupt and frightful clarity of a nightmare. He could feel the water at his neck like powerful hands, choking, suffocating . . .

Scott released the wheelchair and staggered back, clutching his throat, his body faint and tingling with airhunger.

With an effort he managed a breath.

*scratch,scratch,scratch . . .*

*"Stop it!"* Scott exploded, one hand sweeping down like a sword, cutting the clipboard from the old man's grip and sending it clattering to the floor. "Stop it!" He buried his fists into Nicholas Rowe's nightshirt and hauled him upward to the limit of his restraints. "Krista's dead!" he bellowed at the unheeding skeleton in his grip. "Krista's dead and I want my daughter *back!*"

His face livid, Scott bent and retrieved the clipboard. He jabbed it roughly into the old man's ribs.

"Here you sonofabitch! *Draw!*" He sounded absurdly like a cowboy, calling out the town marshal. "Draw my girl normal or I'll kill you!"

The Cartoonist broke wet, rancid, old-man's wind.

And for the first time since Scott had set eyes on him, he seemed to grin.

Scott struck him a whistling backhand. He lifted his hand to strike again, but then something had him by the wrist. He snapped his arm free and whirled to face Jane Copeland, the nursing supervisor.

"Have you gone *mad?"* Copeland shouted, her face an almost comic mask of shock and disbelief.

"Out!" Scott bellowed at her. "Get out of here now!" He steamed toward her like an engine of destruction.

Copeland backed cautiously away. "What is going *on* in here, Doctor? My God, he's just an old man . . . ?"

"Out," Scott repeated, clenching his fists in front of him. "He killed my wife." Part of him knew how crazy that sounded, but he was beyond caring. "He killed my wife and now he's trying to kill my daughter."

"Wha . . . ?" The supervisor stumbled through the doorway into the hall. "I'm going to get Security, damn you! You leave that old man al—"

The slamming door cut off her words. Scott twisted the lock, then dragged the bed across it as a barricade. He turned back to the old man and felt his legs turn to rubber.

The artist gawked vacantly into space, blood-streaked drool oozing from his mouth, the pencil in his hand a twitching blur against the page. Teeth bared viciously, Scott lurched forward to see what the old man was drawing—and fell in a heap to the floor, his legs disconnected from his brain. His chin struck the tiles, and that old wound started to bleed again.

There was no doubt about it now.

The old man was grinning.

Scott began dragging himself toward the loathsome wretch in the wheelchair. The pencil was moving at incredible speed now, whispering like the faraway voices of the damned.

"What are you drawing?" he bellowed. "Why don't you speak?"

The pencil whispered cunningly.

"It was an *accident,*" Scott pleaded. "We were just kids . . . scared kids. We didn't mean . . ."

Nicholas Rowe, lashed to his wheelchair like some dark and terrible lord, stopped drawing and stared into Scott's lunatic eyes. And for a terrible instant, Scott felt certain the old man would speak. Instead, he withdrew a single sheet from the clipboard and let it drift to the floor. It landed before Scott's eyes.

On it were a series of drawings . . .

An old man lying on his back on a stretcher, his toothless mouth agape in an oval of death. Above him, a portly doctor in a white lab coat preparing to apply electric paddles to his chest. In the final frame, the paddles backfiring, electrocuting the doctor in twin, cartoon flashes of fire.

Brian Horner.

Another sheet floated to the floor, the sketches gruesomely detailed.

Jake Laking.

Taking a repeating rifle down from its rack and bringing it upstairs, to where his family sat watching TV. Using it first on his wife, then his two kids, and lastly on himself. . . .

Finally, torn from its brass frame, the family photo from Scott's office drifted to the floor in the lazy arcs of a falling autumn leaf. Thumbed across it was a big bloody X.

The pencil resumed its doom-etching.

Scott, weeping like a child, crawled to the old man's feet. "Stop," he begged through his tears. "Stop . . . it's not her fault. Please, can't you see that?" He dragged himself to his knees, using the chair's spoked wheels for leverage.

Slowly, deliberately, the old man angled the clipboard toward Scott, allowing him a tangential view of the developing drawings. The pencil never faltered. It flashed across the page with superhuman speed, creating shapes so rapidly, they seemed almost to move.

A child in a bed. Kath. Respirator tubes hooked to her neck. Jinnie lying limp on her chest, lifeless doll eyes peering out at him as they had done earlier that day, from beneath Kath's hospital bed.

Scott ordered his hands to move, to grab that clipboard and snap it across his knee, to take those murdering drawings and rip them into so many fat December snowflakes. But his hands ignored the command. They were cold, numb, someone else's hands.

The Cartoonist's pencil blurred. Frame by hellish frame, Jinnie began to shift. Off the bed, onto the floor, behind the respirator. One fingerless hand reaching for the wall plug . . .

"No!" Scott screamed, fighting the slushy numbness in his muscles. *"No!"*

Jinnie's hand inched tormentingly closer to the plug. Scott could see it past the blur of the old man's pencil. It folded around the power cord . . . and then stopped.

Nicholas Rowe stared into Scott's eyes and laughed, a clipped, mirthless laugh that chilled him to the marrow. Then that old and cheated face twisted into a scowl, and a gob of spittle flew into Scott's eyes. Reflexively, Scott shut his eyes. . . .

And there was Kath, in the nightmarish twilight of his mind. Sitting up in bed. Huge black pupils swallowing her eyes. Tracheostomy tube jutting like the blunt haft of a knife from her neck. Hands raised beseechingly. "He's killing me, Daddy," she was whispering dreamily, without passion or fear. "He's killing me."

The artist's hand resumed moving.

And so did the doll's.

Fury flowed into Scott like molten lava, replacing his fear, scorching it into meaningless cinders. He pushed to his feet and the old man paused once again, his expression of triumphant rage faltering into one of stunned surprise.

That pause was all Scott needed.

He drove his fist into the old man's face and felt the splay of fossil flesh, the snap of brittle bone. With his free hand he grabbed the clipboard and yanked with everything he had—but Rowe held on, hissing like a cat through his stubby black teeth.

Outside the room someone thumped on the door.

"Open up!" a muffled voice commanded. "Scott, it's Vince Bateman! Open this door now!"

Scott and the old man battled for the clipboard, tugging it to and fro like lumbermen sawing timber. Vaguely, Scott heard the clunk of tumblers turning over. He lifted his foot and kicked the old man in the chest, almost losing his balance. Ribs snapped.

The door opened a wedge, the obstructing bed scraping

heavily across the tiles. Bateman's shrill voice shrieked through the crack.

"Scott! What in hell is going *on* in there? Open this damned *door!*"

Scott's legs were slackening to rubber again. He looked away from those dark, hypnotic eyes and pulled, beginning to hiss himself with the effort. The old man growled like a wildcat.

And as Scott looked on, horror-struck, the figure of Kath's Cabbage Patch doll came to life within its frame, like an animated character on a miniature, black and white screen. Its stubby hand tightened around the wall plug and pulled. Now Scott could see the metal prongs: halfway out, they gleamed in the light of unseen fluorescents.

Behind him voices grunted heftily, and the barricading bed slid again.

Without warning, Scott released the clipboard and reached for the old man's throat. His scrawny neck felt spongy between Scott's closing hands.

Spongy and good.

*Choke, you bastard,* he thought with idiot glee. *Choke like I did, like my little girl . . .*

Gagging, black eyes bulging like those of a throat-slit hog, the artist stabbed out with his pencil, driving its tip into Scott's left shoulder. Scott cried out but held his grip firm, tightening it by torturing degrees.

*Die,* he thought, and the thought became a chant: "Die, die, die . . ."

The old man swung the pencil again, this time catching Scott in the face. Blood spurted from a lead-blackened hole in his cheek.

*die*

The door scraped open enough to admit Bateman's head.

*"Scott!!"*

Again the pencil gouged—but now Scott had the old man's wrist and he was turning it inward, leaning his full weight and all of his strength against that wasted arm.

There followed a grotesque popping sound, and a gurgling rattle of death, and when the security guards yanked Scott away from Nicholas Rowe's body, the pencil was buried in the old man's throat to the eraser. Blood erupted from the puncture site in an astonishing red jet, spraying Bateman's impeccable gray suit and expensive Italian shoes, spotting his ashen face.

For a moment everyone in the room stood in stunned and silent ranks, Scott and Vince Bateman and Jane Copeland, the three security guards and the two young orderlies.

Then the old man began to howl with laughter, shrill dry cackles that rose and fell in maniacal cycles, seeming to echo from the slag pits of hell. He laughed and blood spurted and Vince Bateman made no effort to step out of its path. The old man laughed and blood drenched his clipboard, that odious slate of his abysmal rage. He laughed and his life ran out on the floor.

And suddenly, behind his laughter, like a far and distant echo, rose the tinkling laughter of a child. Scott heard it and he knew that everyone else had heard it, too. But he saw them shove it from their minds as quickly and efficiently as he had pushed the truth from his own.

Slowly the laughter died.

The Cartoonist slumped forward in his chair, the canvas restraints preventing him from toppling to the gore-puddled floor.

*Kath!*

Elbows bladed like a charging lineman, Scott whirled toward the door. And he almost made it, so deep was the spell that bound the others.

But then Bateman cried "Stop him!" and five men converged on Scott in a tightening pack-dog circle, a strange kind of awe in their eyes.

Then they were on him, all over him. A huge forearm closed around his neck, cutting off his air. Scott bit into it until he tasted blood and the arm was withdrawn. There was a shriek of anger and pain. Then other arms had him, and they were wrangling him down. A fist plowed into his sternum, collapsing his lungs, graying his vision. Now the orderly he had bitten was back on top of him, his massive arms clamped around Scott's upper legs. They were lifting him, lifting him right up in the air . . .

He barely felt the needle when it punctured the flesh of his hip.

*Ketamine*, he thought. *Fast-acting stuff.*

Pure volcanic power surged into Scott Bowman then and he wheeled, kicked, convulsed and flailed until he was free. He vaulted over the bed and out through the door in a single agile movement.

But even as he lurched down the hall and locked the door to the nursing office behind him, the drug began to work on him. The dial on the phone seemed to warp and sag like a clockface in a Dali painting, and the cramped little room seemed to ooze around him like toffee.

He shook his head and found the right numbers and dialed the General Hospital in Danvers.

"Let me speak . . ." he said before anyone answered.

Then he collapsed, his forehead striking the blotter on the desk with a soft, unheard thud.

# EPILOGUE

Maria Falsetto stopped her cart outside room 117 and murmured a prayer in her native Italian. She had heard about the murder through the preshift grapevine, and had known even then that she would end up responsible for the mess. Maria was a cleaning lady. She worked permanent nightshift so she could hold down a day job at the high school—and room 117 was in her quadrant on the main floor.

Marshaling her courage, Maria thrust the cart into the room. The smell struck her first. Back in Italy, her father had worked in the village slaughterhouse. This same smell had been on his clothes when he came home at night. As a girl, Maria had imagined the beasts her father slayed pouring out that stink in an effort to ward off the inevitable steel. It was a combination of odors really: urine, bowels, the sour taint of blood, and something else . . . something not visceral, and very old.

It was the blood that got to her next, and she swooned

as her eyes widened to their normal size, then stretched-out round as china saucers. Bile puddled in the back of her throat, and she uttered a small, sickened whine.

So much blood . . . she had never seen so much blood.

Deep religious fears pushed Maria back to the doorway with a frightened cry. Then she stopped and turned back. If she didn't do this, she might lose her job. And she couldn't afford that, not now, not with Gino starting college.

Breathing in hitches, Maria set about her grim task. She began by mopping the floor. It surprised and sickened her how difficult it was to scour the blood off the tiles. There was even blood on the ceiling.

*Dio buono.*

As she worked, Maria's mind insisted on creating imaginary scenarios of the crime. God, she thought, she knew that Dr. Bowman. And he seemed like such a nice man, even took time to speak with the cleaning staff, made them feel like his equals. She would never have guessed he was insane. But to murder a helpless old man like that . . . and for what reason?

Her stout legs barely supporting her, Maria leaned over to do under the bed. On the third rapid stroke, her mop dragged out a wadded-up ball of paper. She nearly tossed it into the big industrial wastebag on her cart . . . then she paused and unfurled it, remembering that the old man had been an artist.

She studied the drawings for a minute, her expression puzzled, then set them aside. She would give them to the nurse later on, when she was done in here.

*What a crime,* she thought, hoisting her mop to the ceiling. *A helpless, gifted old man . . .*

The balding, birdlike man seated across from Vince Bateman leafed through the thick sheaf of drawings with something like awe. The man's name was Peter Lloyd. He was the psychiatric director at Penatanguishene, the provincial center for the criminally insane.

Bateman, decked out in a dapper houndstooth plaid, paced uneasily behind his desk. "I've interviewed Bowman a dozen times since he committed his crime, and still he insists that his story is true. His delusions are deep-seated, Peter. At first I thought they might simply be reactional—he did lose his wife, and very nearly his only child. But he refuses to let go of the notion that the old man was some sort of evil magician, settling the score for the death of his grandchild . . . or child. He muttered some foul drivel about incest."

Dr. Lloyd regarded Bateman over the half-moon glasses on his nose. "How did he make it into medical school with a criminal record?"

"He ran. He and his friends left the scene of the crime . . . at least, if you can believe even that part of his story."

Lloyd shook his head with a weariness that lay deep in his eyes. "What happened to his daughter?"

"She's recovered," Bateman replied. "Apparently, the team in Massachusetts hadn't expected her to, not so completely anyway. She's staying with relatives for now."

"Has he been allowed to see her yet?"

"No, not yet. He still has episodes of extreme violence, even with all the medication he's getting. Hallucinations and nightmares. He claims the old man is in there with him. I've assured him personally of his child's well-being, but he refuses to believe it. It'll be up to your people when best to allow the girl to visit."

"Hmmm," Lloyd mused, looking back at the drawings. "What's this one?" He turned a badly creased sheet toward Bateman.

Refusing to believe what deep-down Bateman knew these sketches to represent, he only shrugged. "A cleaning lady found them under the old man's bed that night two weeks ago."

In the first frame a grim-visaged judge heard the pleas of a man clad in old-style prison fatigues. In the second, two guards restrained the prisoner while the judge, delivering his verdict, brought the gavel down with a crash. . . .

There were four more frames, and Peter Lloyd noticed absently that the texture of these was subtly different, more like faded Xerox copies than actual lead-pencil sketches . . . but he couldn't make much of it, and he continued to review their content with interest.

The third frame showed the prisoner being dragged out of the courtroom, his twisted mouth uttering silent oaths. In the fourth the man was being forced into a padded cell. In the fifth, bound in a straitjacket, he crouched in a corner on the bare white floor, legs drawn up to his chest, head propped against folded knees.

In the final frame it was nighttime, the man a barely visible smudge in one corner. There was a tragically lonely feel to this frame that made Lloyd shudder a little.

And there was something else, something he almost missed, something which, when he saw it, caught the tag end of his shudder and converted it to a deep, convulsive spasm.

Through a small barred window set high in the wall of the cell, baleful red eyes peered watchfully in.